UNHINGED
A DARK MAFIA STALKER ROMANCE

BRATVA KINGS

JANE HENRY

Unhinged: A Dark Mafia Stalker Romance

Copyright © 2025 by Jane Henry

All rights reserved.

This is a literary work of fiction. Any names, places or incidents are the product of the author's imagination. Similarities or resemblance to actual persons, living or dead, events or establishments, are solely coincidental.

No part of this book may be reproduced, scanned or distributed in any form or by any electronic or mechanical means, including information storage and retrieval systems, without written permission from the author, except for the use of brief quotations in a book review.

The unauthorized reproduction, transmission, distribution of, or use of the copyrighted work in the training of Artificial Intelligences (AI) is illegal and a violation of US copyright law.

Cover Photography by Wander Aguiar

Cover design by Sylvia Frost

ISBN: 978-1-961866-31-7

TRIGGER WARNING

Readers please note: This is a ***dark romance***. *Unhinged* contains kidnapping, CNC, caging, BDSM, dubious consent, and past mention of abuse and graphic violence.

SYNOPSIS

Anissa Laurent is a ghost—a master of deception, a woman who has slipped through the cracks of the underworld. Untraceable. Untouchable. Unclaimed. Until me.

I made it my life's mission to find her, drag her back where she belongs, and punish her for her betrayal.

I traced every false identity until I found her, but I took my time. I studied the way she breathes, the way she moves, what she loves, and what she hates.

She thought she could run. She thought she could hide. She thought she could get away with betraying my family.

But I'm not a man who lets go of what's mine.

She was meant to be broken, to be owned, meant to carry my mark in the most primal way possible. I won't just take her body—she'll have my baby, too.

But I didn't expect her to be as broken as I am. I didn't expect her to fight like she has nothing left to lose. And now, I don't just want to cage her—I want to own her.

She'll curse me. She'll hate me. She'll claw and bite and scream my name in fury and in pleasure. But in the end, it doesn't matter. Because there is no escape from her past... and definitely not from me.

CHAPTER 1

MATVEI

Branding is *not* the same level of pain as a tat, and I don't know why I ever let Rodion convince me otherwise.

But this isn't just my brand. It's my vow to swear my soul to the Bratva, my promise to give every ounce of my being to my Bratva kin.

I sit on a stool, molars locked, my feet hooked under the rungs so I don't topple off. Fucking hell.

"How's that pain, bro?" Rodion, my younger cousin and best friend, stands a few feet away, strategically out of my reach, his arms crossed on his chest.

"*Feels like ink*," I mock. I glare at him. "I'm gonna kick your fucking ass."

It doesn't feel like ink. It feels like penance.

Rafail, the head of the Kopolov family Bratva and my oldest cousin, shakes his head. "He's due," he mutters.

Vadka presses his lips together, a look of concentration on his face. I look away as he presses the brand into my back. I close my eyes and try to mentally transport the fuck out of here, but it doesn't work. The pain is too raw, too vivid. My throat burns from swallowing a scream, the sickening stench of seared flesh filling the room. Someone makes a retching sound.

"What'd he tell you?" Vadka says, doing a piss-ass job of hiding his amusement.

I exhale through my nose. "Said it felt like a tat."

Vadka snorts but keeps his hand still. "You should definitely kick his ass for that, but *you're* the dumbass who believed him. How is a prickling needle the same as a hot iron scarring your flesh?"

If a tat is a paper cut, a brand is severing a limb.

Jesus.

The pain makes sweat dot my brow. I have to take my mind off this.

So instead... I think of Anissa.

The woman who betrayed my family. The woman who's *mine.*

Anissa fucking Laurent.

The runaway. The ghost. The girl who managed to slip the noose off her neck and vanish into thin air like a goddamn myth. But my mind is a vault of every detail I've gathered over the years I've tracked her.

Sister to Polina Kopolova, my *pakhan's wife*. Both of them pawns in a brutal game of life and death, and neither knew of the other's existence. Anissa still doesn't.

She's sometimes blonde, sometimes auburn, sometimes short or dyed black. Her eyes are a striking blue but cold. Always analyzing. Watching. She looks at the world as if it's a threat to her.

I want to be the one who makes her look that way.

Her mouth—full lips that smirk like she knows every secret you've ever kept, smug because she's clever enough to wipe out full identities. And just above those pouty lips, she has a birthmark I'm obsessed with. I imagine resting my finger there when I finally have her pinned beneath me.

"The next part is the hardest. *Breathe*," Vadka reminds me when he lifts the larger brand, so hot I can see steam rising from it in the cool basement air.

"Fuck," Rodion says, paling. Maybe he's the one making the sound like he's about to vomit. I imagine the satisfying feeling of my fist connecting with his jaw.

I close my eyes and breathe through my nose. The problem is, it isn't just the pain, but the way the smell of burnt flesh brings back the worst memory of my life, the one I try to bury.

I remember the way the walls of The Cottage basement absorbed the sounds of my brother's screams, the cement floor slick with his blood. I stood, my arms crossed on my chest as cold decision settled in my veins. My brother betrayed us. I had to watch him die. My younger brother, the one I had protected and half raised, the one who'd give my own life for, committed the unforgivable sin of betrayal. He traded his blood for a pocket full of promises from our enemies.

And now, I'm hunting down the girl who made betrayal look easy.

She ran from my *pakhan*, made a mockery of our family, and then joined forces with our enemies. Made the whole world think we were weak.

Just like my brother.

Gleb hung in front of us, wrists raw and bleeding from the cuffs—a living warning of what happens when you break the *Vorovskoy Mir*, the Thieves' Code.

"Tell us the three laws you took a vow to," Rafail said. When we were younger, Rafail acted as the big brother for all of us. He was stern and unyielding, our guide and friend. Now he was our *pakhan*, the acting leader of our Bratva, the one who called for the execution of his cousin. My brother.

And I vowed I would watch every brutal, soul-tearing second.

I'd failed my younger brother. It was on *me* to teach him to obey the law of the Bratva. *I* was the one who taught him how to ride a bike, how to smoke a joint, how to fuck a girl well and good and keep her coming back for more. I was the one who bailed him out when he fucked up, but that night—that night, I was the one who burned his tats from his flesh before he faced the ultimate punishment for his sins against us.

I took a blood vow when I was eighteen years old. And I'll die before I break it.

Just like Gleb did.

The Thieves' Code was ironclad:

The Bratva comes before all else.

Never cooperate with the authorities.

Never, ever betray your brothers.

There's a reason we're feared, a reason why the mark of the Bratva makes women hold their children closer when we pass and grown men tremble.

"We're done."

My eyes fly open. Someone presses a bottle of vodka to my lips. I drink as if I'm dying of thirst. It helps a little.

I sit up straighter. Every cell in my body seems concentrated on my back, the pain carved into my flesh, throbbing, unrelenting. I grip the neck of the bottle and take another swig.

Vadka lists off instructions for healing the brand. I only half hear him.

I spilled my blood and took an oath. Let them brand me. I did what had to be done.

Now, *she's* the next step. My offering. My proof of loyalty.

My obsession.

I grit my teeth and think of her.

The runaway. The traitor. My ghost.

The one who ran away from my *pakhan* but made a fool out of all of us. Rafail has moved on. Thanks to my brother's folly, Rafail married a woman he thought was Anissa while Anissa ran.

Unpunished.

She's mine. I'm going to own her. Every inch, every breath, every scream. She doesn't know it yet, but she already belongs to me.

I can already imagine her gasping beneath me, marked by me. I want to fill her, breed her, make her mine in ways no one can ever undo.

Rafail stands in front of me, feet planted on either side, his arms crossed. He's dressed in a suit, still wearing his jacket as always.

"I'll let you know when we have our meeting, Matvei," Rafail says.

Though Rafail is happily married, Bratva men don't forget betrayal. Rafail has not forgotten. He knows exactly why the specific date matters. I meet his eyes and nod. "I'll wait."

The others look on curiously, but it isn't time yet to tell them why the dates matter. And Rafail doesn't give a shit who knows what; he'll tell them when he's good and ready.

Even as I'm breathing through my nose, my body throbbing in pain, pride surges in my chest. Ink marks the sign of the Bratva, but branding means something entirely different. And Rafail trusts me.

London.

Perfect. My cousin Semyon has orchestrated a proposal, a coalition of the most powerful crime syndicates in the world, seeking asylum. They all assemble in London.

Keenan McCarthy's Clan from Ireland, now headed by his son. The Rossis from Boston's Italian mob. The Yakuza and the Cartel. We sought the most dangerous, the most powerful.

Our family represents the Bratva.

The Irish would be there, of course. The McCarthy clan didn't miss an opportunity like this. But it wasn't Keenan who bothered me but his fucking rabid dog, O'Rourke. Rumor had it he kept Anissa close. And I don't fucking like that.

"And from London, you're heading to Dublin?" Rafail asks in my ear.

I nod.

Now I know why Rafail chose today for my branding. Word will be released that I've taken the ultimate step of allegiance. My tats tell a story, but the brand means absolute loyalty, proof that I've bled and suffered. Penitence for the crimes my brother committed. A chance to be reborn into Bratva leadership.

Breaking the *Vorovskoy Mir* is a death sentence. Brutal, slow, and inescapable.

Anissa thought she was clever, sneaking under the radar and flitting from one place to another, changing her identity. But it doesn't matter if she took an oath or not—she was promised to my Bratva. She ran, and now I'm going to teach her exactly what happens to runaway brides.

She's not just a target or distraction, a pretty little plaything to take the family name. *No.* She's a fucking craving under my skin. I'll chase her to the ends of the earth if I have to.

She never swore an oath, but she ran from a promise. From my family.

That makes her my responsibility, my obsession. My fucking craving. She's not just a runaway bride—she's the girl who made me invisible, and I'm going to burn my name into her skin like this brand is seared into mine.

She doesn't get to run from us twice.

Everyone but Rafail leaves while I catch my breath. I try to play a mental game to move beyond the pain, but I can't. So I sit with it and let it consume me.

He holds my gaze. Sometimes, I see my cousin. The guy I grew up with, older, who practically raised me when my parents weren't around. Other times, I see my *pakhan*. The ruthless king of the Russian underworld.

My *pakhan* stands in front of me now.

"I want to give her to you, Matvei," he says calmly, but the chill in his tone is unmistakable. "You've earned her. But make no mistake. If you can't bring her in alive and under your control... she *will* be eliminated. If not from us, she's one of Interpol's biggest targets."

Someone whistles behind us. I turn to see Rodion.

"You really think you can tame that one? She'll slit your throat before she spreads her legs."

And just like that, my obsession becomes personal. It's not just about revenge.

I will *own* her.

After I beat the shit out of Rodion.

UNHINGED

CHAPTER 2

ANISSA

I SLICK my long brown hair, the color *du jour*, over my shoulder and give myself a small chin lift.

It's hard to find a decent mirror in these tiny Irish pubs. I miss Moscow. My family in Russia takes their appearances a lot more seriously, and full-length mirrors are everywhere. At least in my apartment here in Dublin—the tiny flat I'm renting because they asked no questions and I could pay in cash—I have my makeup. Here, I'll make do with what I have.

I swipe on some pink gloss and run my fingers through my long hair. Blonde is my natural color, but disguises are my specialty.

Today, I'm in sleek, comfortable clothes—nothing too restrictive. I always need to be ready to run. The black spandex fabric stretches tight across my ample ass, the tiny tank clinging, an oversized white sweater falling off one shoulder. I have on tiny black flats, the expensive kind that fold into your luggage and let you run if you need to. Gold jewelry finishes the ensemble.

I glance at the time on today's burner phone.

Oh, Cillian O'Rourke, you're five minutes late. That will cost you.

I walk to the tiny booth in the back and quickly double-check all the exits. Behind me, an orange exit sign flashes, and I've already confirmed it leads to an alleyway.

"Sorry I'm late, lass," O'Rourke says, but the expression on his face tells me he isn't sorry at all. Spoiled prick. Cillian is one of the youngest of the McCarthy clan—a cousin or a brother, I can't keep track. There are too damn many of them. His head is shaved, with Irish mob ink running down the side of his neck and across his shoulders. Even in a sweatshirt and jeans, he can't hide his bulk.

His gaze skims over me, lingering. I wonder if I imagine that flicker in his eyes. Not business or courtesy, but something I can't quite identify.

I'm lonely, though. And for one sliver of a moment—just enough to pull at my heartstrings but not long enough to embarrass me—I wish I were a more permanent fixture in the Irish Mafia. I'm told the McCarthy men are brutal, vicious, old-fashioned, and heavy-handed... but they're loyal. Filthy rich. Protective. And sexy as sin.

But I'm not their type. I only work for them. I'm a hired contractor and not even paid that well because our deal is simple—they get my excellent forgery skills in exchange for their protection.

Some days, the ability to disappear isn't the superpower it seems. Cillian never asked for more than my work, but I wanted *more*. Power. Protection. Maybe something like devotion. But if any of them were interested in me, he would've made a move a long, long time ago.

"What do you need, *lad*?" I ask, flipping open the tiniest laptop known to man—barely bigger than a tablet.

With an eye roll at my mockery of his brogue, he shoves a piece of paper over, the details scratched down in ink. In the digital age, we've found that paper trails are sometimes easiest. I'll literally burn it after I'm done. I take a look at the specs and nod.

"Doable. I can have this for you in twenty-four hours."

Predictably, he frowns, his full lips pulling down at the edges as he leans forward, his eyes boring into mine.

"I don't *have* twenty-four hours, luv."

I blow out a breath, roll my eyes, and shake my head. Of *course* he doesn't, but it's part of my bargaining power.

His expression's pinched, his jaw tight. He hates having to ask, hates not being the one calling the shots. Ah, well, sucks to be him.

"Buy me a Guinness, and I can do it in four. You'll have to find me a pizza too."

It's always the same. They never have time, never have patience. Everything I do for them needs to be done yesterday.

But they do keep up their end of our deal, so I keep mine.

I've been under the protection of the McCarthy Clan since I betrayed the Kopolov Bratva and ran for my life.

I pull up a browser and begin working. He takes his leave after securing me a Guinness and a shitty excuse for a pizza, checking in every hour to see how it's going. If he wasn't one of the scariest assholes I'd ever met, which comes in handy for a girl like me, I wouldn't want anything to do with the bastard. But being in the pocket of the Irish Mafia is my ticket to safety.

For now. I mean, a girl has aspirations.

I finally hand him over everything he needs to assume a different identity in South Africa, with a bit of unsolicited advice. "Try to tamp down your *accent*, Cillian." I shake my head. No amount of perfect documents will erase his telltale brogue. "Just... pretend you're mute or develop a sudden vow of silence."

He grunts and gives me the middle finger. How quaint. He's practicing.

It's two o'clock in the morning when I make it back to the little apartment. I pop my sleep meds because I want to fall asleep, face plant, and not wake up until I've slept for *hours*.

My eyes are bleary from lack of sleep, but I still find my way to the bathroom because even a nomad in hiding needs to have a solid skincare routine. It will take a few minutes for the meds to kick in. I clean, exfoliate, and moisturize, then slide off the wig and sigh with relief. It's kind of like taking a bra off at the end of the day. Under the wig, my blonde hair sits in a messy bun. I tug it free and watch as it falls over my shoulders.

Sigh. That's better.

I frown at my reflection when something catches the corner of my eye.

Wait a minute.

I may not have a permanent residence, but I have my rituals, and I never put my toothpaste *there*. What kind of a heathen makes the top face the sink? I look down at the tube and touch it with my fingertip as if expecting it to get up and move on its own.

Was I so distracted this morning that I started putting things in the wrong place?

I'm tired. Dammit, O'Rourke.

I go to open the bathroom door and freeze, my hand on the cold metal doorknob.

Wait.

I don't hang my towel on the back of the *door*. I hang it on the rung by the tub so I can grab it when I shower.

The skin on the back of my neck prickles. Was I not paying attention this morning? Or was someone...in here?

I open the door to the bathroom and call out. "Hello? Anyone there?" As if someone's going to just magically appear out of thin air. Still, I wait for a reply, but when none comes, I don't know what to do next.

Should I alert Cillian? I could call the McCarthys if things go south—if I'm in real trouble. But what would I even say? *Someone moved my toothpaste and my towel?* Maybe I'm just being paranoid, but what if I'm not? Still, without better evidence, I can't cry wolf. Not with that crowd.

I shake my head and walk to my bedroom. I stand in the doorway, narrowing my eyes and assessing it carefully.

Bed is made, cheap, cream-colored duvet straightened. Charging station lit up, ready for my devices, shades pulled evenly three-quarters of the way down. Not even a shoe out of place in here. Orange bottle of prescription sleep meds sitting on my nightstand right where I left them after I took tonight's.

I strip out of my clothes and grab the sweats on my dresser. My eyes are so heavy. The meds continue to take effect, but something feels off. My eyes are heavier, my limbs like lead. The pills I take to sleep are usually more subtle than this. Right now, it feels as if my world is shifting.

I close my eyes and let sleep take me. But even in sleep, I dream of dark alleys, rain, footsteps... and a deep voice calling my real name.

Anissa Laurent.

No one has called me *that* in ages.

Anissa.

I crawl into bed and sleep like the dead.

The blaring ring of my phone jolts me awake. My head pounds, and the air smells... off. For a moment, I startle. I sniff the air like a damn dog.

Has someone been in here?

I blink hard, and for a split second, I swear I see a shadow moving across the room.

"Who's there?" I yell into the darkness. But when I blink again, nothing's there.

Shaking my head, I try to clear the fog as the phone rings on and on. I startle awake when I recognize the ringtone.

It's The Undertaker's. If I miss this...

My heart races.

I grab the phone and stab at the screen. I'm sick with nausea, thinking I'm too late.

"Hello?" My tongue feels too thick.

A pause before he says in a low, calm voice that still chills me to the bone. "That was a close one, lass." The unmistakable voice of The Undertaker—Keenan McCarthy's eldest son. I shiver and squeeze my eyes shut, breathing a sigh of relief. If I'd missed a call from *him*...

"Yeah, well, your guy had me at the pub until two a.m., and I was finally sleeping." I feign nonchalance, but my hands are shaking.

"I heard about that," he says. "But you're needed, lass. We have an urgent job at the wharf. I need you there in three hours. Can you do it?"

On the phone, he makes it sound like a request, but I know the truth. If I don't go, they'll drop me. No more protection. I'll be exposed. If I refuse the job, I'll have to run.

Again.

"What's the job?" I pinch the bridge of my nose, willing the ache in my skull to stop. I never get headaches. What the hell?

My gaze snaps to the corner of the room—another shadow in my peripheral vision. But when I look again, there's nothing.

What the fuck is wrong with me?

He fills me in. I nod, yawning into the speaker.

"I'll be there."

"Wear the blonde," he says.

"What the fuck—does one of your men have a blonde kink?"

I don't take direct orders from them.

"Is that a problem?" he asks in that calm way of his that strikes fear in the most hardened of criminals. "Let's just say you might have been sighted last night. I want to throw them off. And honestly, luv, you know better than to question me. I'll see you in three hours. More accurately, two hours and forty-eight minutes."

The line goes dead.

I set a timer on my phone, punch my pillow, and slam my head back down. I'm so fucking tired.

It feels like minutes later when the alarm blares again. "My god. I'm taking a vacation, and you guys are paying for it," I mumble into the void. Thankfully, when I open my eyes this time, the shadows are gone.

What the hell happened to me? I had the craziest, most vivid dreams. I feel worse now than before I fell asleep.

I stumble toward the dresser and open the drawer. I freeze, my hand hovering mid-air.

This is *not* how I fold my clothes. I'm fastidious, always on the go, so I've learned to fold my clothing into neat little packages arranged in a vertical row in my drawer. I fold them that way so I can pack a bag in a matter of seconds. These are *horizontal* and all out of place. Neat, yes, but not the way I left them.

I lick my lips and turn around to face my room.

"Who's there?" I yell into the darkness. But just as before, there's no response.

Someone was in here. I know it. I take a slow, careful breath, my fingers curling into fists by my sides. I didn't flee the controlled, miserable existence I had in Moscow and the threat of servitude to the Bratva only to trade for another kind. *No.*

I keep my heartbeat steady, my gaze focused. I've trained myself to stay calm under pressure.

I exhale slowly, forcing myself to think. The Irish? No. They need me. They keep me on a tight leash, but they don't play these kinds of games. If they wanted me dead for whatever reason, I'd already be floating in the Liffey.

Cillian isn't a man of subtlety. If he wanted me under his thumb, he'd drag me there kicking and screaming. No, this feels like someone else entirely.

Who else could it be? A random break-in? Unlikely. The exits are too well-guarded.

I have to think this through. I'm the one who sees the details no one else sees. I'm the one skilled at crafting new realities. I erase identities. I disappear when I need to.

But this...

A ghost from my past?

My father's gone, and even if he were here, this wasn't his style.

The Irish?

Nah. They need me. I shake my head and walk through my apartment. I've only been here a few weeks, but I set it up the same everywhere I go.

The living room seems fine, though I wonder if I left those books I was reading on the nightstand or the coffee table? I shake my head and move to the little kitchenette. I open the refrigerator and stare. Looks normal.

I *am* losing my mind. There's nothing to see here.

I hit play on the playlist on my phone for some background noise while I go to get ready. I go to the bathroom, when suddenly, my playlist switches from my usual bedtime songs to something... Russian?

Is that a Russian *lullaby*?

I grab my phone.

What the fuck?

I didn't add this song to my playlist.

This doesn't make any sense. *Did someone fuck with my playlist?* Playlists glitch... right?

God, I'm panicking over literally nothing.

No one's coming in here to stalk me, change out my towel, and mess with my playlist. I'm not that important. I'm overtired, overworked, and probably need a drink—maybe I should find some random stranger in a pub, give him a fake name, have a good time for myself, and get this out of my fucking system.

Wear the blonde.

I have to get ready. But when I stumble to the closet and sift through everything, my blonde wig is gone. I yank open a drawer with my props and nestled there in front of me are small boxes of white and pink. I stare.

Are those... *pregnancy tests* next to my pink opal?

What the actual fuck?

Now I'm wide awake, glaring into the closet.

Someone was here.

Last night, I convinced myself I imagined it. But I know.

I do *not* lose disguises.

I do not put my clothes in the drawer *like that*.

Oh, you bold little fucker. You want to play with me? You have no idea who you're fucking around with.

I do not run from shadows. I fuck them up and bury what's left.

I turn and face the room as if my phantom stalker can see and hear me. I give the room the middle finger.

"I am going to find out who you are, and when I do, I'm not going to just kill you. I'm going to erase your entire existence from this planet and make an art project out of your bones. So *fuck you.*"

Of course there's no response.

I glance at the window, my instincts humming. Really, the irony is rich.

I'm not the one who vanished this time.

Someone has found me. And they're making damn sure I know it.

CHAPTER 3

MATVEI

She's catching on. But not fast enough. She's not scared enough.

Not yet.

Good girl.

Right where she belongs. In my sights. Under my control.

I look forward to when she is, but for now, I'm enjoying keeping her off-balance.

It's been twenty-three days.

Twenty-three days since I left Moscow and came to Dublin. Seven days left before Rafail will hold a meeting with the other men invited to form the coalition.

If the alliance is officially formed as planned, Anissa's shit out of luck. If the Irish agree to the terms, she might become a bargaining chip or be eliminated to tie up loose ends. They might not need her anymore.

I don't just want to take her. I have to beat them to it before someone else decides her fate.

I've been watching her. She's made it laughably easy.

McCarthy's son called her to do a job by the wharf, and I knew she suspected I was there. I saw her fear when she stared at the misplaced towel. The way she looked at the toothpaste with curiosity. How she sat up in bed and stared at her playlist.

I heard her pathetic little threat. Cute.

I don't need to barge in and force her hand. A little psychological manipulation will go a long, long way.

I know her weaknesses. I know what she likes. I know she values autonomy and a challenge, and she's skilled as fuck with forgery and speaks several languages fluently.

She thrives on pizza and diet soda like a fucking teenager. I know she gets herself off to filthy, kinky porn.

I know she betrayed my family.

Anissa's father arranged for her marriage to Rafail. She jilted him at the *altar* on their wedding day. And now she's in league with the Irish.

This isn't just about revenge but loyalty, proof of my devotion to my family. This is personal.

Her betrayal stained my family's honor, and I'll make an example of her.

I stare at the footage I have of her on my phone. It was almost a stroke of luck that I found her. I'd been looking with no luck since she escaped. The Irish covered her tracks well, and I had no reason to suspect them. But she grew too complacent with her Irish protectors. Little does she know her time with them has come to an end.

Anissa dresses in wigs, changes the color of her eyes with contacts, and tries to cover up the little birthmark above her lip—her one identifying mark.

I was the one who put her portfolio together for Rafail when they were engaged. I was the one who handed it to my brother Gleb, who handled the rest, but I saw every detail of who she was before she went incognito.

And I was the one who wouldn't let her betrayal lie. Not after what my brother did. Not after what I owe to the Kopolovs.

So one night, as I was poring over video footage involving the Irish, I saw the curvy figure of a woman who looked a bit familiar. I zoomed in and didn't recognize her, but when she turned her head, moonlight glinted on her lip. And I knew exactly who she was.

I pull my knit cap down over my brows and walk with my head lowered, going up to the apartment I'm in directly next to hers. It was easy to... *persuade* the people who lived there that they needed to leave... fast. It was child's play, switching out the glass behind her wall mirror and making it a two-way. Thirty minutes later, I had what I needed. I get a bird's-eye view.

I've left her alone for a few days on purpose. I want her to question herself, to wonder if she imagined it all. I don't need to force the issue. Not yet. Watching her unravel? *That's foreplay.*

I lie back on my bed, staring at her as she moves about her apartment wearing nothing but a pair of tight panties and a tank. Christ, she's fucking hot, all curves and dimples.

I stroke my cock through my jeans, imagining those lips wrapped around me, her thighs shaking as I take my time marking every fucking inch of her. I'll make her beg—not just for mercy—for *me*. Her belly swollen with my child flashes through my mind, and I fuck my fist harder, needing it—needing to know no other man will ever touch her again, because she's already carrying my blood.

I spent weeks here in Dublin before our big meeting, blending into the background, leaning into my natural skills to study my prey. I move through the city's streets without attracting attention. It's easy in a place like this, teeming with people and businesses, tourists and families. Head down. Don't make small talk. I order groceries and avoid the shops, and I don't cause a disturbance anywhere I go. I'm a model citizen. If anyone ever suspected who I really am, my elderly landlord would say with such confidence, "But he was such a decent bloke."

It's ridiculously easy to pretend to be normal and sane.

She walks through her apartment, blissfully unaware she's being watched—straightens a throw pillow, wipes down a counter. I lose sight of her for a minute when she heads to the kitchen, but she comes back later with a pint of chocolate ice cream, sits on the sofa, and picks up her phone, mindlessly scooping large bites of ice cream. When a drop falls on her lip, her tongue quickly laps it up.

Fuck. I'm hard as fuck watching her.

I unzip my pants and stroke my dick, mesmerized as she flicks through her phone until she settles on something, leans back, and watches. It's hard to see her from this angle.

I lift the scarf I stole from her, along with the blonde wig, a bar of soap, and one of her tops. I inhale her fragrance—light and almost spicy, with a citrus edge. I've seen her turning her apartment upside down, looking for them, but after a few days of rest, she's given up.

If she had any idea how close I am to her while she's right here, under my nose, walking free under the protection of the Irish...

She's grown complacent with them. Why?

Maybe she thinks the Irish are just regular clients like anyone else. Maybe she doesn't know what they're fully capable of.

That's what gnaws at me. She's too at ease, moving through their world like she belongs. But there's something else—something that twists in my gut.

None of them touch her. Ever. And they're like us—marrying age and in need of wives. Keenan McCarthy's carried on the family tradition of arranged marriages.

I've watched her interact with them. The men defer to her. They speak to her, joke with her, but they don't get too close. Not like they would with a woman they claim as their own. Not like they would if she belonged to one of them.

Good. Killing one of them would fuck that alliance to hell.

She shifts on the couch, stretching out, then curling her bare legs beneath her. Then, out of nowhere, I see it—something I wasn't expecting.

She laughs. Not a forced laugh or the clipped kind you give when you're keeping up appearances. No. A real one. Her head tilts back, her lips part, and the sound is soft. Unguarded. *Real*. I can't remember the last time I heard someone laugh with such abandon, with such wonder and unreserved humor.

Does she laugh like that with the Irish? Jealousy claws at me and my chest tightens. For weeks, I've observed her—careful, calculating, always watching her back. But right now, she looks... *free*.

It quickly evaporates, but a strange part of me wants to hold onto it, gather it in my hands, and tuck it safely into a jar where I could store it out of reach. But just as soon as it comes, it's gone.

She shakes her head, still grinning at whatever amused her on her phone before she does something that fucking destroys me.

Reaching for a fluffy, blush-colored blanket folded at the foot of the couch, she shakes it open and pulls it over herself. I watch as she nuzzles it like she's seeking comfort. Like she's safe.

She rocks herself, and her eyes close shut. I wonder if she's playing music when I see her swaying slightly. She isn't on guard but... vulnerable.

For a split second, a voice in the back of my mind whispers

—what if she *isn't* what they say? What if she isn't our enemy? What if—

No. I crush the thought as quickly as it comes. The evidence is right in front of my face. She's a liar. And now she's mine.

My cock throbs, and my jaw clenches. Safe is a fucking illusion.

She doesn't *get* to feel safe. Not when she fucked over my family and would do it again.

Not when she belongs to me.

I tighten my grip around my cock, dragging my fist slow and deliberate, my breath coming harder. I imagine her beneath me, frantic, her breathing desperate as she begs for me. My free hand fists the end of the scarf, pressing it to my face to inhale her scent like an addict. It's soft between my fingers, softer than I expected. I imagine it still holds her warmth, and I bury my face in it, fisting it tighter. I jerk my cock, groaning against the fabric like a fucking animal.

She should be mine. She should be curled up in my bed, under *my* sheets... under *me*. Not playing house with the goddamn fucking Irish.

I watch as she stretches again, takes another bite, and settles under the blanket. She shifts beneath it, burrowing deeper, and I shift, too, my grip tightening. She licks the last of the ice cream off her spoon, and my fist strokes harder. She licks, and I stroke.

Lick.

Stroke.

Lick.

Stroke.

It's obscene the way we move together, and she has no idea I'm even here. She sighs and bites her lip.

If she knew what she was doing to me, would she slow her tongue? Or would she lick faster, tease me?

I come so damn hard, biting her scarf between my teeth like it's a fucking bit. I imagine marking her.

She has no fucking idea who I am.

But she will.

She will.

Her guard is slipping.

It's time.

She's mine.

CHAPTER 4

ANISSA

I THOUGHT MAYBE I'd been imagining things, but the dream is always the same.

I fall asleep, and the room is quiet. Empty. But there's breathing—low, measured, too close.

I jolt awake, my pulse hammering too fast. But there's always silence. No movement. No shadow. Nothing out of place except the weight pressing down on my chest.

So I finally cave and call in a favor with the Irish to do a sweep of my apartment.

They must think I'm crazy because no one's here. Just me.

Then why do I hear someone *breathing*?

I tell myself it's just stress, just my mind fucking with me. But I haven't forgotten the little things out of place.

Yes, that was a couple of weeks ago.

Yes, there was no sign of forced entry.

Yes, I have no verifiable proof.

But my instinct knows better.

I've made enemies in my line of work, but I thought I was covered under the Irish's protection.

Now I'm not so sure.

I wake from another night of bad dreams, throw the covers off, and swing my legs over the edge of the bed. My muscles ache, and the effects of too little sleep for too long are wearing on me.

I need to figure out why I'm having these nightmares and why I'm freaking out. I need to get out of this apartment. I can't shake the feeling that someone's been here.

I stand and stretch.

And then I see it.

My stomach drops to the floor.

The far wall—the one I was facing. The one just feet away from where I slept.

Marked.

Slashed across the drywall in thick, dripping red is a single word:

MINE.

A scream locks in my throat.

I stumble back, my calves hitting the bed frame, sending me crashing down.

Who would do this?

I scramble to my feet, my legs shaking, and rush to the front door.

No. I have to grab something to wear before I call them.

"You motherfucking asshole," I seethe at my empty apartment. "When I find out, I'll fucking *kill* you."

Cillian answers.

"Someone's been in my apartment."

"Right now?" he asks, his voice tight and angry. "Any signs of entry?"

"No." My voice shakes. "No signs of entry, but someone painted on the wall."

"I'll be right there."

It takes him fifteen minutes to get here. I'm freezing, trembling in my coat, when he finally pulls up. I walk down the stairs.

"I wanted to tell you guys—little things have been out of place." I fill him in on all the details.

"You look like shite," he snarls. "Like you haven't slept. You need sleep, lass."

How do I tell him I haven't been sleeping because when I fall asleep, I hear someone *breathing*?

I can't. He'll think I'm crazy, and I need their gig.

He takes the stairs two at a time, and I trot in his wake. It doesn't bring me the assurance I hoped it would—this large, muscled man coming to help me.

He's here because he has to be.

Not because he wants to be.

He opens the door and pushes it open.

"Where is it?" he asks.

I point a trembling finger toward my room.

"Where?"

Where? What is he talking about? Isn't it obvious?

I follow him in, pointing at the wall that's now—

Blank.

Clean.

Not a trace on the wall.

What the actual fuck?

"It was right there," I say, and I feel like one of those crazy heroines in a movie where someone's playing a prank on her.

He turns and cocks his head to the side.

"How do you feel? All right?" He watches me carefully. "My boss wanted to bring you in today. Had another job for you. Maybe you need a little time off."

I can tell he's trying to be nice, but questioning my ability to do my job is not the way.

"I'm fine," I tell him, shaking my head.

"You said you saw paint on the wall?"

"Yes."

He shrugs a big shoulder. "What did it say?"

I swallow hard before answering.

"Mine."

His eyebrows shoot up, and he purses his lips.

"Well, it wasn't one of us," he says quickly.

Too quickly.

It hurts.

"I know."

"Listen, take a little time off. Get out of Dodge for a while, yeah? We weren't meeting this weekend anyway."

I nod. That actually sounds like a good idea. When things are going haywire, I don't like staying in one place too long. I never did.

The cool thing about Dublin is how easy it is to leave. In six hours, I could be in America, Iceland, Greenland, or Paris.

"Good idea."

He gives me a brotherly pat on the shoulder.

"That's a lass. Go take care of yourself. We'll have work for you when you come back."

Then he's gone.

And I'm alone in my apartment. Back with my crazy thoughts and fucking stalker.

I snatch my phone off the nightstand. I need to get to the airport and book a flight.

Paris is quick and easy. Too many tourists. No one will suspect I'm there. And it's fun to get dressed up.

I can do this.

I need cash. Once I get a ticket, I'll have a way out.

I quickly pack my bag, but when I find my blonde wig hanging exactly where I thought I left it, I hesitate.

Maybe he's right.

Maybe I have gone bonkers.

I eye the prescription bottle sitting next to my bed, then shove it into the bottom of my bag.

Cash is the easiest way to move. I have a small stash in my safe, and I'll take that with me.

I open the safe.

It's empty.

No.

Impossible.

I have to get out of here.

I grab my purse, shove my hand inside for the ATM card, and walk downstairs. Right across from the little convenience store is an ATM.

I need a way out.

I swipe my card.

Red. *DECLINED*.

I try again. I refuse to believe this is happening.

DECLINED.

I never used it. Never even touched it.

I open the banking app, and a notification flashes in red: *Your account has been flagged for fraudulent activity.*

I go still as a cold sweat prickles over my skin.

My breath comes too fast.

Every option I had…

Gone.

I have no cash.

I lift my chin and make a decision. I have a second burner phone, and I am not helpless.

I try a different site, something untraceable, something that will let me buy a ticket now, but the damn page won't load.

A text pings through.

I don't want to read it, but I have to, *god.*

What if it's O'Rourke or one of his men?

An unknown number.

> **Unknown**
> Mine.

My phone nearly slips through my fingers.

I need a cab, a train—something.

A car slows at the curb, and a driver leans out the window.

"Need a ride?"

I can't see who it is in the car, but nothing about this is familiar.

I tell myself I'm imagining ghosts everywhere I go.

"Yes, I need a ride. Thank you."

The man's wrist rests against the steering wheel.

"Come in. It's open," he says.

He doesn't have an Irish accent.

My stomach lurches.

"Well? Are you coming in?"

He leans over, and I swear I see something Russian tattooed on his hand.

"I-I forgot something," I mumble, forcing a smile.

I turn, walking fast, and duck into the first dark alley I see.

Streetlights flicker overhead.

The pavement feels too quiet.

Everything feels wrong.

I try to shake myself to see if I'm asleep or awake, but I'm definitely awake.

My eyes burn too much.

My stomach churns with hunger. When was the last time I ate?

The car idles at the alley's entrance.

What the actual fuck?

I reach into my coat, and my fingers close around a small blade.

I know even now that it's too small, too useless, but maybe if I—

A shadow moves behind me.

I spin, my heart stuttering.

A hand clamps over my mouth.

Beautiful, furious, unforgettable, stormy gray eyes meet mine.

A voice murmurs in my ear.

"Mine."

CHAPTER 5

MATVEI

I'VE GOT HER. Here, with me, so close I can touch the sweet scent of her skin and feel her living pulse under my fingers.

Mine.

She didn't see me coming. I thought she'd be better than that. I understand though. She was terrified. I got under her skin—just like I wanted to.

It's about fucking time.

She fucked over my family.

She ran from my cousin, put us in a state of turmoil, and set us up to be betrayed. And yes, my brother made use of that time. He fucked us over even worse.

But she deserves to be punished.

Waltzing around, traversing the planet like she didn't screw over the biggest Bratva group this side of the Atlantic.

She's a woman who prides herself on always being a step ahead. Always knowing when the noose is tightening.

But lately, she's been slipping.

Big mistake, *solnyshka*.

She barely has time to inhale before her back hits the brick wall, the impact sharp. I pin her there, my forearm braced against her collarbone, my body caging hers in. I have to hold myself back because of how easily I could hurt her.

It's not time yet.

Her gasp is soft, startled—but it doesn't last.

No.

My girl's a fighter.

I feel the moment the shock wears off, when instinct takes over, and she lashes out. Long red fingernails rake across my forearm, sharp enough to draw blood.

A knee jerks up, aiming between my legs, but I twist just in time, deflecting. My dick's instantly hard when I imagine her pinned under me, fighting, clawing, biting.

Christ.

Her teeth flash, incisors sharp and bared at me.

She swings at my face next.

Beautiful.

Just what I like.

She's like a captured little bird, fluttering her wings. I'd be disappointed if she didn't fight back.

I catch her wrist midair and twist. Not enough to break, just enough to remind her she's not getting away.

I don't want to break her bones.

No.

It won't be *that* type of punishment. Not for my girl.

She's breathing hard, her chest heaving against mine, and I feel it—the feral spark between us.

She's terrified. Furious. But goddamn, she likes a fight. Just like me. I wonder if she'll fight when I take her bare, when I empty myself inside her and fill her, when I give her no choice but to carry my child.

"So vicious," I murmur, dragging a knuckle down the line of her jaw.

She stares at me, her eyes flashing with fury, but I don't miss the way her body responds.

"You're quite the little masochist, aren't you?"

I've been waiting for this, solnyshka.

Waiting to see if she'd run, beg for mercy, or bare her teeth. I'm so proud.

"Good girl."

She spits in my face. "Go to fucking hell."

I laugh, low and dark, swiping my face clean.

"Beautiful, don't you know that's where I came from? I'm here to take you back with me."

She thrashes, trying to shove me off, but it's useless.

I tighten my grip with one hand and let her feel the weight of my control. I want her to know that what's coming is inevitable.

I want her afraid.

I see the moment it sinks in—when the cold realization dawns in her sharp blue eyes.

She isn't getting away.

And no one is coming to stop me.

"You're a fucking predator," she spits. "Are you going to rape me? Is that the plan? Then why didn't you just come into my apartment? Why play all the fucking games? It was *you*, wasn't it?"

"What fucking games? What did I do?"

I want to know. If anyone else got close to her or stepped foot in her apartment, I'd have to hunt them down and make them pay. Anissa belongs to *me*.

"Moved my things. Made breathing noises. Painted *mine* like a fucking psycho on my wall, then got rid of it before I could prove anything."

Good. Yeah, that was all me.

"Why the games?" she snarls. Some women are beautiful when they're angry. She's a fucking goddess. "Why didn't you just barge in and take what you want? Hmm? You like stolen pussy?"

I lean in close, my mouth at her ear. "That's not how I play, beautiful. Make no mistake—I *will* fuck you. But not until you beg me."

"So *you're* the one who's fucking psycho instead of me," she seethes.

I run my tongue along the curve of her jawline. My dick aches. I feel half vampire, ready to suck her blood.

"Maybe, sweetheart, we're a matched pair."

She screams and tries to knee me, but I deflect easily. I love the way she fights me. Hmm. That won't do.

So I shift my grip, grabbing her hair. It feels so fucking good. The number of times I've jerked off imagining her silky hair fisted in my palm, the look of pain on her face and parted lips...

I yank her head back. The impact against the wall makes her wince, but I force her to meet my gaze.

"I've been watching you for weeks. Waiting for you to slip. And now?" I lean in, letting my lips ghost over her ear. "I have what's mine."

She growls, and I feel her coiling up for one last strike. My god, she's feral.

I lick my lips.

I have to end it too soon.

I hold her against the wall with one arm.

"When I tell the McCarthys—" she starts.

"They're not coming to save you," I whisper in her ear. "They don't have any use for you anymore. Why do you think I waited until they were done with you? I've taken away every single block between you and me."

Her eyes widen, and she shakes her head, momentarily taken off guard.

"Who are you?"

I give her a patronizing slap to the ass. I relish the sting of pain in my palm and imagine how much better it will be when she's naked, over my knee. "You know who I am," I whisper. "You know exactly why I'm here. You're a smart girl, aren't you? Sadly, playtime's over. For now."

The needle's in my hand before she can react.

The sharp gasp she releases when it bites into her neck makes my dick hard.

She feels it.

The second the drug hits her system, her struggles weaken. I wrap my hand around the back of her neck, yank her mouth to mine, and kiss her. Hard. Claiming. My tongue touches hers, and her eyes flare with drugged shock.

I've had this drug particularly formulated to work with the pills she's been taking under the guise of sleeping meds.

Her body betrays her instantly.

Her muscles lock, and the fight bleeds out of her.

Our lips are still connected.

She claws weakly at my shirt as we break apart, her voice laced with venom as she begs me to stop.

"Don't," she cries, her bravado slipping from her face. "Please."

"Good girl. There we go." I catch her before she slumps fully to the ground. Holding her against me feels easy. Natural.

Her body fits against mine.

Made for my arms.

It almost makes me feel soft toward her.

"You've been mine for a while, *solnyshka*." I brush my lips against her temple, then her ear. "Your cunt. Your womb. Your whole fucking body was meant to be mine. And now, you'll pay for what you've done."

I carry her nestled in my arms like a baby to where the car waits, idling at the curb. I jerk my head at the driver, and he opens the door.

I slide her inside, tuck a blanket around her, and sit next to her.

Time to take my girl home with me.

CHAPTER 6

ANISSA

Sleep. Blissful, deep sleep. Until it isn't anymore.

I open one eye, groggy. My head hurts and feels too big for my body.

I wake up slowly. The first thing I register is the cold bite of metal on my wrists. Tight.

The second is a smell that's all too familiar—one that's been in my apartment.

Leather. Whiskey. Pine.

My heart beats too fast as memory rushes back. *Him.*

I wasn't imagining things. I wasn't hallucinating. Lovely. My life's become one long episode of a freaky reality TV psycho-thriller.

I did have a stalker—one who had me terrified and running for my life. My eyes snap open.

Where am I? It's dark, and I'm... in a cage. *A cage.*

Oh my fucking god.

The space is dimly lit, one flickering ivory bulb barely cutting through the shadows, the walls bare. If there are windows, they're sealed tight and covered.

It feels like the ground beneath me is swaying. Am I... moving?

Where the hell am I?

Am I in a truck? A ship?

I don't know.

But I do know one thing—

This isn't some damp basement. No duct tape around my wrists. *I'm in a fucking cage.*

I'm lying on a sleeping mat, with sheets beneath me and a heavy blanket over me, but it doesn't change where I am—

A prison.

The very thing I've spent my entire adult life trying to escape. Bile rises in the back of my throat along with my fury, but I have to stay focused.

Calm.

My body aches.

The back of my head throbs.

I close my eyes, trying to remember what happened.

My head hit a concrete wall. My wrists are sore, trapped in heavy-duty cuffs. I'm no stranger to kink—I've played around with handcuffs in my past—but these? These are the real deal. When I tug experimentally, they don't budge.

I open my mouth, licking dry lips.

At least I'm not gagged.

And then I hear it—

That same heavy, deep breathing that woke me in my apartment.

My voice is hoarse. "Who's there? Why did I hear you in my apartment? Why are you doing this to me?" I don't sound as angry as I feel. I could spit venom right now.

There's a shift in the shadows. My breathing stills.

He's here.

He's sitting on the outside of the cage, arms crossed over the sheer mass of him, broad and inked and huge. His hair's dark, unruly, and his eyes—those *fucking* eyes—blue-streaked gray, like fire and ash.

I hate the way my stomach clenches when he stares at me as if he... as if he *knows* me. Calculating. Assessing. Like I'm a problem that needs to be *handled*.

The cut of his jaw is too sharp, his features unforgivingly violent and raw, his mouth cruel.

A thick neck covered in ink that snakes down his chest and over his shoulders, the type of shoulders built for hard work and heavy lifting.

He leans forward, his body massive. Broad-shouldered, with a quiet intensity radiating from every inch of him.

But it's the way he watches me that makes my skin crawl and burn at the same time. Like he already *owns* me. Like the chase is over, and he already knows exactly how this ends.

He has ten minutes, give or take, before I make him regret not kidnapping literally *any* other woman but me.

I should hate him. *I do*... I do hate him. But somewhere, under the hate, is something worse. Dangerous.

Something that feels like... fascination.

I stare before I ask again, "Who are you?" I pretend it takes all my energy to say this, like I'm more drugged than I am. I have to play into this if I'm going to escape, and I *am* going to fucking escape.

No one cages Anissa Laurent and lives to tell about it.

He doesn't answer. Just watches me, taking up space in a worn leather chair, legs spread, one arm draped lazily over the armrest—like he has all the time in the world. Like he's about to crack open a beer and watch a game.

My stomach tightens.

His voice is low, rough, and full of dark amusement. "Finally awake? Makes sense; I guess you were sleep-deprived."

I glare at him. The weight of his gaze bears down on me. I wait, but he doesn't move. Doesn't snarl. Doesn't gloat or threaten.

Just watches. Unmoving. Patient. Like a wolf who's already sunk its teeth in but enjoys the struggle too much to end it yet.

This hunt is over.

That's what he thinks.

I force my breathing to steady. Panic is useless. I've been here before. I had to wait, bide my time until I could run.

I need information. A plan. My eyes flick to the corner of the room, searching.

He chuckles, low and lazy. I shiver. "Looking for an exit, little witch, so you can cast your spell?"

I roll my eyes at him. "Cute."

His eyes narrow, even as he lets loose another chuckle that curls around my spine.

"Go to hell," I snarl.

"Sweetheart," he drawls, "I already told you." A slow smile spreads across his face. "That's where I came from. Do you want me to take you along with me?"

Right. I try to hide the shiver that rolls through me.

I don't know who he is. I don't know why I'm here. But I will not break.

I will not let him win. I *will* find a way out.

I can't fucking wait. Finally, a chance to do what I do best, but to save my own damn hide.

Little does he know he's in for the fight of his life.

He tilts his head, watching me as if he can hear my resolve, before he stands.

Of *course* he's tall. Legs like tree trunks. Hands as big as fucking dinner plates. None of that lankiness I've seen from other men. A full-grown man where others are boys.

"Let's get one thing straight, little witch." His voice is low, soft—almost gentle. "There's no hiding anymore. No more running. Nowhere else for you to go. No one to save you."

Blah, blah, fucking blah. It's what they all say. I roll my eyes and lift my chin in defiance, even as he looms over me. If I had a dollar for every mobster who thought monologuing in chest-beating grunts made him sexy or powerful, I'd be retiring in Hawaii by now.

I shrug. "Meh. You don't know that."

Unless my fairy godmother moonlights as a grifter.

I'm bluffing though. The people who would have saved me? They'd be here by now. I'm not so special that anyone would go out of their way to find me.

Stepping closer, he reaches through the bars. His finger brushes the cuff, slow and deliberate. The metal is cold, but his touch burns. My breath catches before I can stop it.

He notices. His gaze flicks to mine, unreadable. "I know everything about you, Anissa." My name drips from his lips like a taunt. "Every alias. Every safe house. Every escape plan."

Whatever. That's what *he* thinks.

Gold glints on his ears. Little hoops. Why is that so damn sexy on a man like him? My eyes drift over the ink on his arms—Bratva, without question. The markings tell me rank and allegiance. High-level, but not a boss. He takes orders, but he's not a pawn. More dangerous than either. He's the kind of man they trust to make people disappear. To make sure they *stay* gone.

I can only assume my worst fear—the very reason I made a deal with the Irish in the first place—has finally come true. The Kopolov family has come to collect what's owed.

But he isn't one of the Kopolov brothers or the man I left at the altar. I don't recognize him.

I've heard strange rumors about the man I was supposed to marry. Rafail Kopolov is the Kopolov family *pakhan*. I'm told he's now married, which is a relief for *me* because I figured he'd be less inclined to come chase me. The McCarthys never shared details with me, and I didn't want them because I figured the less I spoke of the Kopolovs, the better.

For a while, I thought Rafail wasn't hunting me anymore. But a part of me always knew the reprieve wouldn't last. Eventually, they would come. Not to reclaim me but to punish me.

But... this man isn't Rafail.

He's younger, for one. Bigger, heavier.

I stifle a sigh and get myself together.

Okay, alright.

I know what to do here—if you're out of your element, in danger, and in desperate need of more information and an escape route.

Rule number one: Play dumb.

"I have no idea who you are," I lie.

He tips his head to the side. "You're a pretty convincing liar. What's your pain level?"

Rule number two: Try to gain sympathy for the purpose of disarming.

"It's alright, though I think you gave me a... what do you call it..."—I feign a lack of focus to lean into the *drugged-up as fuck skit*—"concussion."

He crouches in front of the metal bars.

I pretend my pulse doesn't race.

"Did you think I was such a danger to you that you felt it necessary to put me in a cage like an animal? Frankly, I'm honored."

"No, not at all. I'm just a kinky motherfucker and wanted to see what you'd look like behind bars." He gives me a mirthless smile and a wink that sends my heartbeat between my thighs. "And no one can hear you scream in here."

Kinky motherfucker.

Why do I have the literal *worst* taste in men? *Why?*

"Locking me up doesn't make you more powerful."

His lips twitch, and his voice lowers. Calm. Deep. "Of course not. I don't need bars for that."

Heat rises in my cheeks. I wasn't prepared for that answer. "So, are you going to tell me who you are, or do I have to guess?"

"You're a smart girl."

Rule number three: Hold your ground.

I shake my head. "I'm not a girl, you condescending prick."

He drags his eyes down the length of my body, and for the first time, I look down at myself. The shirt I was wearing is ragged, the frayed edges baring my breasts. It's risen up, showing my torso, and the leggings I'm wearing are still taut around my legs and ass.

"My mistake; you're definitely not a girl."

"Glad we cleared that up unless you need a better flash of my tits, or are you good, big guy?"

His look grows feral. I can feel his low growl from here, and I'd be lying if I said it didn't affect me.

I swallow hard. I play a good game, but I'm human. A sex-deprived, twisted, also kinky, self-assured human.

I was a lot more afraid when I didn't know who was after me, and I feared that my mind was playing tricks on me. Now that I know I have been kidnapped and that I wasn't fucking it all up in my mind, I'm actually a little relieved.

I'm not staying here. If he were going to put a bullet through my skull, he already would have. No... Instead, he's put me in this fucking cage, drugged me, and is taking me to god knows where.

Yes, but I was *born* for this moment. I know exactly how to slip out of somebody's grip. I know exactly how to get away. I know how to cut a man's balls off, shove them down his throat, and then choke him out in his sleep. And this asshole has actually given me a reason to do that.

Yay me.

I didn't escape the clutches of my father and his fucking asshole minions—the worst, most painful experience of my life—or marriage to the Kopolovs and danger with the Irish, only to end up dragged back like a naughty little girl who ran away from home.

Nope. Not me.

So I'll bide my time, lean into this "I'm so drugged" shtick, and then, at my first opportunity, I'm getting the fuck out of here.

"Hungry?" he asks. Even though he's speaking English, he has a hint of a Russian accent.

"I could use a little water," I say in my most pathetic voice. I add in a little dry cough for the hell of it.

He takes a little bottle from beside him, twists the top off, and sticks it through the bars. But his hands are too damn big. He can't fit through while holding the water bottle. It actually pleases me to see the way he thinks about opening up my cage, as if the second he opens it, I'm going to flee.

I'm obviously hightailing it out of here, but I'm not so dumb to try and take him now. We could be airborne for all I know.

Still, I watch as he slides a key into a metal hook, unfastens it, and warily hands me the bottle.

"Um, my wrists?"

"Nice try. Do the best you can."

Fine then. He wants to play this game? I take the little bottle between my hands and make sure it's sloppy work. I slosh half of it across my torn top. The soaked fabric goes sheer, outlining my full (very nice, if I do say so myself) nipples. Some of the water gets into my mouth, and it does feel good. I wasn't lying; I *am* thirsty. I'm also hungry, but I don't give him the satisfaction. For all I know, he'll poison the food.

Predictably, his gaze drops to the wet T-shirt contest in a cage as he leans in and takes the cuffs out with a grunt. He stares at me but doesn't speak for long minutes while I take my time observing everything I can. He wears a tank top, and the markings on his neck show me a few things. He's not just Bratva but high-ranking Bratva, for one. He spent time in jail for another. But there's no ink to indicate he's an assassin.

"I'm assuming you know the Kopolovs," I say. My tongue is thick, and my voice sounds strange. I close my eyes to make myself look half out of it. He doesn't answer but just watches me. "If you are, then you would know I have a deal with the Irish."

He nods his head almost amiably. "More accurately, you *did*."

My heart thumps. *What?*

"I'm sorry to tell you," he says in a tone that isn't sorry at all, "we've moved in and given the Irish a better deal. They don't need your services anymore."

"But you do?" I snap. This isn't fair. After everything I did for them, they're just going to ditch me?

"Do I have a *use* for you? Yeah, you could say that," he drawls, his voice dripping with amusement.

I don't flinch. He doesn't own me. And the second I get a chance? *I'm gone.*

I'm almost sad I'm going to ditch his sorry ass. Could be fun taking the piss out of a guy like him, and I've been bored for a while. But I did not come this far only to be put back in a *literal* cage.

Asshole.

I'm going to play the long game. He might be motivated, but I suspect he's done what most men have done—underestimated me. And since he obviously thinks he's already caught his prey, it's only a matter of time before I can make my move. Every man has a weakness. *All* of them. And this one, despite his control, is no exception.

A door opens, and someone stands on the other side. I'm momentarily blinded by bright white light. Okay, so we're not flying, then, but in some sort of transport vehicle.

"Matvei."

With a growl, he turns his back to me and snarls at his visitor. Ha! He doesn't want me to know his name.

Matvei. Nope, definitely not one of the Kopolov brothers. I knew their names. But his name is unfamiliar to me. One of their friends? Associates? Hmm.

The Irish never kept me in the loop of what their plans were, and for my own safety, I kept my nose out of details. They gave me a job, and I did it, no questions asked unless I had questions that were directly related to my job.

I watch the way he moves, slow and deliberate, which

makes sense for a guy of his size. Despite Matvei's control, he still has a weakness. But I'll wait.

"I'm a little nauseous," I say in a low whisper. "Can I have something to eat?"

He eyes me suspiciously, definitely expecting that I'm going to play him. Of course I fucking am.

"We'll get something to eat once I get you situated."

"Oh," I say with mock excitement. "Do you have a bigger cage for me? Or am I good enough that I'll get let out of my cage and maybe get a little fresh air? Spread my wings a little bit? Please, sir?"

He now has his eyes on me and doesn't respond. I'm a scrapper, but he's obviously larger than I am, and larger usually means slower. He's the goddamn linebacker for the Bratva, too big to move with any speed, and either way, too damn proud to send someone else after me, or... this is personal.

Incapacitating a man this big takes precision.

I will not get a second chance.

He comes closer to me and bends. I draw in a breath, and I move. A quick jab to the throat, followed by a knee to the groin. I lift the water bottle and smash it against his skull. He stumbles, caught off guard, and he's so big that when I kick his kneecap, he falls hard. He reaches for me with a growl, but I have the key in my hand already.

Stay calm, stay calm, stay calm.

"You little bitch," he says. He almost grabs a fistful of my hair, but I quickly evade his grip and elbow him in the neck before I kick his groin. He could have grabbed me just now, could have manhandled me, but either he's afraid to break me or too surprised by my sudden movements. I take the water, splash it in his face, and when he turns and blinks on instinct, I dive out of the cage. I slam it, turn the key in the lock, and take a moment to gloat at the sight of him in there. He grabs my wrist straight through it. I bite down on his finger until I taste blood. He screams, shouting in Russian, but I shake my head at him. "Did you forget? Nobody can hear you screaming in here."

I smile at him. I've won this battle. I am so fucking out of here.

It was dirty, brutal, but effective. I make my way to the front as he curses at me from behind, yelling.

"Oh, honey. Settle down," I purr.

Sure enough, there's a small latch that allows me to open the door from this holding place to where the driver sits. Outside this door, I see four armed men, but the dumbasses are staring at the entryway to the back, not this way. I have seconds to make a move. Right on the console, I see a faded leather wallet and a gun. I take both, slide out of the driver's seat, and then tuck myself beneath the largest wheel.

I can hear Matvei screaming and swearing from here, and I can't help but chuckle a little to myself. I blink at the bright sun overhead and assess my situation. We're in a gas station. Excellent. To my left, about six feet away, is a large pickup truck with bales of hay. All I have to do is hide there, and I have enough cash to bribe my way out.

I wait until there's a shout behind me, and I make my escape. They're going to look everywhere for me. I'm thankful I'm small and lithe. None of them think to look here. When a truck pulls up beside me, these guys aren't even pretending to be good guys anymore. They're scouring the gas station, looking for me with their weapons drawn.

D'awww. I'm so dangerous.

Dummies.

I shake my head, crawl unseen into the back of the cargo truck, and to my delight, find that it's loaded with junkie snacks for delivery. I open up a bag of cheese puffs, sit in the way back, and happily munch. Two minutes later, the cargo truck is on its way, and so am I, with orange-tipped fingers, stolen cash, and a gun at my side.

CHAPTER 7

Six months later

MATVEI

I SIP MY BEER, not paying attention to my cousins.

"You alright, brother?" Semyon is not one to observe emotions, but he doesn't miss details either. I've been keeping to myself, not talking to anyone.

It's been six fucking months since she slipped through my fingers, leaving me caged like an animal. Six months, while I swore that I would find her, make her pay, and make her pay dearly.

Six months, while I've lost sleep trying to find her, while I've fallen into a dismal routine of work, hunt, lift, sleep. Prowl.

She's still out there. Running. Hiding. Thinking she's safe.

My woman.

She's mine, and she's nowhere to be fucking found.

Rafail shit bricks when he found out she'd escaped. Fun times. He may be happily married and forgiven the *fuck you* she gave him, but he doesn't forgive disloyalty to the Bratva. None of us do.

Her contract with the Irish has long since expired.

At first, I thought she could be anywhere in the world. A woman like her, with her skill set—she's a chameleon. Easily managing to evade capture, she'll become anything she wants to be.

In the past six months, I have watched the members of my Bratva group form their alliance. None of them knew I was after her, but they know why I'm on a vendetta now. Maybe she thinks she's safe out there, running, hiding.

Maybe she gets a thrill out of running. Maybe her kink is the chase.

Maybe mine is, too, as long as it ends up with a capture.

I drag a hand down my face, exhaling as I study the map spread across the worn table in front of me. Red strings, pins, notes scribbled in Russian—my obsession laid bare. Every lead, every sighting, every whisper of her presence documented and analyzed.

I should have found her by now. I should have her on her knees, begging for mercy I have no fucking intention of giving.

But Anissa Laurent is a slippery little ghost.

And the truth is... I miss the whole game.

I looked forward to listening to the little sounds she made in her sleep. Stroking my cock to the image of her licking a spoon dripping with ice cream. It's not the same when it's sheer memory. And that one day, I finally had her in my clutches, her snark and banter...

I want her back.

I *need* her back.

And worst of all, if she isn't with me—if *my* woman isn't with me—that doesn't keep her safe from any other fucking predators out there. Who knows what enemies she's made?

When I lie in bed, I imagine her lying beside me. It's too cold. I don't sleep; I just lie there, remembering the way her breath hitched when I touched her throat, the way her pulse jumped between my fingers. The wicked gleam in her eyes when I said I was a kinky motherfucker.

Even now, I can still smell her, just a hint, nothing too floral, but a soft hint of citrus and spice. My sweet little ghost. My venomous, little, traitorous thief.

I need to find her again. Break her. Crack her open and teach her the consequences of her actions. Cage her in my sheets, wearing nothing but my marks. My teeth in her skin, my hand on her throat, my cum dripping from her hot, sweet cunt, my name on her tongue.

She's not safe out there—not from the Irish, not from the Bratva, and especially not from me. Because I'm not just going to take her back—I'm going to make sure she never even dreams of running again.

I'm the only man who sees her for who she truly is. And I'm

the only one who can destroy her for good... or worship her forever.

My phone buzzes with a text.

> **Aria**
> Hey. I've got something.

I've been working with Polina's sister-in-law Aria Romanova, the best hacker in the damn world. Anissa is slippery as fuck, and I called in every favor I had.

My pulse kicks up. If it's what I think it is...

I tap the speaker. "Finally."

I stand, muscles coiled, barely restraining the anticipation clawing at my spine. "Where?"

"Little village outside of Paris. Forged documents flagged at customs. She's careful, but she fucked up." Aria pauses. "She's too good for something like this. A part of me wonders if she *wants* to be caught. Maybe she's tired of running..."

A slow smile spreads across my face. *Got you, little ghost.* This time, when I get her, I'm not going to play so nice.

"Send me everything you've got."

I get a good cut of my family's wealth being a member of the Bratva, but I've spent thousands tracking her down and paying Aria. I'll take it out of Anissa's ass and enjoy every fucking second.

The call disconnects. I glance at the single photo pinned to the center of the board. Anissa. Smirking. Defiant. The same look she had in her eyes when she locked me in that fucking cage. The cage that I've now moved into my bedroom and decorated with pink fairy lights and luxury bedding. Just waiting for her.

I shake my head, running a thumb over the image. "Hope you had your fun. Enjoy your last little croissant, you stunning little bitch." I shrug on my coat and slip my gun into its holster. "My turn."

Now it's time for me to don a disguise. I can't hide my broad shoulders or my bulk, but I've learned how to blend in when I have to. A different coat. Slight limp. Lowered gaze. Details matter. I tweak them just enough to pass unnoticed.

Lucky for me, the Irish want nothing to do with her anymore. No allegiance. No ties. There's a reason why none of them would touch her romantically. Rumor has it they like their women submissive.

Heh.

I land in Paris at two o'clock in the morning, and I'm going to take my fucking time—just like I did the first time.

This time, instead of sneaking from one place to the next, offering her services, she's actually settled down a little bit. She bartends at a local pub.

Oh, this is too rich.

I'm not going to grab her right away. No. That would be way too fucking easy. Instead, I'll study her. Watch her. I'm going to—

There she is. There's that little birthmark right above her lip that I want to bite. She almost crumbled the last time I had her, all her cleverness unraveling under the weight of my hands. Psychological warfare? She's a natural victim for it.

And I'll do it again.

What's the fun in swallowing your prey whole? Nah. You bat them around a little first. Tear off little pieces. Scrape them with your teeth before you bite. Let them think they've escaped, just to remind them they haven't.

She's my favorite little game.

I'll wait until she's walking home one night, her grocery bag in hand. And this time, I have everything planned... down to the last detail.

I watch her as she goes to work. She looks almost happy. Normal. Like she's moved on.

Even now, after six months of chasing her, my pulse kicks up when I see her, the way that red wig frames her sharp jawline. My fists clench—anger or desire, I can't tell anymore; they're almost one and the same.

I've memorized the way she lifts her chin when challenged, the way she smirks like she knows exactly how to drive me crazy.

She's too fucking smart. Too slippery. And damn if I don't respect that, even as I plan exactly how to make her regret what she did.

She was in trouble before. Now? She has no idea.

She makes me furious. She makes me reckless. And worst of all... she makes me *want*.

The red wig bobs around her shoulders, and my blood boils watching her. She thinks she's free. That she's not going to suffer for what she's done.

But I watch her.

I want her to feel me before she sees me.

I watch her for weeks. I *want* her to think she's free. I want her looking over her shoulder.

Humans are ritualized creatures. Even the most unpredictable tend to walk the same way, buy the same things, and eat the same foods. So it doesn't take long for me to memorize the way she heads home from tending bar, how she doesn't cook for herself but manages to somehow subsist on bread, cheese, and wine and some quirky little foods.

I know what makes her relax—the few occasions she lets her guard down—when she laughs at something, takes a sip of whiskey at the bar in a rare moment of relaxation, how she runs a hand through her hair.

I want to know everything about her, the kinds of things I have to dig beneath the surface to find out.

I want to know what makes her laugh. What makes her cry. I want to know how her eyes look when she comes and what makes her toes curl in bed.

I brush past her in a crowded place, literally rubbing elbows, but never look back. Just enough to make her wonder.

I make a shadow move in an alley when she's coming home from work, making her question her own sanity. But this time, I've already marked her as mine.

I try to listen in on her conversations… but she has none. She has no friends. She doesn't use her real name at work, of course, and spends no time with anyone outside of the bar.

I wonder if she's lonely.

Why do I care?

I walk past her window, over and over, just to make her look. I think she sees me on the third day, but I could be wrong.

I want her. I fucking want this woman.

Then one night, I unlock her door while she's sleeping, and in the morning, when she checks, she does a double take.

Good.

Keep her guessing.

I pick the lock of her apartment and leave a cabinet door open before she comes home. But instead of leaving it vacant, I stock it with her favorite little foods. Pain au chocolat—buttery and flaky, layered with dark chocolate. Gummy bears—she chews on them when she's thinking or watching TV. She picks out the yellow ones and leaves the red. Instant coffee because, despite being in Paris, she's too practical for the whole French press thing. And a tin of sardines in olive oil because she's weird like that.

That night, I'm rewarded with some good old-fashioned cursing. She's on to me. I know she's been looking over her shoulder, and I'm afraid if I don't make my move soon, she'll slip away again, just like she did before.

I watch her from the shadows. Her habits, her routines, her weaknesses—I know them all. And I want her to know by now that I'm watching her. Finally, it's time. This time, she is not getting away from me.

I follow her one night, staying just out of sight, close enough to hear the sound of her breath quickening when she feels me behind her. When she looks, I'm wearing a hat pulled low to cover my eyes and a long coat.

She goes to the bar for work, and I help myself into her apartment. I sit on her bed and run my fingers over her sheets. Inhale her scent. *God*, she's addictive.

I go through her closet, feeling the fabric of her dresses, breathing in her scent. She has a tiny place tucked away where nobody would ever suspect she's here. And I steal things—a half-open jar of pink lipstick, a silky black hair tie, a small pair of ivory panties that easily fit in my pocket. And I watch her.

I watch the way she moves. I note that the only thing she does for fun is watch videos on her phone when she's alone in bed, the same way she did before. She laughs at silly jokes and reads a few books, but lately, she's been agitated. Nervous.

Time to move in.

The second I get there, I send her a message at the bar.

<handwritten note>*You look beautiful tonight. You can change your name, your face, your voice even—but I still love the way you bite your lip when you lie...*

I watch the way her fingers tighten around the paper, but when she looks in my direction, she only sees an empty chair. I'm waiting in the hallway. When it rains, I stand just outside beneath the glow of a streetlamp, knowing she'll look out the window—but she won't see who's there.

I plan on controlling her before I take her.

I'm the one steering her exactly where I want her. This isn't like before, when I went after her and drugged her. No.

This time, I'm going to punish her.

This time, she's not going to get away.

The next night, I watch her from the far end of the bar, nursing whiskey, my eyes locked on her every movement. She's still sharp, cautious, but there's a softness about her now. And then I see it. Some drunk asshole leans over the bar, too close, slurring something in her ear. I know the second it makes her uncomfortable because she stiffens and pulls away—but he grabs her wrist.

And the words I wrote in blood, the ones I texted her, the ones I whispered to her, surge into my mind. I'm half blinded by red-hot fury.

Mine.

I watch as she forces a polite smile as if trying to de-escalate the situation, but he doesn't let go.

I don't think. I move. Before I realize what I'm doing, my hand is locked around the asshole's throat, slamming him against the bar. The glass rattles. Conversations stop. Anissa's eyes widen.

"You've got a problem?" I keep my voice calm, even—but there's no mistaking the threat in it. I press a knife where no one else can see, just below the hollow of his collarbone. He gasps, his hands scrambling at mine, but I don't let go. I want him to feel it, to understand the cost of putting his hands where they have no fucking place.

"Leave now," she says. "Before I have to call the police."

"Why don't you do that, doll?" I tell her. Interpol's got a file on her an inch thick, and I've already paid off locals. I've thought of everything before I came here.

"Let me go," the guy says, smacking at my hands. I pin him down and whisper in his ear.

"Stay the fuck away from her. You touch her again, and I'll slit your fucking throat."

He nods frantically before bolting out of the bar. The room is silent as she watches me, her blue eyes unreadable. I lean in just enough for her to hear.

"You need to be more careful, little ghost."

I hold her gaze. I have every exit monitored, everything I need on my person.

"Close the bar. Send everyone home." I lean in. "Do it now."

CHAPTER 8

ANISSA

I SHOULD BE TERRIFIED, but it isn't like it was before. The last time he came for me, I practically ran from the shadows, waiting for him to make his move.

But this time... I can't even explain it. The moment I saw him at the bar, standing with his bottle of whiskey, I should have felt terror claw up my spine. But instead, something inside me exhaled.

Relief.

As if I needed further proof that I'm fucking losing my mind.

For months, I've been running. Forging new names. Slipping through cracks. Changing disguises and burning bridges before they could even be crossed, and it's exhausting. Always having to look over my shoulder. Never feeling at ease. Never knowing if the next breath is my last—somewhere along the way, it wore me down.

Maybe I got sloppy.

Maybe I did it on purpose.

And now he's here, Matvei Kopolov.

Yeah. I've done my homework.

I outplayed him once before, but he swore he would make me pay.

I've thought of him every fucking night since I escaped. I remember the way he looked. The way it felt under the heat of his intense glare. I remember staring at the marks of ink that showed him to be Bratva.

He looks even more raw now, like he just spent six months subsisting on a diet of pure vengeance. He still has an aura of quiet, controlled rage. But there's something else—I don't know.

I clench my fists.

I *knew* he was here. It wasn't a phantom that stocked my shelves with food.

The bar is still full of people. I could try to slip out the back, but he'll find me.

And I am so tired of running. So fucking tired.

Even if I escaped him, what next?

He'll find me.

I have to play along for now.

I'm done trying to pretend that I won't have to face what I've done.

I've never been weak, and I won't cave now.

Even when I escaped him, I did so on my terms. I don't know what he's going to do with me, but I know this—I'm not getting away a second time.

So I don't fight. Maybe he wants me to. Maybe he wants me to kick and scream or force me into submission. Perhaps he wants me to realize there's no escape.

I know this: He gets off on my fear, so I won't give him the satisfaction. Instead, he just tells me to clear the bar.

Of course he does.

I reason with myself... if he were going to kill me, I'd be dead by now. Instead, he meets my eyes...and winks.

Winks.

"Bar's closed," I say out loud with finality. I try unsuccessfully to hide the tremor in my voice because I know shit all about what he's up to next.

I shut off the taps and fold my bar top—indications that I'm done. "Everyone has to go home for the night."

Some businessman with a briefcase and half a glass of whiskey still in front of him shakes his head. "You don't close till ten," he snarls at me.

"We close when she fucking tells you we do," Matvei snaps. "Get the fuck out of here before I make you."

I stare at him.

I was never free. I was just delaying the inevitable.

But I am not surrendering. I'm not breaking. I'm choosing—to take whatever consequences come, even if he kills me.

"You heard her." Matvei goes over to the door, opens it, and escorts everybody else out. "*Out.*"

"I'll sweep the bathroom," he says in a low growl.

I nod and swallow hard like we have some sort of fucked-up agreement to work together.

God.

I gasp when I spin around and find him right there, so close I can feel the heat of his body next to mine. He grabs my wrists, holding me in place as if waiting for me to struggle—but I won't.

I hold his gaze. "This is where you tell me some kind of bullshit about you taking care of what's yours? How you're going to punish me for what I did? Go ahead, Mr. Cliché. It's your turn. But I promise you're not going to get a chance to break me." I smile and cock my head. "Kinda missed you."

His grip tightens as if in warning. I just smirk at him, but he's got a glint in his eyes that looks familiar. Comfortable.

He's close now. Too close. The air between us is charged with electricity, but I won't flinch. I won't shrink back. That's what he wants—to gain the upper hand, to punish me for escaping him the first time.

But the way he looks at me—his eyes fiery, his grip firm, his nearness making me shiver. Hatred coils between us. But there's something else, too, something I can't put my finger on.

Something darker.

He leans in, his fingers brushing my chin, forcing me to look up at him. "You're more beautiful than I remembered, *solnyshka*."

Sunshine. He calls me sunshine.

Awww.

I smile. "It's because I ran, isn't it? You *are* a kinky motherfucker." I lower my voice and eyelids. "Got a primal kink, big guy?"

He steps closer, the wicked smirk confirmation.

Well, damn.

He *does*.

I can't move. There's nowhere to go when the walls are closing in.

No. *He's* closing in, his presence suffocating. And as the silence stretches between us, it's like he savors it.

"Finders keepers," he croons. "There are no cages to shove me in this time."

"Shame," I say with a shake of my head. "A face like yours really does belong behind bars."

The door slams shut, the heavy lock clicking into place. My stomach twists. The bar's empty—no backup, no witnesses. Just me and my hot, furious, wicked stalker. Matvei.

"Matvei Kopolov," I say by way of greeting, but I quickly stutter to silence when his hands find his belt buckle.

Uh-oh.

It clinks as he leans back against the bar, lazy and predatory, like he has all the time in the world to decide what to do with me—even as his fingers unfasten the buckle and tug the leather through the loops.

My pulse beats too fast in my throat. I've faced killers, survived interrogations, and outwitted men smarter than him—but none of them ever looked at me like this. Like they wanted to ruin me, own me, and devour me all in the same breath.

"I'll give you ten seconds to run," he says softly, eyes glinting.

I shake my head. "I don't want to."

"*Now* you decide to stay? Ha. *Go*. It wasn't a request," he says. "Ten. Nine."

His voice drops deeper. So he wants to chase me first. Chasing me through the streets of Paris wasn't enough? No. I'm not going to play that game. Plus, I know there's nowhere to run in here. It's a stupid fucking bar in Paris— you have to pull down a rope just to get to the basement, and they stock the damn liquor bottles outside in an alley so narrow he couldn't even fit his left arm in it.

"Eight, seven—"

When he gets to three, I decide—what the hell.

Too little, too late. I know I won't get far because—fuck me —I don't want to.

I turn around, and the second my feet move, he says, in a rush of words, all in one breath, "*Three, two, one.*"

Holy shit.

He grabs me by the hair, yanking me forward and tossing me across the bar. My hands go flat on the glossy top, scrabbling for purchase where there is none.

"What's your plan, *solnyshka*?" I taunt, the word twisting my mouth, mocking his affectionate term. "You gonna beat me into submission?"

I feel the slow stretch of his smile across those beautiful lips when I look over my shoulder.

"No, beautiful. I'm going to whip your ass raw for your first punishment. Because you're as fucking kinky as I am, and it's gonna make you wet. Because I don't just want you, Anissa. I own you. I want my cum dripping from your hot, wet, needy cunt."

Oh fuck. Oh *fuck*.

I blow out a breath, dizzy and a little nauseous. I wasn't expecting *that*.

I can hardly hear my own words from the blood pounding in my ears. "You're such a gentleman. Tell me how you really feel."

My hips hit the bar, and I twist, trying to break his grip—but his hand is already in my hair, shoving my face down on the surface. My cheek scrapes against the wood, my breath catching—and I am so fucking wet. Not one goddamn porn scene I've watched in years has made me this wet.

Fuck. *Fuck*.

I can't see him, but I can feel him—his heat pressed close, his breath skimming the back of my neck. That breath I've heard in my dreams, for whatever fucking reason he gave me.

"Let me go," I snarl, but it's half-hearted. Part of the game. I have to push back so he pushes with me. I elbow him and connect with skin—he lets out a surprised little grunt—before the belt loops over my wrists.

"Naughty, naughty," he chides, shaking his head at me.

"Aww. You're not as predictable as I thought. I really thought you'd whip me with that first, with all your big-guy talk of punishment and all."

I'm wet at the very thought. God, I love a fucking belting.

As if answering a prayer, his hand slaps against my skin hard. Welting.

I gasp, hating how wet I already am, how my pulse pounds between my legs.

I feel the loss of his heat at my back and crane my neck to see him bent over the pool table. When he prowls back toward me, he has a long pool stick in his thick hands, his predatory gaze pinning me in place. In one swift move, he snaps the stick in half over his knee. The sound alone makes my stomach drop—and my pussy clench.

Oh no.

He grabs my neck, pushes my face onto the gleaming bar top, and slaps the thin part of the stick across my ass. Even over my clothes, it stings like *hell*.

The second slap lands.

The third.

The thin end of the pool stick whips across my ass, sharp and merciless, and I let out a scream. I try to wriggle away, but he pushes one broad arm across my back and holds me in place, his grip like iron. The next lash whistles through the air before it hits so hard the sting makes me see white. My hips crashing into the bar, a startled yelp escaping my lips.

I hate him. I hate myself even more—because I fucking want this.

"You know you deserve to be punished," he says, his voice dark silk. "You broke a promise. You played games. You thought you could get away with this, didn't you?"

The next strike lands right where my ass meets my thighs. My knees buckle—and my panties are fucking soaked.

"You thought you could get away from me, didn't you?"

"Of course I did," I snap, my voice ragged. "You fucking sadist."

His low, dark chuckle makes my nipples hard. My thighs tremble, my face burns, and I'm desperate for friction between my legs. The need claws at me, tinted with shame.

I should be afraid—but what I'm really afraid of is that he'll tie me to this bar and leave me.

I expect him to stop, to pull back.

"Good girl," he murmurs in my ear, dragging the thicker end of the stick down my spine. He slides it on the bar as he reaches for my leggings and rips them down. "Give me that wet cunt. Give me *my* wet cunt so I can fuck it. Own you. Mark you."

He kicks my legs apart with one booted foot, and the sheer force of it—the casual ownership of it—makes me shudder. I'm scared, I'm shaking, and I've never wanted anything so badly in my fucking life.

He doesn't tease. Doesn't ease me into it. The pool sticks in Paris are thinner than other ones, but still—this thing isn't—is he—*no*.

The glossy, thick end of the pool stick presses against my dripping heat, forcing my body to stretch around the unyielding wood. I gasp, half pain, half pleasure. The wood scrapes just enough to remind me that this isn't gentle. This isn't romantic.

This is punishment.

CHAPTER 9

ANISSA

AND THEY SAY men can't find the G-spot.

Holy *fucking shit*, he's found it, and he's assaulting it with the wooden tip of the pool stick. A spasm of pleasure rushes through me, and my hips are off the bar, my breath strangled in my throat.

"Fucking soaked," he growls, half approving, half angry in my ear. "You act like you hate me, but this fucking greedy little cunt knows who owns it. *Good.*"

I bite my lip to hold back. I don't wanna give him the satisfaction, but the wood inside me's unyielding, pushing me to the edge, pushing me closer to bliss. It feels so fucking good. My cheek presses against the cold wood of the bar as my body stretches around the thickness of the pool stick.

"You wanna come, little witch?" The varnished end of the pool stick throbs inside me.

In.

Out.

In.

Out.

My back arches in my throes. "Little brat's been playing fucking games for weeks, but the second I've got her pinned down, the second I get this greedy little cunt's attention—she's fucking dripping all over my fingers."

Part of me wants to tell him to fuck off, but all that comes out is a whimper.

He leans over me, his breath hot in my ear, and he nips my earlobe hard on his exhale, and a shudder of pleasure runs through me. "Beg me. Fucking beg me," he growls.

"Fuck off," I spit, my voice shaking. A part of me wants this, and a part of me wants to fight. I'm confused and aroused, and I want him so fucking bad.

Slowly, with agonizing deliberateness, he pulls the stick out until just the end rests at the edge of my pussy. I can feel the varnished edge, and my body clenches to be filled. But even now, I want his thick heat inside me—not just the damn wood. "Try that again, you fucking little brat."

I squeeze my eyes shut and bite back a grin. I love getting under his skin.

"Please," I say in the smallest, tightest voice I can.

A sharp slap lands across my ass, his palm rough and mean. "Fucking pathetic. Not good enough." He bites my shoulder, a punishment that sends a delicious shiver spiraling through me.

"Please, fuck me. Please let me come." My voice breaks, little raw sobs tangled in the plea. I'm laying it on thick. "I need it. Please."

"Is that better?" He slides the stick back in deeper until I'm pinned between it and the bar, so full I can barely breathe. His free hand slides under my body, fingers curling around my clit—rough. Ruthless.

"That's my girl," he purrs. "My lying, running, fucking little bratty girl." The combination of the crude pressure of the wood, the brutal circles over my clit, and the weight of his body pinning me in place—it's too much. I explode around the stick, screaming loud enough to rip my throat raw, my body convulsing. He fucks me through it, working me like I'm his personal plaything until I'm slapping at him, begging him to stop and never stop, all in the same breath. I don't know what I want. It's too much. It's perfection. And then my legs give out, and I'm nothing but a limp, ruined mess on the bar.

He pulls the stick out, dripping and slick, and tosses it to the floor with a crash. His fingers tangle in my hair, dragging my face up to meet his. Holding my gaze, he licks his fingers, savoring my taste. "We're not done here yet," he says, wicked promise in his eyes as he yanks the belt off my wrists. "That was your first lesson."

I'm still shaking, my body boneless and fucked out, when my survival instincts kick in and my brain catches up.

Shit.

Run.

I slide one trembling leg off the bar, then the other, my fingers fumbling for balance. My thighs are soaked, my pussy ruined, my skin hot and raw. *Fuck.*

But I only need to run.

I lean across the bar, grab a bottle, and, in one quick motion, smash it. Liquid pools over my hands, but I quickly swivel the broken glass in my grip and swipe across his arm. Blood instantly wells at the site.

"What the fuck?" he growls, but it's all I need. I slip again, and I run. I run as fast as I can. I'm smaller, faster than him, and there's no way he'll get through that tiny bathroom window.

I dive into the bathroom just as I feel him at my heels and slam the door in his face. I press the flimsy lock, knowing it's not enough to keep him out for long. I only have seconds. I leap onto the sink, heave myself up, standing on the porcelain edge, and reach for the window above. There it is—my *freedom.*

I go to hoist myself through the window, but it's locked. I hit it with my elbow. Glass shatters, and I push myself through just as I hear him breaking the door below. He's gotten in. He tries to chase me, his fingers snatching at my ankle. They clamp down just as I kick him hard. I scream and twist, and I manage to shake him off me just as I drag myself through the tiny window and out into the street. I barrel-roll, ignoring the pain as glass bites into my side.

"Going somewhere?"

This guy in front of me is young, cocky. We're in the dark alley behind the bar, alone. I'm on my feet, panting like a victim—like a fighter about to jump into the ring—when the guy reaches for me. He wraps his hands around my wrist and drags me closer.

"You're not getting away," he sneers. I look for an escape, but there's none. I dive to the side, but his grip holds me back.

A gunshot.

No hesitation.

I scream as the man drops to his knees, blood gushing from an open shoulder wound. Matvei stalks forward slowly, his vicious gaze narrowed on the man in front of him. Measured. His knife is already in his hand. I back up until my spine hits the wall, and my skull smacks concrete.

Déjà vu.

We're back where we started.

"I fucking told you not to touch her." His voice is calm. Flat. Terrifying. The kind of voice that speaks truth, not threats. "I told you to fucking watch the exit and *not to touch her*."

"Please! Please, sir, I didn't mean—"

Boom.

The gunshot shatters the silence, followed by the wet crunch of bone and flesh. Howls of pain and pleas for mercy fill the small alley. No one comes as Matvei advances.

"I told you *not to fucking touch her*."

Boom.

The pleading dissolves into whimpers and gurgling. Blood pools beneath the man's trembling body as he frantically tries to stop the inevitable.

Oh god. I should be horrified. But all I can do is stand there, my breath shallow, and *watch*. I should be trying to find a way to escape instead of staring, with my jaw unhinged, as Matvei Kopolov punishes the man who *touched me*.

Because I'm *not* scared. I'm fucking mesmerized. His brutality doesn't disgust me. It doesn't terrify me.

It *owns* me.

He did this... for me.

"I don't. Fucking. Repeat. Myself."

Every word is punctuated by another bullet.

The man screams, then drops, flailing.

Matvei's moving closer to him.

He looks up at me, his eyes locking on mine.

Cold. Certain. *Possessive*.

My hands are flat on the wall behind me as he grabs the man's wrist, drops his gun, and, in one quick movement, takes out a knife.

Oh my god.

One clean slice—and the hand drops to the pavement. Blood spurts fucking everywhere, a rivulet of crimson.

The man howls, writhing in pain, but they're the sounds of a dying man. Hopeless.

Matvei unfolds his huge body, stands, and steps over him like it's nothing. Then he turns and looks at me.

His eyes meet mine.

We stare at each other. I don't know how to explain the way I feel right now.

I should be horrified.

I am. I am horrified.

Am I?

I should be wanting to get away from him.

But all I can think is... I'm a fucking psycho.

Have I met my match?

He moves until he stands in front of me, so close his breath kisses my cheek. Then he brushes a thumb over the apple of my cheek, smearing blood. "You belong to me, Anissa. Get that through your pretty little head." He leans in, voice softer now. Almost intimate. "You like this game, don't you?"

Do I?

He turns, grabs the man by the shoulder, and shoves him through the broken window. His body topples onto the porcelain sink.

Oh god.

My hand is suspended in the air in front of me as if frozen in time. I'm not reaching for him, but I—

Will he walk away? After whipping me, making me come, and viciously murdering a man who dared to touch me?

"You think you're clever, little brat?" His voice is low, almost amused. "You think you can cut and run, and I'll just chase you like some rabid dog?"

I say nothing. My breath is caught in my lungs, my eyes locked with his.

"Let me explain how this works." He leans in until his lips brush my ear. "You don't run because you want to." He pauses, dragging me toward him until I'm arched into him. "You run because I tell you to."

That's what *he* thinks. Still, I'm curious where he'll go with this. I'm frozen in time, eager to hear what he says next. "You want to play games?"

"Of course I do. It's my favorite." Why does my voice sound all husky and flirtatious?

His teeth scrape my throat, a mockery of affection. "Good girl. I'll teach you the rules."

My heart thumps even as my fist clenches in defiance.

I want this.

No, I don't.

Yes, I do.

And then his mouth is on mine, and his fingers are in my hair, his second hand on my throat. He's covered in blood, and I can still feel the slick heat between my legs. Our tongues touch, and when I bite his lip, a low, masculine hum of approval makes my pussy clench. The kiss is rough, consuming, punishing.

And I want so much more.

"First rule," he whispers in my ear, hand still at my throat, "*I decide when the game begins.*"

"Of course you do." I shake my head. "Control freak."

"You have no fucking idea." He shakes his head. "Second rule," he says, backing away. "You can run, little brat."

His smirk is deadly.

"But you can't hide."

He's not a captor. He's not a jailer. He's the goddamn game master.

"*Run*, little ghost. I'll catch up."

In a flourish, he's gone, I assume to clean up the mess of the mutilated body of *the man he just killed for touching me*.

Right, right.

My mind races.

I could run, and I could even have some fun with it. I'm damn good at it. But he *wants* me to.

And if I get away? It's not freedom.

It's a head start.

And I've never been more thrilled in my life.

So I'll go home.

For now.

To wait for him.

I'm a fucking mess, so I pour myself into a cab and go back

to my apartment. I feel like I'm in a daze. This time, he didn't drug me. This time, he didn't need to.

I walk to the kitchen and open the cabinet to get a glass for some water.

And I see it—all of my favorite foods, neatly arranged just for me.

My stomach twists.

He cleared the bar and fucked me up against it with a pool stick. I wonder.

Is he still hard?

Does he want to fuck me?

He said I belonged to him. That I'm his little brat.

His voice was low. Intimate.

Why do I love that?

And then he told me to run.

This is fucking *unhinged*.

But I'm not afraid.

I should be.

I can still see the man's hand—his fucking *hand*—falling to the ground, blood spurting out like someone opened a fire hydrant of blood onto the street.

I didn't flinch or scream but watched the blood pool on the ground, tilting my head to the side like I was studying art.

That man who was writhing and gurgling in pain?

He wasn't even important.

My eyes went back to Matvei.

Not the hand.

Not the blood.

Him.

He did that *for me*.

My whole life, I've been used and discarded. *Replaceable.*

He did that for me.

How romantic.

If this is a game, it's the exact kind of game I like to play. With a wistful sigh, I open the cabinet and reach for a snack.

And then—the lights go out. I'm in pitch dark.

Not just in my apartment but the whole block.

"Wow, buddy, you don't do shit in half measures, eh?"

Outside, I hear a car alarm shriek and a distant yell. Voices, the muffled thud of something hitting the concrete. My breath catches.

This isn't just a power outage. It's *him*. Coming for me. He loves the game, and so do I. But what's going to happen when I can't get away anymore?

I was under control once—I was hurt and abused, and I won't ever let that happen again. But this is... god, this is so different.

My ass still aches from where he spanked me. My pussy clenches at the memory of the pool stick sliding in and out of me. And if I had a light and a mirror, I'd still see where he bit me. Matvei left his mark on me, but it doesn't feel the way it did before.

I stand, glass in hand, water sloshing over the sides, and take a long sip.

When I initially got to Paris, the first thing I did was get in touch with the Irish. "Our deal is over," O'Rourke told me, his voice chilling. "Don't call again." I'm told The Undertaker had my name scourged from their files as well.

I know it's not personal. It never was.

That's the problem.

What now?

I could flee to the depths of the earth and change my whole identity. *Again.* But I wasn't created for a nomadic existence, moving from place to place and never putting down roots. I have no friends and a list of enemies a mile long.

I set the glass down so quietly it doesn't even clink.

The front door is locked, as useless as that is. But I can *feel* him. And just as before, I can hear him breathing. My skin prickles, and my stomach flips.

Why does he say I'm his?

My thighs clench because I know what's coming, and a sick, twisted part of me *wants it*.

I take a step toward my bedroom, treading lightly, listening for any sound that he's near, and the second my foot touches the cool wooden floor, a hand clamps over my mouth.

Hot. Rough.

Familiar.

I grin around the calloused palm.

Oh, hello.

His other hand slides around my waist, jerking me back against him as my ass is pressed to the thick line of his cock. Already hard. Already hungry.

"Little brat." He breathes in my ear, his voice a low purr that drips down my spine. "I wanted to see where you'd go while I cleaned up my job."

I lick his palm, causing him to flinch, but he holds me tighter.

Did he like that?

I bite his palm hard enough to taste copper.

Growling, he spins me, shoving me onto the bed, where he pushes my head down hard.

"You like blood, Anissa?"

"Depends."

"You think you're funny."

"I know I am."

Flipping me to my back, he grabs my jaw roughly in his palm and kisses me... hard. Punishing. Teeth against mine, fingers digging into my throat until I'm gasping. His tongue fucks my mouth with possession.

I want to fight him.

I want to fuck him.

I want to slit his throat.

So naturally, I kiss him back.

When we break apart, we're panting. I feel the smear of his blood across my chin from where I bit him.

"Coward," he says, shaking his head. "You don't want freedom, do you?"

He's right, and I hate him for it.

I love him for it.

I'm confused as fuck.

But I know what I *don't* want.

"Was that for me, Matvei? What you did in the alley? Are you in trouble with Rafail?" I lower my voice, having fun. "Are you going to get a spanking for being a bad boy?" I sigh. "You cut the man's hand off. How romantic. Tell me something." I lean in closer to him. "Would you have done that if he'd just looked at me wrong? Or was it the *touch*?"

His hand grabs my jaw, fingers pressing just enough to hurt. "You think this is a game?" His voice is low, almost amused.

My eyes have gotten adjusted to the darkness. I blink and smile up at him in the dark. "Isn't it?"

Maybe he wants me to break. I know he wants me to beg.

Instead, I tilt my chin up, exposing my throat to him. If he were a vampire right now, he could sink his teeth into my skin and never look back. "You like hurting people, don't you? But I think you like it more when they deserve it."

His thumb presses against my neck. My pulse beats faster. In the dark, his lips curl as he shakes his head. "You're not scared, are you?"

The tension between us snaps, burning.

Hate.

Fascination.

Lust.

He shakes his head with a sigh. "You're going to be so much fucking fun to break."

That's what he thinks.

You can't break someone who's already broken.

In seconds, he has my wrists wrapped in one of his while he ties them with rope.

"Hey—"

"Patience, little brat," he says as he stalks away and leaves me.

I shake my head, and my heart beats faster. I can't predict what he's going to do or when, but I know this game is only just beginning.

I'm not trapped. I'm playing the long game.

He thinks he's in control.

But *I'm* just getting started.

CHAPTER 10

MATVEI

Every fucking time she fights me, I want her more.

Every time she outsmarts me, I *need* her.

I started out hunting her down to punish her for her betrayal and drag her back to where she belonged. But now—the thought of anyone else near her makes me rage. I cut off a soldier's fucking hand before killing him for touching her. The idea of anyone else touching her—*god.*

I don't just want her.

I want to own her, every inch of her.

But I owe my allegiance to my Bratva, and I can't let even the most beautiful, intriguing, captivating woman who's seared herself into every cell of my being sway me from what's right.

She's in the back seat of my car, her wrists red and raw from the restraints. I check them, frowning. I didn't mean to tie them that hard.

Her hair's a tangled mess around her face. She isn't drugged, not this time. She's just asleep. When she sleeps, she looks fragile and almost childlike, but there's nothing fragile about this woman.

When I undo her restraints, she wakes with a start. Blinking up at me, her baby-blue eyes meet mine. "Where are we?" she whispers. Her voice is sharp around the edges.

Fuck.

She's not afraid. She's planning.

"Home sweet home," I murmur, more to myself than her.

The gates swing open to my property, then close behind us with a satisfying click.

She turns to me, her eyes calculating.

Beautiful.

I'm sure she doesn't want to be here, but this is where I live. My home is outside of Moscow, not far from my parents.

"Lovely," Anissa murmurs, taking in the large estate. Cold stone, high balconies, windows too high and narrow to escape. "A five-star hostage situation."

I give her a shrug. "If you behave."

The house seems to swallow her whole when we step inside. I've dismissed my guards for the day. After what happened in Paris, they seemed eager to comply.

I want her alone.

I don't want anyone else coming anywhere near her. Eventually, I'll have to bring her back to the Kopolovs, but I want to wait until she's not as wild… after I've had time with her.

She doesn't know she has a sister. I don't know how she'll react to that.

I catch her wrist before she pulls away, rubbing gently at the chaffed skin. I watch as she scans the room with those thief's eyes, already clocking exits.

Clever little brat.

"Don't forget, you run, and I'll find you." I kiss the damp hair at her temple. I can't help myself. "Faster than last time."

"Thought you had a primal kink," she says, her voice low. "Really, you think this is the first cage I've been in?" Rolling her eyes, she goes all wistful, her voice soft. "There was this guy…"

I freeze. Blood pounds in my ears, and my vision blurs.

No. She watches me. Waiting. Testing.

I let her go. I like her roaming free, ready to run. I like being ready to pounce.

"You think catching you was the endgame?" I shake my head. "That was only the prelude." I lean in, my voice against her ear. "You think fucking you was the endgame? We'll get there, but that's not the endgame either."

She huffs out a laugh. "Then what is?"

I shake my head. "I've already told you."

Staring up at me, something like fear sparks in her eyes. "Owning me, right, right." She winks at me. "Just like that guy in Paris..."

And then she smirks. The smirk *destroys* me, and I snap. I don't think. *I act.*

One second, she's standing there, all cocky and defiant as fuck, and the next? She's over my fucking shoulder. I smack her ass so hard she howls. She kicks and fights, and it's satisfying as fuck, spanking her again and holding her in place.

"You want to test me?" My voice is low, lethal. "Go ahead."

I slide her down my chest, one arm wrapped around her back like a vise, my hand against her throat. I could bruise her soft, creamy skin. I could *break* her, and she knows it.

I press closer, my mouth against her ear. "Tell me about Paris. Tell me his name."

She doesn't.

Smart girl.

"You sure you've got nothing else to say?"

She could be bluffing, or I could be making a list of men who need to be erased from the face of the fucking earth.

Her gaze flicks to the bolted main entrance and the locked windows lined with security glass. She presses her lips into a thin line. "That's what I thought." I push an errant hair behind her ear. I blink, and I can see clearly again. Then I bury my nose in her hair and breathe, and my heartbeat settles.

"Now that we've got that cleared up, let's get cleaned up before we order dinner."

She's quiet now but not defeated. She's thinking... planning her next move. I could strip her naked and chain her to the bed, and she'd still be ten steps ahead, planning her next move.

So I don't mind taking my time. I'll let her play her little games, let her think there's a way out of this.

I hold her hand, take her upstairs, and lead her to the bathroom, where I turn the water on warm. She watches me warily, but this isn't a time when I'll hurt her. Slowly, methodically, I strip her. I run a hand over the fading welts across her ass, and she hisses in a breath. I can't help it. I drop to my knees.

Holding her hips on either side, I run my lips across the welted skin, committing it to memory. I bite her ass, earning me a scream.

My fingers skim her ribs, her waist, her hips. She shivers but lets me.

Maybe she's brave. Maybe she's resigned.

Maybe she wants this.

I get to my feet and lead her into the shower before I undress and join her. Water sluices over her skin, washing away sweat and dirt. I lather her scalp and rinse it, then use conditioner on the ends. I take a washcloth and slide it down her breasts, over the swell of her stomach and the curve of her hips.

I imagine her belly pregnant with my baby. We'll get there.

Fuck. She's so fucking gorgeous.

"You take care of all your prisoners like this?" she asks, her eyes tracking my every move.

"No," I say simply, wiping between her thighs, spreading her slick with the soap as if there's nothing at all sexual about this. Her breath stutters. "Not every prisoner will have my baby."

My cock aches. Her gaze grows deadly, her voice tight. "Lucky me."

Will she feel like she's lucky when she's pregnant with my baby? When she's tethered to me, our DNA knit together? When we'll be aligned as parents to our child, whether she likes it or not?

Then—to my surprise—she reaches for the soap.

I watch her long, thin fingers as she pours some into her palm and then lathers my hair.

Next, she rubs it on the washcloth and spreads it across my shoulders and down my chest.

My cock throbs.

I want her.

Even as a part of me still whispers guilt.

Bring her back here for punishment—that was my job. That was the order.

No one said I couldn't enjoy it.

I grip her hips and drag her closer, wet skin sliding against mine. She cups some water and pours it over my shoulders, washing the bubbles away.

I watch them drip down her arms... down her breasts.

I make sure they land right here—where I want her.

I grab her hips again, bend her over, and line my cock at her entrance.

I slide the head of my cock into her pussy, and the feel of her—hot, slick, clenching like her body's trying to pull me deeper—is fucking magic.

I thrust into her.

Her hands slap against the tile, and her moans echo off the walls.

I thrust harder. Punishing. And her greedy cunt tightens around me like she can't decide if she wants to push me out or pull me deeper.

She's so fucking tight.

I reach around her, rough fingers twisting her nipple until she gasps.

I want her to feel this.

I want her to know exactly what it feels like to come on my cock, on my hand, on my face.

I want her to crave it. Crave me.

I want her to come back for more—crawling if she has to.

Anissa loves sex.

Now she'll love sex with *me*.

She can run, but I'll always find her. I'll always give chase.

But the way I'll truly tether her to me is simple.

I'll make her addicted to me—to my cock, to my tongue. To the way her body feels after I've filled her with my seed.

Pregnant.

Ruined.

Mine.

That's how I'll prove myself to the Bratva.

I watch her body as I drive into her. Watch the muscles in her back tense and flex. Watch her neck arch and her breath stutter.

I sink my teeth into her shoulder, and her moan breaks apart like she's falling.

I cup her breast, palm heavy and rough against her skin. She doesn't flinch—doesn't move. But when I flick her nipple, her body jerks.

And when I press my thumb to her tight little asshole while I fuck her...

That sharp cry? That's the sound I'll replay in my head every time I close my eyes.

"Kinky, beautiful girl," I purr, licking the sweat from her throat. "Look how dirty you fucking are. You want me to take your ass, too, don't you?"

She shudders, her voice low and seductive. "What you're doing right now? It's perfect."

My cock throbs inside her, watching the red welts bloom across her ass. My teeth mark is dark on her shoulder.

I want her wet with my cum.

Dripping with it.

Owned by me.

I thrust into her again. And again, and again.

Until her fingers claw the tile. Until her whole body locks and shatters around me, and I spill inside her.

I slide my fingers over her clit, circling, rubbing.

She comes again, hard and breathless, screaming into the steam-filled air. Her scream ends with a sniff.

Is she... crying?

I stop moving inside her, still seated deep.

I wait.

But when I look at her, I can't tell. Her face is pink, but it's warm in here.

I take the washcloth and clean her, then clean myself, rinsing us under the water before I shut it off. My stomach growls.

"Hungry?" she asks.

"I've been going from one place to the next, barely stopping to eat. I'm fucking starving," I tell her. "You?"

"Famished."

I hand her a towel, and we dry off; then I take her into my room.

"You live here alone?" She looks around. My bedroom is small and clean, but not immaculately clean like my cousin Semyon's place or messy and quirky like Rodion's. It works. I only sleep in here.

I watch as her gaze falls on the cage just waiting for her in the corner, the pink lights twinkling, the bed on the floor made and ready for her. She has the audacity to *smirk*.

"I like what you've done with the place," she says in a low purr.

I open my mouth to retort when the sound of someone else's voice stops me.

"Hello?" a voice calls from downstairs.

"Are you *fucking* kidding me?"

Her eyes fly to mine.

"I thought you just told me you lived alone."

"I do," I tell her through gritted teeth.

"Then who's that? Are we even in your house?"

She doesn't look vulnerable like some women would, standing in a stranger's home, still flushed from getting fucked hard, wearing nothing but a towel, hair still wet and dripping down her face. No, she just looks pissed off.

"Those must be my parents. They're the only people who have access to my house. Except Rafail. He has access to everything."

For the first time, a glimmer of fear flickers in her eyes. She doesn't want to see Rafail.

Tough shit.

"You let your parents just walk in like that?" she asks, tipping her head to the side, curious.

"Yeah, they have keys." Because I feel guilty that their youngest son is dead, and I'm the one responsible. Because they're the black sheep of the Bratva, and I owe them something for giving me life. Parental guilt's a brutal bitch, and I'm not immune to it.

"Interesting," she says. "So do you want me to go out there in a towel and scare them away?"

My vision blurs red. If my fucking father saw her in a towel, I'd have more than my brother's blood on my hands.

"No. You need to wear something."

I open my drawer. I should've thought of this, but I wasn't planning on bringing her back so soon. I'll have to call my cousins.

"We need to get you clothes," I mutter.

"Funny thing about kidnapping someone and bringing them against their will to your house, isn't it?" she says.

Jesus. This woman.

I open the bedroom door and stick my head out. "Give me five. I just got out of the shower, and I'm getting dressed. Don't come upstairs."

I slam the door with a click and turn to find her holding up a pair of boxers and a small, ivy-green T-shirt I don't remember leaving there.

"What's that?" I ask, already grumpy as fuck.

"It was the smallest thing in your drawer," she says, rolling her eyes, but when she shakes it out, something twists in my chest.

No.

That's Gleb's. A shirt I stole from my mother before she got rid of all his clothes. Rafail would kill me if he knew I still had it.

She can't wear that.

I take it from her hand and shove it back in the drawer. "Not that one."

Great. Just fucking great.

She raises her eyebrows but doesn't say anything.

I yank out a plain white T-shirt and toss it to her. "Tie it or do whatever the fuck you need to do."

"What I need to do is wave my magic wand and shrink it, but since I'm the only witch without a wand, I guess I'll wear it like a dress."

She pulls it on, and it hits the tops of her knees. She looks adorable. Beautiful. Too fucking good in my clothes.

"Put the boxers on too."

"Why? Afraid of a little thigh action?"

I cross my arms. "Afraid I might have to break the kneecaps of any asshole who steps near you, yeah."

She whistles. "Oooh. Possessive. You sure you're Bratva and not some overgrown dragon hoarding shiny things?"

I smirk. "You think you're shiny."

"Oh, honey," she says. My heart turns over in my chest. "I'm *radiant*."

"Put them on, little witch." I narrow my eyes at her.

With a shrug, she slides my boxers on, then holds out the waistband to show me a full foot of material between her waist and the boxers.

I grunt. "Fine. You win. Take them off."

"I could just pretend I'm asleep or something if you wanna see them alone."

Good idea unless she decides she's going to run again.

"Yeah. They're not staying long."

"You sure about that?"

"Fucking yes. Go. Lie down. I'll be back." I hold her gaze. "Do *not* come out of here."

Shit. I don't trust that glint in her eyes. What do you do with a girl who loves to be punished?

I throw on a pair of shorts and a T-shirt, my stomach growling.

"Note to self—Matvei gets *hangry*."

I ignore her, grumbling as I open the door and shut it behind me.

From the top of the stairs, I can see my dad already helping himself to my liquor cabinet and my mom rifling through the snack drawer.

Make yourself at fucking home.

"There you are," my mother sings in that high-pitched voice that grates on my nerves.

She's wearing one of her signature sweaters, hanging off one shoulder, skinny leggings painted onto her legs, and a gold belt cinching her waist. She's standing in three-inch platform heels, her blonde hair pinned at the top of her head. But even bottled blonde and trendy clothes don't hide the bags under her eyes. The sag of her skin. The way her lips pinch down in a perpetual scowl.

The son she loved most of all, the one she coddled and spoiled to his own demise, was taken from her, and she'll never forgive any of us for it.

"It's about time. We've been calling and texting, and you haven't responded at all."

I walk down the stairs, shaking my head. "I've been busy." I eye the top of the stairs as if the little ghost followed me, but the bedroom door's still shut tight. For now. I don't trust her.

I get to the landing and go to get myself a drink.

My father raises an eyebrow. "Rodion said something about that. Did your busyness involve a certain traitor?"

"Hey. The name's Anissa."

Jesus. She didn't wait long. I give her a heated glare, but she only smiles at me with a shit-eating grin and a finger waggle.

"Well, look what the cat dragged in," my mother mutters. "You couldn't get her in decent clothes? Ugh."

Anissa stiffens.

My father stares at her. Unblinking. Cold.

"Name's Anissa, and yours is—?" She looks expectantly at my mother. "You must be his grandmother, right?" She blinks so innocently, she almost looks sincere. I stifle a groan, and my father coughs into his drink.

My mother gives her a scathing look through narrowed slits. "Why don't you just tell me you two fucked without telling me? And it's *mother*, princess."

"Because I think it's weird you want to know your son just fucked his prisoner," Anissa answers with another smile. "Ew."

I should've locked her in her cage.

"As far as clothes go, surprise, surprise—your mammoth of a son doesn't have clothes that fit me." She shrugs. "I could've put on the clothes I wore on the way here when he kidnapped me, but they're covered in blood and dirt and—" She covers her mouth, eyes wide. "Oopsie. You probably don't want to know the rest."

My father's drink clatters to the table. He stares at me wide-eyed.

"Is there a reason you're here?" I ask, my voice tight.

"We heard you were back in town," my mother says, eying Anissa up and down. I know that look. She's planning something. "She *does* look a lot like her sister," my mother says, a wicked gleam in her eyes.

Jesus fucking Christ.

"My sister?" Anissa blanches as she turns to me, eyes wide. "I have a sister? What is she talking about?"

My mother looks at her, all fake innocence, just like Anissa herself. "She didn't know? You really don't know the reason Rafail hasn't come after you?"

"Jesus," I mutter. But now that the cat's out of the bag, there's no point hiding it.

"I heard he got remarried," Anissa says, coming to the bottom of the stairs. She walks to an overstuffed chair and sits, tucking her feet up under my shirt like some kind of teenage brat. She's fucking adorable.

I blow out a breath. "My brother betrayed our family. Did you know that?" My mother flinches.

Something like sadness flickers across her face, but it's gone just as fast, replaced with that ice mask she wears so well. "I didn't."

"His betrayal involved a woman named Polina Romanova. Does that name sound familiar?"

She shakes her head, staring at me.

"My brother convinced Rafail he found *you*, after you ran. So Rafail took her—or who he thought was you. Turns out, it wasn't you but someone who looked exactly like you. Because she's your sister."

For the first time since I started stalking her, Anissa actually looks shocked. Guilty, even. I don't blame her. It's a hard fucking pill to swallow. She stares and doesn't respond. I think it might be the first time I've seen her dumbfounded.

There's a lot more to that story, but I'll tell her when we get there. Not now. Instead, I turn the force of my gaze to my mother. "That's enough for now."

"Why do I feel like everything you've told me might've been a lie, except this?" Anissa asks, her voice quiet.

"Because it's not."

She swallows. Vulnerable.

I hate my mother.

"And when do I get to meet my sister?"

"Tonight. When you meet Rafail."

She blanches. I don't blame her.

My father clears his throat. "So you're all coming to the Kopolov house tonight? Zoya cooking?" he asks, always trying to score a free meal.

My mom's jaw locked the second I mentioned Gleb's name, and it hasn't relaxed since. She'll never forgive me for what I did.

Neither will I.

I take another sip of my drink and shake my head, watching Anissa's reaction. "No. Rafail and Polina are coming here."

Anissa stares at me but doesn't say a word.

I turn to my parents. "I still don't know why you're here."

"We can't just come see our son?" my mom asks, voice sticky sweet.

"You could." I shrug. "You don't."

My mother shakes her head and lifts her chin high, but something like sadness flickers across her face. "It would've been your brother's birthday today. Did you forget so soon?"

A stab of pain hits my chest. I don't want to look at Anissa right now. The memory of Gleb leaves me vulnerable, splits me bare, and I don't want her to know. My voice is husky, affected, when I shake my head. "No. I didn't forget."

Unlike her, I don't celebrate any of those dates.

I turn my back to all of them, suddenly gripped with the desire to be alone. Alone, just like I've been since the day I buried my brother's mutilated, traitorous body.

It's safer being alone.

Instead, I pour myself another drink. I jerk my head toward Anissa. "Drink?"

Wordlessly, she nods. The room is silent as I pour her a shot of vodka and hand it to her. The face she makes when she sips it is adorable, like a little kitten who's drunk soured milk.

I sip mine slower, leaning against the wall. The drink makes the dull aching in my chest bearable.

For now.

"You came here because it was his birthday?" I don't want to speak his name.

Did they expect me to fucking celebrate?

My mother sniffs, but she can't hide the tremor in her voice. "We're feeling nostalgic. Sad. Thought we'd see our other son. Maybe that was a mistake."

She gets to her feet, heads to the kitchen, and starts rifling through my cabinets like she owns the place.

"How do you even stay alive?" my mother mutters, shaking her head. "There's no food in here."

I clench my molars. "I just got back from Paris."

She mutters something under her breath before turning to my dad. "Honey," she says to him, "let's get food. I'm starving." She looks at Anissa. "And I don't want to be here any longer."

"Oh," Anissa says in a fake-ass voice, "please. Don't go. I was just starting to get to know you."

She holds up her empty glass to me, her eyes on my mother. I refill it.

Jesus Christ.

"Nice, you got yourself a cute little bitch, didn't you?" my mother says, cold as ice. If she were a fucking man—

"That woman," I begin in a low voice, fury pounding through my veins as I clench my drink. My father knows better. He's already moving to stand between us like he could stop me if he had to. "Is mine," I finish, my voice lethal. "Rafail gave her to me. That woman's going to be the mother of your grandchildren. Is that clear?"

My mother's face turns beet red—but not from embarrassment. Not her. She's pissed.

"I get it. You've had to let a lot of shit go, haven't you?" she spits. "A lot of expectations. Hopes. Dreams. We've let you get away with plenty, and the only reason Rafail still lets you hang around is because you have some respect left for the rest of us."

I lean in, voice pure fucking ice. "I might not be so nice."

"Be careful," my father growls. "You're loyal to a fault."

I turn to him, eyes narrowing. "I don't have a brand seared into my back with *your* name on it, do I?"

He swallows and shakes his head.

Anissa whistles.

"Irma, let's go."

"Don't let the door hit you on the way out," Anissa calls sweetly as the door shuts.

We look at each other in silence for a long minute. She doesn't speak, just traces her finger along the rim of her glass.

"Got the shit end of the stick with parents, eh?" But her eyes are pained when she sips the vodka.

I shake my head. We drink in silence for long minutes. The sun has begun to set outside, but I don't move to turn any lights on. I like the dark.

"When were you going to tell me about my sister?" she asks quietly, her throat working up and down.

"Tonight."

"Before or *after* I met her?" She doesn't hide the note of sadness in her voice. "No wonder he didn't come after me. Jesus. *A sister*." She shakes her head. "That's so fucking weird."

"You have a mother too. She's in New York. Matriarch of the Romanov family."

Her eyes widen. She's never had a mother. I have no clue how that lands.

"And when were you going to tell me about your brother?" she asks. "There's more to that story, and it sounds fucking brutal, Matvei."

"Eventually. Probably when we were snuggled up on the couch, sharing our hopes and dreams." I shrug a shoulder. "Funny, we haven't gotten there yet."

She chews her lip. Thoughtful.

"Any other siblings?"

I shake my head. "Not anymore."

She blows out a breath, meeting my eyes. "Another story for another day?"

"Yeah."

I sip my vodka, and the alcohol surges through my veins. I need to eat. We both do.

Her gaze drifts to the kitchen clock. "When are Rafail and Polina coming?"

"We've got two hours."

She nods. "Enough time for me to wash and dry my clothes, right?"

"Yeah. Or we can buy you new ones."

"Maybe another day. This one's been long enough."

No fucking shit.

I lean against the wall, sipping my drink. "Do you think the small talk will help me forget that I told you not to leave the room? How long did you last? Thirty seconds?"

With a shrug, she looks away. "More or less. I didn't like the tone of voice they were taking with you."

I narrow my eyes at her. "You're still in trouble."

Her heated gaze meets mine. "Is that a promise?"

I shake my head. It's a fucking prophecy.

CHAPTER 11

ANISSA

I have a sister.

A sister.

The revelation circles my head like a vulture waiting to swoop. Another secret. Another twist.

This is the strangest turn of events I could have imagined. Just when I think I have control of the situation, even the tiniest little modicum of control, he throws me another curveball.

And now his family. His parents are assholes. I've seen his mother's type, the kind of shallow, brittle woman who goes to charity galas for the accolades but hides her venom behind the glitter.

Yet another thing we have in common.

Great. We could start a club. *Children of monsters.*

I have a mother too? And I'm going to meet the man whose life I apparently destroyed in a matter of hours. I didn't think I could ever get back to a place where I was insecure or afraid. I run head-on toward fear, toward discomfort, because I've found that's what makes me stronger. But now, my mind is spinning with the most mundane question: *What am I going to wear?*

And why is he not really afraid of me running anymore?

I also heard him loud and clear when he told his mother—that *catty excuse* for a mother anyway—that I would be the mother of his children. Dear god. *Children.*

Ha. I'll have the last word on *that* one.

"Hmm. With no real time to go shopping," I say, working my lip. "I can't exactly go to the shop wearing the elephant-sized T-shirt."

I don't normally mind standing out, but this is different.

He nods, scowling, thinking.

"I'll call Rodion."

I know that Rodion is his cousin—Rafail's younger brother. Maybe they're close.

"Rodion's going to have women's clothes?"

"No, but his wife probably will."

His wife.

Maybe choosing ignorance over the Kopolov Bratva wasn't my smartest strategy.

I nod, thinking.

"That's probably the best option. I don't even think the clothes I brought will be ready in time."

I look down at my nails—short, chipped, clean because of the shower, but barely presentable.

I washed my hair, but it dried into a frizzy mess. I have no makeup, no jewelry. I don't even have a razor.

What am I thinking? Since when have I cared about this bullshit?

Since now.

Since I'm back in Russia with women who dress well and take pride in their appearance, that's when.

I get up to use the bathroom. "Where's your bathroom?"

"There are four. Closest is here, off the kitchen."

This is a nice home. The Bratva do take care of their own.

I walk to the bathroom and splash water on my face. It's a start. My reflection stares back at me—bare-faced, no makeup, no jewelry.

No armor.

For the first time in years, I'm just *Anissa*.

And I hate it. I hate it so much.

Matvei's voice echoes behind me. I hear him talking to Rodion, filling him in, asking him for a solid.

There's that little pang again—the one I pretend not to feel. The reminder that I never bothered to wonder what kind of man Matvei is when he's not hunting me. Turns out, he's the kind who has family dinners and inside jokes.

And yet, he's barely afraid of me running anymore.

That's what keeps twisting the knife. What's given him so much confidence?

I'm losing my edge—or worse, he's getting inside my head, rearranging my instincts until the sharp edges dull and the exits blur.

I feel Matvei behind me before I even see him. "Any luck with Rodion?"

He shakes his head. "They're out of town. I forgot."

"Well, I can't exactly meet them in this."

Matvei's gaze drags down my body, slow and heated. Not even trying to hide it.

"We'll figure it out."

That's the difference between us. I survive by planning ten steps ahead. He survives by deciding no plan is necessary—because he *is* the fucking plan.

I grip the counter, forcing myself to breathe. My reflection stares back at me, daring me to break first.

"You're still in trouble," he says.

"Mm. So you say." I manage to keep my voice coy even as my pulse thunders.

I can't decide if I want him to punish me—or if I want to make him bleed first.

Maybe both.

Hmmm.

I stand in front of the mirror and pull my shoulders back. I guess a little bit of makeup or something couldn't hurt. "So do you always let your parents talk to you that way? You didn't seem the type."

"What's the type?" he asks.

"The type to let your parents control you. And you didn't answer my question."

"My parents are ruthless, mean. But they're the reason why I'm here, so...yeah."

I catch his eyes in the mirror and narrow my gaze at him. That is not the answer, and we both know it, but I'm not going to pry. Eventually, I'll understand the truth about him.

And eventually, he'll know the truth about me too.

Because at this point, I know for a fact that what he said about chasing me is true. And even if I could erase my existence—disappear off the face of the earth, never to be found—I know that's not what's tethering me to him right now either.

Deep down, I'm intrigued. Curious. No one has ever made me feel as alive as he does, even when that feeling is laced with danger.

And I can't help but wonder—have I finally met my match?

I was interested in the Irish, only inasmuch as what they could offer me. But I didn't like any of them. They're too old-fashioned, too set in their ways.

And I thought I actually didn't have a romantic bone in my body.

Maybe I was wrong. Even now, when he tells me that he's going to punish me, excitement curls in my belly. Will he hurt me again? I want him to. It's strangely cathartic in a way I can't explain, and I'm not sure I would want to, even if I could.

"I'm going to get my clothes and wash them," I tell him softly, then mumble under my breath.

"What's the matter?" he asks.

"I just wish I had my... clothes and things."

"Your disguises?" he asks, eyes cold.

"I like to dress up." I shrug. "So maybe I like a little cosplay."

When he crosses his arms on his chest, his eyes grow colder. "Maybe you like to hide."

My heart thumps. I get the message loud and clear: *There is no hiding here.*

"It doesn't matter what you wear, Anissa. You could walk around in a fucking sack for all I care, and it wouldn't matter. My parents will still hate you because you're mine. And Rafail won't forgive you for what happened, but he'll eventually forget."

How does he see right through me? How do I see right through *him*?

I freeze as our eyes lock. This is fucked up and inevitable, and I don't know how to handle it. This is some kind of freaky soulmate-level shit I'm unprepared for.

I shake my head, feeling uncomfortable.

We're wasting time.

"Where's your washer and dryer?"

"I might as well give you the tour."

"Yeah."

He doesn't touch me but stands so close I can feel his heat licking up my spine. My hands are eager to touch him, to ground myself in the reality of Matvei, the man who... owns me.

I could lean into this.

My heart beats faster, and I hate myself for it. I've been dragged through hell by the men who thought they owned me. I've been beaten, abused. It forged me into who I am today.

I won't think of that now.

I look away because I don't want him to somehow read my mind. I'm afraid that if he meets my eyes again, he'll see the replay of that night over and over and over again... just like I do when I close my eyes to sleep. When I run my hands over the scars on my belly.

I follow him as he points to the kitchen, the entryway that leads to the garage, a large sitting area, and a paved patio on the other side of glass doors, barely visible now that it's dark out.

And as he gives me the tour, he looks over his shoulder at me from time to time.

It's unsettling. No one's ever looked at me like this—like I'm a challenge and a prize, an answer to a question he didn't know he was asking. And I know then that if somehow I did manage to escape tomorrow, he would burn down the world to find me.

For better or for worse...

"Since you live here now—"

"I live here?" I interrupt. My voice is dry and mocking because if I don't make it a joke, the truth might slip out—and I can't have that. "Bold of you to assume."

He doesn't blink. "It's a fact, and you know it, you little brat."

"You're very bold, Mr. Cliché. *She's going to have my babies; she's mine*," I mock. "Yeah, I got you ever since the time you wrote on my wall in that red." I tip my head to the side. "How did you get rid of it so fast anyway?"

He shrugs. "A magician never shows his hand."

I point my finger in the air with a dramatic flourish. "So you admit you did it."

His eyes darken, his lips pressing into a thin line. "Yes. Any other motherfucker did that, I'd kill him."

I swallow. He's telling the truth.

There's no bravado, no need to raise his voice. His control is a blade pressed to my throat, and the worst part is... I crave pressing back. Feeling the metal scrape my skin.

I want to see if he'll cut me. I want him to bleed for me too.

This is not how this is supposed to go.

"The tour," he rasps.

I nod, hyperaware of the fact that I'm naked under this ridiculous T-shirt and we're somehow standing toe to toe. "The tour," I repeat.

I trail after him, cheeks flaming no matter how hard I try to control my reaction as he moves through the house, my bare feet silent on the gleaming hardwood floors. The house is exactly what I'd expect from him—dark wood, expensive, brutally elegant. Not a single soft edge anywhere. Maybe I'll be the soft edge. Once I get my hands on one of his credit cards, I'm getting some fucking pink in here. Maybe even some witchy crystals—a little rose quartz to soften his edges and some obsidian to give me some goddamn protection.

He opens a door off the hall, revealing a laundry room—modern, spotless, efficient. Shelves are stacked with neatly folded clothes, softener and detergent lined up like soldiers. Even his damn laundry room looks like it's ready for war.

"Housekeeper?"

I just want to fill the silence, but I also want to know who's going to come in and see me half-naked because that's definitely what's going to happen. Some people drink to relieve stress. Others take drugs.

Maybe Matvei *is* a drug.

He shrugs. "Sometimes, yeah. Mostly, it's just me. I'm not here a lot."

"Oh?"

"But that's going to change."

That throws me. I look down at his massive hands, the same ones that pinned me down and held me, and imagine him carefully folding... towels. It's disturbingly intimate. Domestic. Because now I can't stop imagining those hands back on me, peeling my clothes off instead of washing them.

I swallow hard and wish I had a pile of dirty clothes to wash, suddenly eager for distance. I need a break from the intensity already. His gaze drops, dragging down the curve of my back, and I feel it—his desire, a little hum between us.

"I'm surprised you care as much as you do," he says suddenly, his voice low, cutting.

I straighten slowly and turn to face him. "About what?"

Don't tell me he's seen through my fake nonchalance already.

He takes a step toward me, closing the space until my back hits the dryer. "About how you look. About what my family thinks. About what I see when I look at you."

Fuck.

"Okay, get over yourself, Matvei," I snap, but my voice betrays me. "I don't really care about any of that."

He bares his teeth at me, and it would be a smile if it didn't look so much like a threat. "Liar."

So what if I do care? So what if I like the disguises because they feel like armor? So what if I like the fact that I can move from place to place without ever putting down roots—because when I do, *if* I do, someone always comes along and rips them up again.

So what?

How does he flay me open without even trying?

And the scariest part? *Why do I like it?*

He leans in, one hand braced beside my head. His eyes are stormy and beautiful. My heart beats faster. I want him to touch me, and I don't want him to be gentle.

He smells like vodka and soap. I lick my lips.

"Why do you think I'm not afraid of you running anymore?" he asks in a whisper.

The truth is, he should be.

He should be waiting for me to slip up, but instead, he watches me.

The air between us snaps like electricity.

I roll my eyes to hopefully hide my reaction to my pounding heartbeat. "Because you know how to track me."

He touches my chin, tracing the line of it. My breath hitches for a second.

"Yeah, little ghost. But we both know that's not the truth. Not all of it anyway, is it?"

He's just as fucked up about me as I am about him.

He's supposed to hate me. Even his parents hinted at that.

I can't look away. I can't stop myself. My fingers curl into the front of his shirt, dragging him to me. His body presses up against mine, and I crave being closer, connected. Flesh against flesh, mouth against mouth, tongues tangled. Because I've never been more attracted to someone in my life.

I don't know what the hell that says about me.

His hands skate down my sides, rough and possessive, leaving a trail of heat behind.

"How long is the wash cycle?" I whisper.

His low, dark chuckle makes my nipples harden. "Long enough."

I sigh and close my eyes as his lips meet mine.

His kiss isn't soft—too much wanting, too much need. His hands fist in my messy hair, keeping my mouth locked to his, and I feel it... *I feel it*.

The way he's holding back.

The way his control slips through his fingers like sand.

Fuck it. I want to make him *lose* control. I want to see exactly what happens when Matvei Kopolov snaps.

"The tour," I tell him. "You going to finish giving me the tour?"

"Right."

I feel a giggle bubbling up because—god help me—he's kind of cute when he doesn't know what to do with himself.

"So this is the laundry room. Down the hall are some guestrooms, and upstairs is the bedroom. Our bedroom," he says in a rush of words.

"That's great, but I hope you know I'm gonna buy something pink. Maybe lots of pink."

He makes a face. "Pink?"

"The ultimate feminine color, and it's my favorite. Don't judge."

"I don't want pink in my bedroom." His nose crinkles.

"Challenging your fragile male ego? I thought it was *our* room?"

He growls and pinches my ass.

"Fine then. Creams, golds, neutrals. Is that better? Your whole house is like some kind of control freak manifesto."

He shakes his head. "You're unbelievable."

I smile at him sweetly, and my stomach growls. Still starving.

Something buzzes between us.

"Either you're packing a vibrator or someone's calling you."

"Option two."

He answers his phone, lifts it to his ear, and, with his other hand, keeps me pinned against the wall, holding me there like I might vanish if he doesn't keep a grip.

I watch his eyes while he talks, and for no reason at all, I lick my lips. His fingers tighten on my shoulder, a silent *don't you fucking start*.

Yum.

I swallow hard.

"Yes. No problem. Yeah, she knows because my mother's got a big mouth, so we need to get together soon. Of course, yeah. Bye."

He hangs up and looks at me. He shrugs, all nonchalant, but his hand is still on me. "Guess they're not coming after all."

My stomach knots. I don't know what to do with the swirl of conflicting feelings.

On one hand, I'm disappointed. I have a sister, and I wanted to meet her. Surely no one can be as bad as his mother?

On the other hand, I have exactly zero desire to see Rafail anytime soon, so yeah—relief.

And I'm still starving.

"I guess I have a little more time to get some clothes."

"Or not."

My pussy throbs.

"And some food," he says. "I'm about five minutes away from throwing shit."

He pushes away from the wall, but his fingers lace through mine.

He's holding my hand.

I'm not a hand-holder. I'm not a cuddler. But I like holding *his* hand.

"Here," he says, handing me his phone. "Order what you want."

I take his phone in my right hand while he leads me down the hall.

"Anything I want? What if I want a pony?"

He grunts.

"A pink pony?"

"Guestrooms," he mutters, jerking his chin toward a few doors. "Bathroom. This one's nice—it's got a waterfall... thing. Whatever you call it."

He speaks with quiet pride. This is his house, one he crafted in some way for himself, one that's all his—away from his parents' suffocating bullshit. Even if they're still circling, waiting to pull him back under.

"And I really don't give a fuck what you order. Just get me some food. Fast."

I pull up the app, scroll, and place an order for the greasiest takeout I can find. I throw in a side salad to appease my conscience.

I press the button. "Are you a big tipper?"

"Of course. They're bringing me food, and I don't have to cook. Tip them whatever the hell you want."

I like that.

I tip big and hand him the phone back.

He opens a door at the very end of the hall. "And this room here, it's—"

He stops. I do too. Instead of moving forward, I stare.

Inside, the walls are lined with shelves. Books—old, worn, their spines cracked with use. It smells of varnished wood and aged paper.

A framed quote hangs over the desk.

"Even in the grave, all is not lost."

I freeze.

"Edgar Allan Poe?" My voice comes out soft.

Matvei shrugs, but there's something guarded in the set of his jaw. "Yeah. So?"

I stare at him, heart racing. "You know I like Poe."

His head tilts. He doesn't respond. Did he put this here for me? Or...

My skin crawls, that familiar flash of *how long has he been watching me* bubbling up. Of course he knows. Of course he's been in my shit.

Except—

I haven't read Poe in years.

Years.

But when I did, I didn't just read, I *consumed*. Memorized. It was all I read because, for the first time in my life, I felt seen. Someone else understood the complex emotions of being human, of wanting to live and sometimes hating every second.

But how would he know?

I didn't leave that trail for him to follow. I didn't post it, didn't leave a book lying around, barely thought about it... until right now.

"So how did you know?" I whisper.

His eyes darken. "I didn't. Are you giving me shit?"

I shake my head.

We stare at each other, and the air between us shifts. Not just hunger. Something stranger. Older.

"Maybe you've been stalking *me*," he says, his voice low and dangerous.

My breath catches. "Is that a joke?" I laugh to cover the way my pulse spikes. "You wish."

But my hands tremble when I touch the book lying on the desk. My fingerprints have never been on this one—but it still feels like it's mine.

Or his.

Or ours.

"*And so being young and dipped in folly...*" My voice trails off.

"*I fell in love with melancholy,*" Matvei finishes.

My head snaps up.

Something behind his gaze flickers. Sharp. Knowing.

Vulnerable.

My pulse beats faster. Maybe he's been watching me longer than I thought? But no, that doesn't make sense...

I glance down at another page, my voice quieter now. "*Deep into that darkness, peering, long I stood there...*"

"*Wondering, fearing, doubting, dreaming dreams...*" His voice trails off. I mentally complete the line.

...no mortal ever dared to dream before.

The doorbell rings, soft and delicate, like wind chimes. It doesn't belong in a house like this, too pretty for all this dark wood and sharp edges. I glance at him, curious.

He shrugs. "Food."

Oh. Right. I almost forgot. I've been too distracted by him—his hands, his voice, the weight of his attention.

Our shared madness.

He locks the door behind him and double-checks it like a man who's never been safe a single day in his life. And when we head for the living room, his hand finds mine again... like it belongs there.

"Sit on the couch," he orders. "Hands in your lap, where I can see them."

He tries to sound sharp, but some of the bite is gone. He's not as angry anymore—just possessive. Watchful.

I nod like the obedient little brat he thinks I am and give him mocking servitude. "Yes, sir."

He doesn't trust my obedience. I can feel his eyes drilling into my back as I walk to the couch, which means—he's exactly where I want him. I wink over my shoulder, and his jaw ticks.

He checks the peephole. Checks the cameras. Touches the gun at his hip before unlocking the door. He doesn't trust anyone—not the delivery guy, not the air, not the night itself.

It should be sad, and it is, but mostly, it's familiar. *Too* familiar.

A few minutes later, I'm sitting cross-legged on his couch, a spread of food in front of us. Greasy, messy chicken wings, hot, salted fries, and sticky rice. None of it belongs together, but I want all of it.

"Hands off," he says.

I blink at him. "What?"

"Put your hands behind your head."

I stare at him, but his face is pure control. Cold, quiet authority. I do it. My fingers are laced behind my head like I'm under arrest, my chest arching just a little. His eyes flick down and back up.

"You just want my nipples pushing against this tee, don't you?"

With a noncommittal grunt, he picks up a wing.

I expect him to pass it to me. He doesn't. He holds it up to my mouth, and for one long second, we both just breathe.

"Open."

I do.

He slides the meat between my lips, slowly, watching every second like he's committing it to memory. I take a bite, tongue flicking out to catch the sauce, and his pupils blow wide.

"Good girl," he murmurs.

Mmm. I like that.

He wipes his thumb along my lower lip, collecting a streak

of sauce, and holds it up like a dare. Without thinking, I lean forward and lick his thumb.

His breath hitches.

My tongue flicks along the calloused pad, tasting salt and grease. I mean to pull back after, but his free hand tangles in my hair and holds me there—his thumb slipping deeper, just past my lips.

"Messy little thing," he mutters.

I bite down on his thumb, just enough to make him feel it—and his control slips, just a crack. He drags it along my tongue before pulling away.

"You like teasing me," he says, low and dark.

"You like feeding me," I shoot back.

His smile is sharp enough to cut. "You've got no idea."

He picks up a fry next, dragging it slowly through the pool of ketchup, and brings it to my mouth. I take it—lips brushing his fingers, sucking the salt right off his skin. He watches, transfixed.

"More," I whisper.

He feeds me rice next, and I take it from his fingers, deliberately licking the grains off his skin one by one, my tongue tracing each knuckle. His breathing turns rough, his jaw tight. It's messy and raw, and I'm loving every second.

"Careful," he warns.

"Or what?"

He shakes his head in response. "I won't be able to hold myself back anymore, and we'll have to skip dessert."

His voice is all gravel and promise.

"Depends. What's on the menu?"

I didn't order dessert.

He grabs my ankles, dragging me down the couch until I'm sprawled beneath him. My shirt rides up, and his hand slides along my bare thigh, his thumb tracing slow, lazy circles.

Oh.

He bends his head and kisses me hard, licking into my mouth like he's still feeding me—like he's tasting the salt and grease and hunger right off my tongue. I moan into him, fingers curling in his hair, dragging him closer and closer.

His mouth leaves mine, sliding down my throat, teeth grazing my pulse before he drags my thighs apart and settles between them.

"Hands back behind your head again," he growls. "And stay fucking still."

I obey, but my breath is ragged. My pulse races under his mouth as he kisses lower.

"You gonna lick me like you did the fries?" I whisper.

He flashes a wicked smile. "I'm gonna do a lot more than that, little ghost."

And then his mouth is on me, and I forget all about food.

He spreads my thighs, slow but deliberate, fingers digging into my skin just enough to make sure I know who owns me now.

"You were teasing me," he murmurs, lips trailing fire down the inside of my thigh. "Licking my fingers like you wanted to be fed something else."

My breath stutters, my hands aching to touch him. He notices.

"Keep them there," he orders, his voice sharp. My hips jerk, moving close to him, desperate for pressure, for him to taste me.

I let out a shaky exhale, arching slightly against the couch. He's still fully dressed. I'm half-naked.

His mouth ghosts over the crease of my thigh, where the skin is sensitive. He bites, just enough to make my legs jerk. Enough to leave marks. I stifle a moan.

Matvei hums against me, as though he likes the way I react... like he's already memorizing it.

He licks right next to where I want him, teasing. I feel my arousal dripping.

I won't beg. Nope.

But oh my god, in my mind, I am screaming. I want his tongue, I need pressure, I need—

Ahhh.

His tongue flicks over the bite—soft, soothing, making me shiver—and then lower, pressing wet heat right where I need him most.

I moan. I can't help it. My god, it feels like heaven.

Matvei groans against me, his grip on my thighs tightening like he wants to bruise me there and keep me spread open forever.

He works me over slowly at first, with long, lazy, torturous licks, his tongue flat and unyielding. I want to grab his hair and force him deeper, rougher. I want to make him lose control.

I know he's waiting for me to break first.

He flattens his tongue and drags it up, slow and deep, one hand moving between my legs so he can curl his fingers inside me.

Oh fuck.

I whimper.

"That's it," he praises, and fuck, his voice alone is enough to ruin me. "That's right, little ghost. Let me hear you."

He wraps his lips around my clit and sucks, and I don't just moan this time—I cry out.

Matvei growls in approval, pressing me down when my hips jerk. He's holding me open for him, keeping me there so he can take his time.

I don't want time. I want him to devour me.

"Matvei—"

He bites me again. Punishing.

It's harder this time, right on the inside of my thigh, where no one else will ever see. Where only he will know.

I swear I almost black out. The pain, the pleasure, the possessiveness of it—it's all too much and not enough.

He licks over the bite, soothing it, then moves back between my legs, tongue flicking, teasing, circling.

"More," I beg.

He groans like he's the one unraveling, and then he gives it to me.

He eats me like a man starved.

The suction, the flick of his tongue, the scrape of his teeth—it's all too much. My back bows, my fingers knotting together behind my head, my body straining toward him as heat coils low, tighter, tighter...

"That's it," he rasps against me, his voice dark and wrecked. "Come for me, little ghost. Come on my mouth."

And I do.

Hard.

He doesn't let up. He keeps working me through it, lapping and sucking until I'm sensitive and boneless.

"I can't—it's too much. Too much. Please stop, I can't—Please—"

Then, finally, he pulls back, his gaze on me wicked and cruel. "I told you to stay in that room, didn't I?"

Oh shit.

His lips are slick, his breath heavy. But his eyes—those dark, greedy eyes—stay locked on me as he licks his lips.

"Maybe you did," I say in a small voice. He bends and licks my sensitized clit. I cry out.

"No maybe," he growls, biting the inside of my thigh. "I told you to stay, and you didn't. Naughty, naughty little ghost."

And then his teeth are on my clit again, scraping against the sensitive skin, and I know intuitively that moving my hands will compound my punishment. I jerk my hips, trying to squirm out of his grip, but he holds me tight, fingers digging into my skin hard enough to leave marks.

"Bad girls get punished." He breathes against my thigh before he plunders my pussy. He licks my core, groaning as he laps up my arousal, then drags his tongue to my clit again, suckling hard.

My hips arch. It's too much, too sensitive, bordering on painful.

Releasing my clit, he licks lazy, slow circles over and over, and now... now I want more. Now I *need* more. I can feel another climax rising. I whimper, a spasm of ecstasy rippling through me until he licks me again, and I fall apart.

This time, when I come, I shatter, breathless. Ecstasy floods my limbs. I scream until I'm hoarse, and still, he licks and sucks until I fall, slumped against the couch.

"Did you learn your lesson?" he growls, his breath hot between my legs. He gives me one more warning swipe of his tongue. I stifle a scream.

"Yes, yes, god, okay," I say in a rush of words so he doesn't decide to push my body to the point of breaking. My god.

"Good," he says. "Because it's bedtime."

I nod my head.

Bed. Yes. Bed.

We walk up the stairs to his bedroom. I'm boneless as he holds me, pressed up to his chest, carrying me as if I weigh nothing at all.

It's dark, but for some reason, bright lights illuminate one corner of the room. Are those... fairy lights? In Matvei's room?

But as we draw nearer, I see. I shake my head and huff out a laugh.

"Aw. Just like old time's sake."

"Just like old time's sake," he repeats as he kicks open the cage he first used to capture me and lays me on a soft, thick mattress. "Sleep well, little ghost."

The metal door clicks with an audible snap. The lock is the last thing I hear before I close my eyes to sleep.

CHAPTER 12

MATVEI

I don't sleep well.

I set up the fucking cage for a reason, but now that she's in it, her light, waffling snores indicate she's out—and I want her next to me.

And I'm hard as a fucking rock. After tossing and turning, I get up and rub one off in the shower because I can't fucking sleep when I'm hard as fuck. It doesn't bring the relief I'm craving. I don't want my hand when her hot, tight cunt is *right there*.

In my room.

So I sleep fitfully until the morning light streams through the window, and I finally give up. I look over the edge of the bed and see her beautiful, sweet body splayed out on her back, the blanket askew. Sunrise kisses her bare legs.

I want to touch them.

I watch her, waiting to see if she'll wake up afraid. But instead, she rolls over and stretches, her fingers brushing the cold metal above her head.

Her eyes meet mine.

"Morning, *solnyshka*." Always taunting.

I growl at her. "Morning."

She watches me as if waiting to pounce. Something's shifted between us.

I push myself out of bed and unlock the cage.

"I knew if I looked pathetic enough, you'd come back and unlock it," she says, pushing up on her elbow. "Pity you're far too big to get in here with me. It's so warm and cozy." She presses her hand against the mattress. "Memory foam?"

This woman.

I try to remind myself this isn't about her but about me. About loyalty. Making her suffer.

Then why do I have to stop myself from hurting her? Why do I crave seeing her eyes light up? Why do I love that little smirk on her face?

And why can't I shake the feeling that she's playing the long game? Gaining my trust. Manipulating me?

I can't trust the little brat.

She doesn't immediately jump out of the cage, and that... throws me.

Instead, she *stretches*, slow and sinuous, like a cat waking in the sun. Her arms reach high above her head, back arching just enough to make my sex-starved, sleep-deprived brain take note. My gaze drags along every curve and valley, the creamy softness of her peach-colored skin, the elegant curve of her neck still marked with my bites, though they've faded to dusky pink. Her hair, the natural white-blonde, fanned over her pillow like sunrise.

God, I love the way she's comfortable in her body, even knowing she's made enemies everywhere she turns.

I should yank her out by her ankles, drag her to her feet, and make her remember *exactly* who owns her now. I try to remind myself why I hunted her, what she did, and remind myself that she's dangerous as fuck and can't be trusted.

But I don't. I don't do any of those things. Instead, I fucking *watch*.

She knows. She has to know how she affects me.

When she finally sits up, it's deliberate, the queen arching her back and meeting my gaze. "Slept like a baby," she says with a yawn. "Oh, wait." She presses a finger to her lips. "Was I supposed to be scared? Being caged and all?"

She tips her head to the side.

Baby. I'm stuck on the word baby. I've been so obsessed with the idea of her carrying our baby, anchoring her to me, that just hearing the word plants the vision of her heavy with pregnancy, carrying *my child*...

I grunt and reach for her, but she's already sliding out of the cage, unfurling like she has all the time in the world. Her gaze is amused. Calculating.

"I figured you'd fucking like it."

Standing in front of me, she blinks long, long lashes at me and drawls as she reaches a hand to trace my bare shoulder. "The question is, big guy. Did *you*?"

"Enjoy you caged?" I grab her hair and tug it back, baring her neck. I imagine what it would be like waking up to this woman curled up to me, her body rounded and full with my child, my palm pressed to her swollen abdomen. I lick my lips and swallow hard. "You know I do. You know I love having control over you."

But something's changed.

She's not just playing the game anymore. She's *enjoying* it.

And fuck me. I am too.

We head to the kitchen to make breakfast. She asks me questions about my routines, who works for me, and what I do for the Bratva.

"You know," she says, after learning that I'm the one who manages cyber security and hacking, "our skills paired together would be straight-up *fire*."

She's not wrong. Cyber security and forgery? We could rewrite history. Dark, twisted history, but it would be history nonetheless.

"I want to know how you left things with the Irish." I spread butter on toast and cut it into triangles before I push the plate to her. She eyes it thoughtfully and doesn't eat it.

"If I were going to poison you, I wouldn't do it in *toast*," I mutter. Would've poisoned the vodka last night or just skipped formalities and jabbed her pretty little neck again.

Her bright blue eyes meet mine. "Wait, you thought I was afraid of being poisoned?" She takes a huge bite.

I shrug.

"Nah, I just read something somewhere about cutting toast that way, triangles instead of rectangles, and I—" She shakes her head as my phone rings. "Nothing."

She's perched on the barstool, happily munching toast as if she hasn't spent the last month fighting for her life.

I answer the phone with a scowl. Rodion.

"Yeah?"

"You talked to the Irish?"

I scowl at the phone. Anissa chews her toast, but her focus is narrowed on me.

"No. Why?"

"O'Rourke's in town. What the fuck does he want to do with us?"

I shake my head. "I thought we were allies now."

"We are. Allies who have each other's backs, but you don't just show up unannounced. We're allies, but we're not *friends*."

"Where is he?"

"Sighted at the Wolf and Moon last night. Ruthie told us."

And by us, he means Vadka, Rafail's best friend. Ruthie's his sister-in-law and bartends at the Wolf and Moon. It helps having an observant ally in the local bar. There's a reason we know everything. Lips loosen over drinks.

"So he's not hiding. Interesting."

I can *hear* Rodion's smirk on the other end of the line. "Ask your girl," he says.

I scowl. "She's not my girl."

Anissa feigns being affronted with an exaggerated open mouth, her hand splayed across her chest. She holds my gaze and shakes her head.

"Right." I can hear the note of derision in his tone.

Just a girl I keep locked up, feed by hand, and growl at whenever another man so much as breathes on her.

Totally normal behavior.

I grit my teeth and growl.

"Hey, I'm just saying, if it walks like a duck, fucks like a—"

"Shut the fuck up."

"Oooh. Touched a nerve?"

Touched fucking all of them.

"I'm just giving you shit. You're one of the last to fall, and this woman's gonna do you in. Mark my words."

She will *not*. She's here because I forced her, not because she wants to be.

"Fuck you."

"It's alright," he says, snarky as fuck. "You can do this. Be a big boy. Use your big boy words."

I exhale through my nose. "I fucking hate you."

"Nah, baby, you *love* me. Now go take care of your girl and figure out what the fuck Cillian O'Rourke wants here."

I hang up the phone as Anissa polishes off the last of her toast. "You men show affection so strangely," she says, shaking her head. "Probably your bestie on the line, eh?"

I glare at her.

How'd she know?

But when she busts out laughing, I huff out a breath. "I tease, I tease," she says, drinking from her steaming mug of tea. "I saw Rodion's name pop up on the caller ID." Her gaze levels with mine. "You don't think you're the only one who knows how to stalk, do you?"

I definitely fucking don't.

The perpetual glint in her eyes fades a bit. "Did he say something about the Irish?" I note the way she moves without meeting my eyes, standing to rinse her dish and put it in the dishwasher. She takes out a mug and pours me a cup of coffee. "Cream? Sugar?"

I shake my head and take it black.

"Cillian O'Rourke's in town."

Something flickers in her gaze. "That's strange. Why?"

"That's a good question, isn't it?"

She wipes crumbs off the counter and doesn't meet my eyes. "Thought you were friends now."

"We're allies."

She looks over her shoulder. "There's a difference?"

"Yes."

Leaning her ass up against the counter, she looks genuinely curious. "How?"

"You lay down a life for a friend. A friend calls you, you drop everything and go to them. A friend has a kid—they're your blood. An ally means you don't fight, doesn't mean shit about actual loyalty."

You take a brand for a friend.

You bury the body of a guy you fucking loved out of loyalty because he broke the code.

No. Cillian O'Rourke is no friend of mine. I don't like that he's sniffing around, asking questions about their missing forger.

"I love how you frame it all so generally," she says with a sad smile. "And no, people don't treat each other that way for friendship. *You* do." Her gaze flickers away. "That's you, boo. Not everyone."

Doesn't matter.

She goes on. "Alright, so today we buy me clothes, and we go find Mr. O'Rourke. Make small talk. We meet him, and I'll tell you exactly why he's here." She smiles sweetly and clucks her tongue. "And here you thought you were just bringing me back for my pussy."

Jesus.

But she's right. Who better to ferret out O'Rourke than the woman who worked by his side for years?

"So I need clothes. Makeup. Nighttime eye cream before I develop *bags. God.* Shoes. Maybe a mani-pedi. Do they have gel polish here?" She winks at me. "Lingerie. Can't exactly keep wearing nothing but your oversized tees, can I?"

No, no, she cannot.

"So what's around here? I want options. You *do* want me to look presentable, right? And go ahead, tell me your greatest fantasy. School teacher? Sexy librarian? I can do that too."

My greatest fucking fantasy is standing in my kitchen.

"Why the long face?" she asks curiously. "Afraid the brutal Brava enforcer's become a glorified shopping assistant?"

My fucking god, I will tattoo my name across her ass before she steps foot outside of this house.

She's playing me, but I already know I'm going to let her win.

Anissa's back's to me as she's rifling through my fridge. She spins around with a carrot stick in her mouth. "And also, this might be the *only* time I ever admit your mother is right, but you do have a serious lack of food in this house. Can we get some food?"

I should've left her in the cage. Could've fed her fucking triangles of toast right through the metal bars.

The dryer buzzes down the hall.

"Go get changed. We're heading into town."

UNHINGED

CHAPTER 13

ANISSA

IT'S KINDA interesting going into town with a guy like Matvei. He parts the crowd with a look. I'm not even sure he knows he's doing it.

His hand rests on my lower back, a sign of possession. Men don't even look at me. Women stare at him, then me, wide-eyed and fascinated. And *many* obviously recognize him.

I've never been in this little town outside of Moscow before, but I've heard about it—small, tight-knit. Ruled by Bratva. They're known for their excellent food, curated shopping, and Bratva enforcers.

He walks beside me as we look for O'Rourke under the pretense of shopping, but he's nowhere I'd expect him. The bars, the alleyways, the usual haunts. He's a big guy, hard to miss.

"You sure Rodion was right? He was heading out of the country and definitely not here."

Matvei's lip curls into something like a half smile, but his gray-blue eyes are steely. "I'm sure."

Maybe I should be afraid. I should definitely be planning my next escape, but instead, something dark and dangerous and seductive tempts me. Because for all his talk of punishment and retribution, he hasn't really hurt me. Not yet.

He says it's about loyalty, about making me suffer. But then why does he stop himself when he *could* break me? Shove me in a cage as well-furnished as a luxury hotel? Why does he feed me, wash me, and make my body sing? Why does he look murderous when anyone so much as glances at me too long?

I'm playing the long game, earning his trust. But then, why do I watch him when he isn't looking? Why do I notice everything about him?

Why does something dark and thrilling curl in my stomach when he says I'm his? I need to be careful.

He isn't the only one losing control.

It's time I changed the game.

I know exactly how to play it.

"Here, first, please. Do I have a budget?"

"Of time or money?" he asks, stormy eyes narrowed.

"Uh, both?" My eyes light up at the glittering rows of cosmetics and lotions, lip gloss and eyeshadows. It smells like heaven in here. All that's missing is an excellent little cosplay shop where I could get some wigs and trendy little outfits. I'll have to go hunting online.

"The quicker we are, the better."

I nod, lifting a tube of my favorite lipstick, a neutral stain that gives me just a hint of color.

He hasn't said anything about money.

So I have a little fun. I grab the best skincare products, my favorite makeup. I treat myself to a luxury box of haircare products and a few of my favorite scents. It's a shopping spree funded by the Bratva. It feels like poetic justice. And even though he doesn't look at the total at the register, he definitely notes the creepy guy at the exit who scurries away with one look from Matvei.

I buy the prettiest panties and the most comfortable, silkiest bras. A variety of clothes and shoes for comfort and style. And every store we go to, I step up my game.

I lean in too close when he isn't expecting it, close enough to catch the hitch in his breath.

I brush my fingers over his wrist, light as silk, when I'm looking at options by the lotions. I pretend I don't notice the way his fingers twitch as if eager to restrain me.

I bare my neck when I spritz on body spray, tipping my chin just so. "Like this one?"

I tilt my head just enough when I speak—letting my voice dip, my lips part. Just enough to make him notice.

And he does. My god, he does.

I can see it in the way his fists clench when I get too close. The way his breathing shifts when I touch him. In the heat of his wicked gaze. *Wicked.*

He wants to hurt me, but he... doesn't.

Instead, he shadows me. Watches the way I move. Takes his sweet time threading his fingers through my hair and doesn't even bother hiding it when he inhales deeply.

"You like that scent?"

He only growls low in response.

Affirmative.

"You see O'Rourke anywhere?" he asks.

I'm frowning at my phone. The text I sent Cillian shows undelivered. "No, and he *always* read my texts."

Matvei makes a sharp, irritated sound. "Maybe he finally figured out you were *mine*."

I glance up, arching a brow at him. "Yours?" I lean in closer. My breasts brush his chest. I ghost my fingers over the swell of his bicep.

"Tell me otherwise, *solnyshka*."

I'm used to arguing, pushing back, but the way he says it—nah. I'm going to sit with this a little longer.

He's watching me. Not just the way a hunter watches prey. No... this is different. Deeper. Like he's memorizing my pulse in my throat, my movements before I make them.

"Don't know what you're talking about," I say with a smirk.

We're standing outside a shop. He's laden with shopping bags in each hand.

Now might be a good time to run.

"You play dangerous games."

I feign innocence. "I don't know what you mean."

Run.

Too late.

He moves before I can blink. He doesn't grab or pull me but shifts—hard—so that my back meets the brick wall behind me. Two young women walking past stare, their conversation coming to a stuttering halt. One gives me a look of pure jealousy, and I shake my head at her.

You have no idea.

"Do you think I don't see it?" His hand comes up, and for a moment, I think he's going to grab my chin. Instead, he skims his knuckles over the curve of my jaw. I shudder and move closer. I'm wet.

I want him to hurt me.

I want him to push me against the wall until it hurts, until he's crowded me in, nearly suffocating me, his hand flexing around my neck. I want to scrape my nails over his tats and take pleasure in his groans, to push him so hard he nearly stumbles before he pins me beneath him, face down, pressed into the bed while he spanks my ass before he rails me from behind.

I swallow.

"You, testing me. Teasing."

I don't deny it. Instead, I smile. "You're the one obsessed with this whole concept of *ownership*. Keep saying *mine* and all that, half a breath away from smacking your chest like a gorilla."

His nostrils flare, and his eyes darken.

Hahaha.

"There y'are, lass." We both stiffen. Matvei's eyes narrow on mine, as if assessing whether or not I planned it. I give him a shrug just to keep him guessing.

I tilt my head over Matvei's shoulder to see O'Rourke, feet planted on either side of him, his eyes fixed on me. "Been looking for you," he says as if a wall named Matvei Kopolov isn't standing directly between us.

"Have you?"

Matvei turns around and jerks his chin at him. "O'Rourke."

"Kopolov."

Their glares are assessing and pointed, but neither makes a move.

Boys.

"You didn't waste any time, did you, Kopolov?"

"Not something I generally do," Matvei retorts. "Rodion says your boss met with Rafail yesterday. Looks like everything's going as planned, no?"

They share a look I can't quite read before O'Rourke nods slowly. "Aye."

"Something you need?" Matvei asks, his tone sharp enough to cut diamonds.

"No. My visit today had shit all to do with you," Cillian says. "I was needed nearby and fancied I'd grab a cuppa before I headed home." He winks at me, and I swear to god, smoke comes out of Matvei's ears.

When he turns back to me, his gaze is feral, his voice a low growl. "Fucking tell me what went on between the two of you. *Now.*"

I stare at him, taken aback. "Nothing." I narrow my gaze. "But if it *had*, it's none of your fucking business."

Leaning in so his mouth is up to my ear, his voice is tight and low. "None of my business? Anyone who touched you before me is my fucking business."

Oh *really*? I shake my head and roll my eyes, but only to mask the sudden fear that courses through me. I *wish* he knew who touched me before and what happened. It wouldn't be what he thought it was. Not at all.

How can a memory scare me more than the dangerous man standing in front of me now?

I close my eyes at the flashback, the pain still vivid all these years later.

Pain. Blood. Cruel laughter. I was sixteen years old, running for my life, only to be dragged back and overtaken. Beaten. None of the blind rage I'd experienced before. This was slow. A lesson, but I was only the messenger. A boot to my ribs. A knee driven between my legs. Tearing. A heavy boot to my belly. Blood. So much blood.

I try to blink it away. The memory clears like the foggy remnants of a nightmare. His gaze narrows on mine.

"Were you and O'Rourke a couple?"

I grit my teeth and glare at him. Just when I think he's got some redeeming qualities, he shows his true colors. "No, you *asshole*. I wanted to be with the Irish so I could have their protection, but they kept me apart from them. O'Rourke treated me like one of his men but with less respect." I roll my eyes. "*God.*"

It gnaws at me. I wanted more than they gave me, and it doesn't seem fair. The memory of what happened—the rejection from the Irish, knowing they have no allegiance to me anymore, that they don't owe me anything—it aches.

And the man in front of me now—one second, I feel like he cares, but I know it's only attraction. He doesn't care about me. He wants to punish me, to hurt me.

When he leans in and buries his nose in my hair, I freeze, curious. He inhales, deep and long, as if allowing my scent to invigorate him.

"What are you doing?"

A lazy smirk tugs at his lips. "I like the way you smell. I had a dream about you last night."

"Did you?"

"Yeah. Can't get you out of my fucking mind."

He says it like a confession. Like a curse.

"Let's finish shopping."

I don't like being outside in public for long. But before I can argue, a shadow behind him catches my attention.

The entire square is alive with movement—noise, shuffling, voices. I've seen chaos before. Thrived in it. But there's something about today that sends a cold shiver sliding down my spine.

Matvei has enemies. So do I.

A flicker in the crowd—eyes locking onto mine. A shadow where there shouldn't be one. A face too familiar. Too wrong.

My breath hitches.

For the first time in years, I feel real fear.

Not even with Matvei did I feel like this.

My muscles tense.

"What is it?"

"Nothing. I saw something that unnerved me, but I couldn't tell you what."

His voice is low, unreadable. "Try."

His grip tightens just enough to ground me. Just enough to force me back to the present.

Swallowing hard, I glance back to where the figure had been. But there's nothing.

Maybe it's just paranoia catching up to me.

I shake my head. "I'm okay."

He doesn't press, just nods. Then he takes my hand, leading me forward, on the outside of the road, as always. Close enough that our arms brush—a silent shield between me and the rest of the world.

And then, I continue to shop.

I love it. I come to life when I shop—the fabrics, the scents, the colors. Something new and shiny.

"Can I help you?" a woman asks, looking down her nose at me.

But before I can respond, Matvei's voice cuts through.

"Scratch that."

I blink at him.

"We're done here," he says. "Let's go home."

And for the first time, I like hearing him say the word *home*.

It's not home.

But why does it feel that way?

Why do I like the way his fingers tighten around mine?

Why does it send a thrill through me when he leans in and smells me?

Why do I love the way he opens the door for me and gestures for me to go in first?

I love all of it.

But my mind is back on my past, the rejection from the Irish, the pain that took away my choices.

I stare out the window, fingering the edge of the bag in my lap.

"You spoiled me today," I say.

"If buying you what you need is spoiling, then you and I have different definitions of the word."

"Really? What does it mean to you?"

"Letting you get away with everything."

I smirk. "Then I'm definitely not spoiled."

Matvei doesn't let me get away with anything. Not even the things I should.

By the time we reach his house, the unease I felt in the square hasn't left me. If anything, it's worse.

I'm breathing hard when we make it to the front door.

He stands behind me, watching. "You're shaking." His voice is steady. Controlled. "Why are you shaking?"

"I told you—"

"I don't care what you told me."

That's the worst part. He doesn't lose control, and somehow, that makes him terrifying.

He leans in. "What did you see back there?"

"Nothing."

I snap away from him, wrapping my arms around myself, shielding. Grounding. "Just let me go in. I want space."

Silence.

I don't expect him to listen.

But then, the door opens, and I step inside when he gestures for me to go first.

It's warm in here. Bright. Clean. And I immediately feel my pulse begin to slow.

I wasn't prepared for the way the word home would hit me.

But I've been living a nomadic existence for so fucking long.

And I'm angry with myself for even wanting this.

What I love about being able to change my appearance and slip from place to place is that I don't have to put down roots.

I've spent my life running—from control, from the identity forced upon me by my father before he died.

It's made me put my guard up. Made me use my skills in deception and forgery to craft my ultimate escape plans.

It's forced me to trust no one.

Maybe... maybe I'm tired of running.

Maybe I don't want to anymore.

Does that mean I'm giving up?

I won't give up. I can't.

I need to stay until an opportunity comes. Until I can run again.

Matvei doesn't love me.

I'm only a tool to him.

A prize.

I need to remember that.

Then why do I watch him when I think he isn't looking?

Why can't I help but notice the nervous energy he hides by tapping his foot or checking his phone?

Why does it feel so dark and absolutely *thrilling*... when he calls me his?

CHAPTER 14

MATVEI

SHE KNOWS what she's doing.

For days, I've kept us secluded at my house, and she doesn't seem to mind it. I don't know why. Maybe she has a mild case of agoraphobia—she was fun at first when I took her shopping, but something changed. She got uneasy. Unsettled. And she wouldn't tell me why.

She's made no mention of wanting to leave, and instead, she's making herself at home. She knows she can escape. But she doesn't. Not that I'm complaining.

She's beautiful. So fucking beautiful, my girl. And she knows exactly what she's doing.

I made love to her the night after we went shopping. That was several days ago. Since then, I've been busy and let her roam through my house, adding her signature touch. At first, I didn't understand what she was doing. It wasn't like she changed anything major, but I started noticing—the throw blanket over the couch, the diffuser filling the air with something calming, the stack of kitchen towels where I used to only use paper.

Anissa knows how to cook.

"The fact that you have a kitchen like this and don't use it is an absolute travesty," she said, tying on an apron. It was ridiculous. Adorable. She didn't look like the domestic type in the slightest, but then she rolled her sleeves up and got to work.

And she knows what she's doing. They say the way to a man's heart is through his stomach. I never believed that shit, but every time she puts a meal in front of me that reminds me of my childhood—something warm, something familiar—I fucking feel it.

She's doing it on purpose.

She leans too close when she's not supposed to, just enough for me to catch her scent. I still put her to bed in her cage every night, but at this point, it's just for show. If I really wanted to keep her here, I have other ways. And she knows that. She likes it.

She brushes her fingers over my wrist when she takes dishes from the table, a light touch—like an afterthought. But it's not. It's calculated. I know better.

She tilts her head just so when she speaks, her voice dipping soft, getting under my skin.

And it's working.

I want her in my bed. Not just when I fuck her. I want her there when I roll over in the middle of the night. I want her soft skin, her scent, her heat. I want to shove her against the wall and make her stop this game she's playing—but I don't. Because deep down, I don't want her to stop.

I watch her too closely now, memorizing every flicker of emotion, every micro expression. The way her lips part slightly before she lies. The way her eyelids droop when I threaten to spank her. The way she bites her lip when I do.

The way she smells—fuck, the way she smells—like something sweet beneath sharp steel. I could be separated from her for fifty years and still smell that and think of her.

But this is all an act. She isn't real with me. She's spent so much time shifting from disguise to disguise, I doubt she even knows who she is anymore. Authenticity terrifies her. At least, that's my theory.

If I wasn't so fucking dead set on getting revenge and proving my worth to the Bratva, I might find it amusing. But I don't. It's fucking infuriating.

She's in my dreams.

I wake up angry. Unsettled. My cock hard as fuck. I bury myself inside her, and *even then*, it doesn't satisfy me. I don't just want to fuck her. I want to own her.

But it isn't up to me.

I can say the words, claim her, but until she gives herself to me—truly submits—it's just noise. It's just a lie.

And then she does it again. Turns too slowly when I speak. Lets her fingers linger too long on my forearm. Holds my gaze just a second too long. Bites her lip. Breathes too deeply.

And finally, at breakfast, after she sets a fucking feast in front of me, I look up at her.

"What game are you playing?"

That smirk. That fucking smirk makes me want to grab her by the hair, yank her back, and punish her.

Slow and knowing, she leans in, her breath sweet and warm against my ear.

"What are you talking about, big guy?" Her voice is teasing, dangerous. "What if I told you I'm not playing at all?"

And then something in me snaps.

I grab her wrist and yank her onto my lap, her breath hitching just before I seal my mouth over hers. She meets me—teeth and tongue, hands in my hair, nails biting into my scalp like she wants me to feel it.

I do.

She gasps when I grip her hips and drag her against me, making sure she feels my erection pressing into her ass so she knows how badly I need her. My fingers dig into her thighs, my control hanging on by a thread.

"Go ahead, little ghost," I growl against her lips. "Keep lying to me. Keep telling me you're not playing games. Like you're not fucking biding your time until you can run again."

She grins, slow and wicked. "I thought you liked it when I ran," she whispers. "I thought you loved to chase me."

"You know I fucking do."

I wait for her to run. I want her to. I want to give her a head start, chase her down, pin her against the wall.

But she doesn't.

Instead, she moves—rocking against me, rolling her hips in a slow, devastating grind. My grip tightens, and she fucking moans, and that's it. That's the last snap of restraint I have.

I stand, lifting her with me, carrying her to my bed. Our bed.

I throw her down onto the mattress, tearing off her clothes and then mine. She looks up at me, eyes dark and hungry, lips swollen from kissing.

She dares me.

She tests me.

I crush my mouth to hers, dragging my teeth over her bottom lip before moving down, biting at the sensitive skin of her throat. She gasps, thighs squeezing around my waist.

I press my knee between her legs, forcing them open.

Claiming her.

My hands leave bruises. Marks she'll feel tomorrow. And she likes it.

She fucking loves to hurt.

And I fucking love to hurt her.

My hands find her wrists, pinning her down, keeping her exactly where I want her. And still, she twists under me, but it's just another one of her games. She wants me to overtake her.

She wants me to make her submit.

So I do.

I fucking do.

I take my time breaking her apart—holding her hands down, licking her nipples, dragging my teeth over her skin. Savoring every gasp, every whimper, every desperate push against me.

She slaps at me when I let her go for even one second, and I let her come undone before I grab her hair, yank her head back, and bite her neck.

She groans, shaking, panting, her hands clawing at me.

I welcome it.

Just when she looks like she got her way, I roll onto my back and pull her on top of me.

"Ride me."

I slap her ass hard—until she squeals, until my handprint blooms on her naked skin.

She looks at me like she's won.

And maybe she has.

I don't just want her.

I need her.

"You keep fucking pushing me," I growl, my voice barely

holding together. "Do you really wanna see what happens when I stop holding back?"

Her lips part, a slow smirk curving at the edges.

My god, she's gorgeous.

My little ghost. Just a shimmer of a person in front of me—untouchable, elusive, a fucking witch.

"That's the thing, Matvei," she whispers. Mocking. Inviting. "I don't think you want to hold back, do you?"

My grip tightens in warning.

But her gaze holds mine.

My mouth crashes against hers.

This is war.

Brutal. Claiming.

She's never been the kind of woman to yield—so she bites back.

Her nails rake down my arm, leaving angry, red welts in their wake.

I flip her back over on the bed, my body caging hers. She knees me and gets seconds of leverage before I push her down again, my hand wrapping around her throat.

The mattress tips beneath us.

She looks alive.

Her eyes alight, her grin wicked.

"You like this," I murmur. "Maybe I should punish you."

Her eyes burn into mine, my control hanging by a thread.

"Be careful what you fucking tempt me with, you little witch."

She's casting a spell on me.

My hands on her are rough, unyielding. She wants to wear these bruises like a brand—like my brand.

And I want to mark her.

Every movement is like a battle—nails dragging, teeth clashing, grips tightening, bodies colliding in a war of pleasure and pain. Violence. Need.

I grab my cock. "Play with your fucking nipples," I order.

She pauses, eyes wide, breath hitched.

Her hips arch while I fist my cock, pumping, eyes locked on her belly, her fucking gorgeous body that will bear my children and tether her to me irrevocably. I might be obsessed.

I'm not sorry.

"Get on your fucking knees. Head down. Ass up."

She scrambles to obey.

I reward her with a hard, punishing slap to her ass. My handprint blooms, so pretty on her skin, and I can't help but lean down and kiss it. She rocks on all fours.

I thrust into her in one brutal move.

Claiming.

She arches her back, her fingers digging into the bed.

"Matvei." She groans as I slam into her, her body welcoming me.

I thrust into her, again and again, until she moans and arches into me.

My body is heavy above her, and my breathing is ragged.

I continue thrusting, hips slamming against her ass.

I spank her hard, the satisfying crack of my palm against her ass. Once. Twice.

It doesn't bring the relief I crave.

I spank her again, just to hear her scream.

I fist her hair and yank her head back as I move, my grip tightening.

She moans, right on the cusp of relief, and I feel the first spasm of pleasure rip through her.

I come.

I fucking come.

Spilling into her.

Groaning against her skin.

Kissing the bite marks I left on her neck and shoulders as she screams her own pleasure.

CHAPTER 15

ANISSA

His body is heavy against mine, his breath still rough against my neck. I should feel trapped. Instead, I feel... something way more dangerous.

Understood.

Complete.

And it scares the fuck out of me.

When he lifts his head, his eyes dark and unreadable, he stares down at me. "This doesn't change anything."

I grin at him and roll over, running my fingers along the lines of welts and scratches down his back and arms. "Oh, honey." I wink at him to distract him. I don't want to let him know how raw and vulnerable I feel right now. "You keep telling yourself that."

I wince when he looks down at the bruises he's left on me. Fingerprints on my arms, scratches on my inner thighs. Bite marks and welts. Where others may look down and feel abused, this is mine. I *own* it.

Hurting like this when we have sex is the most freeing experience of my life. I've never wanted anything more. Other people, even the Irish, treated me like I was a delicate fucking flower. And I'm not. I like being pushed, prodded, broken. I can't explain it, but there's something about being flayed open like this that makes me feel so satisfied. It's as if his pain makes mine more bearable. It's controlled.

"We should probably put... some antiseptic on that?" Now that the haze of lust is lifting, I see that I scratched the fuck out of him like a cat.

He reaches for my shoulder, and I wince. What the hell? I look down to see a bite mark that's already bruising.

"Oh my god. Fucking hell. I overdid it." His voice cracks as he says, "I'm sorry."

I put my hand on his shoulder and push him back a little. "Stop that. Don't you dare fucking apologize. That was brilliant."

The heat of his body, the ragged way he breathes against my skin, the weight of what we just did presses down on both of us. I know it does because of the way his forehead meets mine, and he breathes heavily.

He shakes his head. "I could've hurt you."

I meet his gaze. "I could've taken more."

Silence.

Heavy.

Charged.

Then, a shift—so small, so lethal. His grip tightens, his thumb dragging over the inside of my wrist as if checking for a weak point, needing to feel my pulse thrumming like something caged. "I know," he murmurs. It feels like a confession. His voice is quieter now but no less dangerous. "That's what terrifies you, isn't it?"

My breath catches. I can't look away. Because... he's right. I've spent my whole life running, outthinking, outmaneuvering the few men who ever got close to me.

Until... him.

He doesn't just chase me—he's caught me. And he might just break me.

He stares into my eyes, and I worry he can read me, that he knows what I fear worse than death.

I breathe out a sigh of relief when he nods toward the bathroom. "Shower. Now. I got a text we need to respond to."

But he doesn't make a move.

"Oh?"

My limbs are heavy, my body aches, and my skin is raw where he spanked me, bit me, and held me down. I should get up and move, slip away like I always do. But this time, I don't. I can't. Because he's still here, and something's wrong.

"Matvei?"

I half expect him to roll away, put on that cold mask, that calculating detachment that reminds me I asked for this. Because I did.

But he doesn't. Instead, he touches me. Not rough or possessive. His fingers trace over my skin, over every bruise and mark he left, as if memorizing the damage. His breath hitches, and when I glance up at him, there's something in his expression I don't understand. Regret? Guilt? It's almost like he's ashamed of himself. Like he hates himself for the way he just fucked me.

A part of me thinks about throwing it in his face, laughing at him, taunting him. But I won't. I can't. Because when he moves, when he leaves the bed, I feel his absence like he just took a part of me with him. What the fuck is that?

I sit up slowly, my body sore, my thighs shaking. He fucked the hell out of me, and he was not gentle.

And then—warmth. Gentleness. A cloth pressed to my skin, wiping away the sweat, the mess, the evidence of what we just did. I freeze. There's nothing he could've done that would've taken me off guard as quickly as this.

I don't know what to do. He kneels in front of me, his expression unreadable as he cleans me and takes care of me. Carefully, delicately, like I'm something fragile. Like he cares.

I bite my lip hard enough that it hurts because something inside me is breaking open, and I can't handle this. I don't want him to know that his tenderness undoes me in a way his roughness never could.

I can handle his cruelty, his punishment. I can handle the way he holds me down and takes me like I belong to him, tosses me around, slaps my ass, bites me, marks me. But this? This tenderness? This fucking gentleness?

I want to shove him away, tell him to stop because it's making me sad. My throat is tight, my chest is hollow, and my hands curl into fists in my lap. His fingers skim over my skin, his touch light.

"Anissa." His voice is low and strained.

I shake my head. I don't want to look at him because if I do, I might cry. And I don't cry. Why is he treating me like I'm something precious?

For the first time... I don't want to run. I want to stay right here.

"We're going to the Kopolov house," he says with a self-deprecating smirk. "You should wear... long sleeves."

"I should wear a strapless, backless top," I snap. "I'm not ashamed of the marks you left on me. Are you?"

For one second, the momentary softness evaporates, and in its place is my ruthless captor.

"I'm not fucking *ashamed*," he says in a low voice. "But any fucker in that house will take one look at you and know what I did, and I'd fucking have to kill them. *I'm* the only one who touches you. I'm the only one who fucks you. *I'm* the only one who knows when I fuck you. Understood?"

I nod as my brain catches up to me. "Wait a second. You said Kopolov house?"

Shit. Shit. No. Fucking shit—

"Yes. You're going to be okay."

I shake my head. I'm not ready for this.

Doesn't matter.

"Rafail called us to him. He and Polina were traveling. They had to leave for an emergency, and now they're home. He wants you to meet your sister, and he wants to talk to you."

Oh shit.

I blanch, and I don't know what to say.

"Excuse me?" I say, raising a brow. He has the audacity to smirk because it's not often he catches me off guard—but he just did. The absolute nerve.

"You heard me." He leans back against the headboard, completely at ease, stretching one arm behind his head. "It's time to meet the family."

My stomach turns to ice. No. No, no, no. Not the Kopolov estate. The lion's den.

Rafail.

I don't want to see the man I ran from. I don't want to see him, or the rest of his wolves, waiting. Watching. Judging. I burned that bridge years ago. I set it on fucking fire. I walked away and never looked back. Matvei came for me, but... what if they still see me as a traitor?

I would rather be a vagabond, running from place to place. I would rather be without any ties at all than under the thumb of Rafail and his brothers. What if they make an example of me?

My pulse pounds in my ears. I scramble off the bed, the sheets tangling around my legs. I shake my head.

"I don't—I don't feel good. Tell them I'm sick. I can't—I can't—"

He's on me in an instant. One hand snaps around my wrist, yanking me back against him. I fall onto the bed, and he pulls me into him, his chest solid and immovable against my spine. His breath is hot at my ear, his voice low. Dark.

"You. Are. Mine."

A shudder wracks through me, and I hate myself for it. I hate myself.

"I found you," he continues, his grip tightening. "I took you. I've punished you."

His lips graze along my jaw. His next words steal my breath.

"No one is going to touch you, my little witch. No one is going to hurt you. And if anybody so much as fucking lays an eye on you, I'll deal with them."

I want to fight him, push him away, snarl that I'm not his possession, that I don't belong to anyone—but the truth? The bold, honest truth?

There's a part of me that's been running, hiding, being nothing but a ghost, that wants to believe him.

So I play it all off like I always do because being serious and honest is sometimes painful. "What if someone cut in front of me in line at the checkout?"

His lips twitch. "Toast."

I almost smile back. "What if I were driving and someone cut me off?"

"I'd slash their fucking tires."

"What if—"

He tilts my chin up until my eyes lock onto his. I close my mouth. "You're mine now. Do you understand me?"

This should terrify me.

Okay, it does.

And yet, a dangerous, reckless part of me exhales at the weight he just took off my shoulders.

Still, I shake my head and give him a curious look. "That's not exactly how this works."

"It is now."

He's so certain.

I stare at him, at all that ink and those stormy, brooding eyes. I can't decide if I want to slap him or kiss him.

My fingers curl into the sheets. "And what if they don't accept me?" I feel like a child on her first day at a new school.

"They'll have to," he says, letting out a dark, quiet laugh.

"And if they *don't*?" I press, my voice sharper now. Wobbling. I hate that it wobbles.

His jaw ticks. "I thought I made that clear. Then they answer to *me*."

I know exactly what it means to answer to him. It's a damn good threat.

Dangerous warmth creeps across my skin. I hate that it makes me feel so safe. I swallow hard, my voice barely above a whisper.

"I'm still a little scared."

What it takes for me to admit that... I've never told anybody I'm afraid. Ever.

He exhales sharply, then cups the back of my neck, dragging me forward until our foreheads touch.

I close my eyes. It feels so fucking right, and that terrifies me.

"Good." His voice is quieter now, rougher. "That means you still have something to lose."

I'm lost. He's caught me.

"If it makes you feel any better, a part of me feels like an outcast too. My brother was once one of us."

"Once?" I ask. "What happened?"

Matvei's eyes darken to storm clouds, more gray than blue. His brow furrows, and he runs his thumb along my cheek like it soothes him. Like I'm his little good-luck charm. His fidget toy.

"He betrayed us. Suffered the ultimate punishment."

"I'm sorry."

"I'm not. It had to happen." He looks away. "My parents will never forgive me. *I'll* never forgive myself."

So his brother betrayed them. And Matvei was the one who acted as the enforcer. Served the punishment.

That's fucking brutal. My heart aches.

I whisper, "That's why your parents hate you."

He shrugs and smirks, but it's not a real smile. His eyes are sad. And a part of me wants to make it better.

"Eh, they always liked my brother better."

I wonder what the ultimate punishment is for betrayal when you're one of them. It wouldn't be a fine, or jail, or something civilized. No.

They must hurt them, beat them, do something physically painful. And then kill them or something. Right?

His own little brother.

My mind is spinning a mile a minute. I'm about to meet my sister. What if she hates me? What if we're nothing alike?

And my mother... I have a mother.

I'm an absolute ball of nerves thinking about facing Rafail and Polina in their own house.

"Do we have to do this?"

I've never been this vulnerable around him. Not after everything we've been through.

When he brushes his thumb along my cheek again, I feel wetness.

I'm crying.

Oh my god, I'm crying.

I hate that.

"Are you really that afraid, beautiful? My little witch?" His lips twitch. "Cast a spell and protect yourself."

Then, softer. "And trust me. You'll be fine."

The depths of his loyalty—it's hard for me to understand. He killed his own brother? For love of the Bratva?

"When do we have to go?"

He glances at the little alarm clock on the bedside table. "We have about an hour."

I leap from his lap, but he catches me midair, tugging me back down.

I fall onto his lap with a quick thump.

"Come here," he murmurs, pressing a soft kiss to my forehead. "Don't go so fast. We just went over a lot. Are you all right?"

He needs to stop being so sweet.

"I'm fine," I huff out. "Can you go back to being an asshole, please?" I shrug. "It makes me more comfortable."

I scoot off the bed just as his hand connects with my ass.

I squeal, smiling, as I head to the bathroom.

I have to get ready for my grand entrance.

CHAPTER 16

ANISSA

I TAKE my time making sure I look perfect. This is what I'm good at—an impeccable physical appearance that masks everything else. But we don't need to dwell on that right *now*.

My hair, my natural color now, hangs down well past my shoulders in thick blonde waves. I miss my wigs. The long, white-blonde feels unnatural now. My eyes are cornflower blue, so I wear thick black mascara to bring them out, but I opt for a sheer pink gloss and a spritz of my favorite body spray. Thanks to our little shopping spree, I am pretty well decked out with clothes.

"I'm guessing business casual?" I yell through the door toward Matvei, who is lumbering on the other side, opening drawers, likely getting changed. He's a big guy. He does nothing quietly or gently.

"What the fuck is business casual?" he says.

"I don't know, skirts, dresses, something like that? Something you'd wear to, like, a business meeting."

Of course, he has no idea what business casual is. He's Bratva. Why would he?

"No, probably just casual-casual. We're not going to a restaurant; we're just going to the family home."

Then something occurs to me. Oh *fuck*.

"Are your parents coming?"

"No, not today. My mom has some kind of book club or something."

Can't think of anything less fun than reading a book with his mother.

"Alright, okay. Just need to grab clothes." I cinch my robe around myself and open the door, finding him standing on the other side, looking like sin in a pair of denim jeans and boots.

My *god*, Matvei.

My ovaries practically self-combust just staring at him. His black hair slicked back, his eyes piercing. The gold hoops in his ears glint under the overhead light—subtle. *Badass*. My eyes roll down to the ink creeping up his neck, disappearing into a fitted black Henley. Heavy black boots.

"You look good enough to eat." I swallow hard. I'm not joking.

The corner of his lip quirks up. "Unfortunately, we don't have time. But I'll take a rain check."

Oh, hell yes, you will. I imagine myself getting down on my knees in front of him, unbuttoning his jeans, pulling out his thick, veined cock, sliding it into my mouth—fuck. I'm wet. And he's right, we don't have time.

"Yes, sir. Rain check it is." I frown at my options. "I'll pick out something for you to wear."

I give him a curious look. Interesting. Alright then. "Go ahead."

I know he wasn't asking my permission, but it's fun to play. He settles on the most modest garment I own—a three-quarter-length sleeve black, fitted top and a pair of dark-colored flared jeans.

"You want us to match, Matvei?"

He looks at what he's wearing, then back at what he picked for me. "That wasn't on purpose, but I think I did it subconsciously. My friend told me that it's a good idea to match your woman."

Your woman.

"Maybe your subconscious was agreeing with him. Which friend was that?"

"Vadka."

I try to remember him. I know he and Rafail are tight. He's married with a kid. His wife Mariah is separate from the Bratva, and even though some of the Kopolov women are active participants, she wants no part of it.

And now I know that her husband likes to match her. Well, that's kind of adorable.

Maybe they aren't all monsters.

Then I remember the stories I've heard of Rafail, the very reason why I ran from this type of captivity to begin with. And my heart is all a flutter. Shit, I'm nervous as fuck.

Nah, not just nervous. *Terrified.* Because Rafail Kopolov isn't just some name whispered in the dark but a legend. I've spent years building my life as a ghost, and this is the very man I ran from. Now I'm walking straight into his den.

I don't know what to expect from them. What if they all hate me? What if the women all gang up on me? I'd rather face a firing squad than a coven of women who actively hate me. Been there, done that.

With the Irish, they kept me intentionally apart from their women. Not sure why. Maybe they were afraid I'd corrupt them. *Ha.*

Matvei is close. Too close. His hand presses against the small of my back, and he leans in and wordlessly kisses my shoulder. Heat skates down my skin, and I wrap my hands around his waist. The corner of his Henley lifts, and I find my hand on the bare skin of his back.

There. That's where he was branded.

"Let me see."

He turns and quietly lifts his shirt to bare his beautiful, muscled back, and right in the lower center part of his back —the Kopolov family brand.

I can imagine it—the pain and raw red flesh when they gave it to him, the way the skin scabbed over and flaked. I shiver. The way the new, tender layer beneath it shone when light hit it, marking him. This is a man who literally let himself be wounded to show his allegiance.

He brought me back as a trophy, the spoils of war. And I know what he's said, what he's planning. Children. A shared bond that will solidify his allegiance to the family. With *me*.

A shiver of fear slides through me when I think about what I can give him... and what I can't.

How will he react?

I brush my thumb lightly over the scar. I don't want to hurt him. "It doesn't hurt anymore," he tells me, reading my mind.

"But it hurt like a motherfucker when you got it." I flinch at the idea of hot metal searing my flesh.

"Was the second most painful thing I've ever experienced."

I swallow hard. "And the first?"

I'm glad his back's to me when he answers because his voice is choked, and I don't want to see the expression he makes. It might break me. "Killing my brother."

I close my eyes when the memory of the most painful night of *my* life flashes before me.

No. That's a closely guarded secret no one will ever know. The shame still burns my cheeks, even as I try to push the memory back down.

I was sixteen. Still under my father's control when he finalized the deal to sell me. I didn't know the full details at the time—only that the man who came to inspect his "purchase" was twenty years my senior, his face etched with the kind of raw cruelty that made my skin crawl. I tried to fight him when he put his hands on me. He laughed and told me I'd be broken in soon enough...

I circle the brand with my thumb.

"Then why did you do it?"

"Because my family's been absolute shit toward the Kopolovs. I wanted to prove my allegiance."

"Do they all have this?" He shakes his head. "No, it's more of an old-fashioned tradition. I was the one who, you might say, brought it back."

I want one.

I blink. What the actual fuck?

I kiss his brand. The mutilated flesh is softer than I expected. Turning, he cradles me in his arms and kisses me. The memory of the night I was attacked fades to white.

His phone buzzes.

"I have to take that."

He steps out of the closet, already answering the call, his voice dropping into something lower, more clipped. I don't hear the words, but I hear the rise and fall of his tone. The sharp curse.

When he comes back, his face is a mask. I wonder if this is what it will always be like with him—these moments of intensity, interrupted by things I'll never be privy to.

"If you decide to run the moment we step foot out of this house..."

I smirk. "I know, I know. You'll come and catch me."

But for the first time in a long time, I don't want to run. Not from him, anyway. From the Kopolovs? That's another story.

The Cottage is quaint in name but not in reality. It's ostentatious in the way that only men with something to prove build their homes. Old money—cold, quiet, powerful—but beautiful. So beautiful. It stands against the darkening sky like a beacon, flanked by sprawling grounds, roses still in bloom.

I wonder, for the briefest moment, what it would have been like if I had lived here.

I almost did.

I would've been the new matriarch of the family.

That's why I ran, of course.

O'Rourke was the one who warned me. Told me what the Kopolovs were really like and what to expect. What Rafail was like—cold, merciless, commanding, the undeniable patriarch.

Argh.

The late afternoon air is cool on my skin as I step out of the car, but it does nothing to ease the nerves curling low in my belly. I am not the kind of woman who gets nervous. I've been in rooms with killers before, in spaces where every breath was measured, every word weighted.

But this?

The knowledge that I was supposed to marry this man—the knowledge that he replaced me with my own sister—makes me uneasy in a way I can't shake.

Matvei parks. We are the only ones outside.

He walks over to open my door, takes my hand, and meets my eyes.

"You don't belong to Rafail," he says, and I don't know if he's convincing me or himself.

"I don't belong to *anyone*," I counter.

Hello.

When he leans in, his eyes locked on mine, he gives me a wicked grin.

"We'll discuss that later, won't we?" He shakes his head at me. "My little witch, always casting spells."

I step out of the car. He's close. Too close. His hand presses against the small of my back, the warmth bleeding through my top like the brand on his own skin. I tense, and he feels it —his fingers flex slightly. Not reassurance—a warning.

"Tell me again, who's here today?"

"Rafail, obviously. And his wife, Polina, who I'm sure you're eager to meet."

I'm not sure *eager* is the right word. I'm nervous as fuck.

"My cousin Semyon, second oldest and second-in-command. His wife, Anya. Her brothers are here often, but they're not here today."

Anya. Pretty name.

I nod, trying to keep track as he goes on. "That's all?"

"It's an intimate gathering," he says quietly. "Vadka will be here as well. He's one of the family's enforcers, not related by blood."

I know the name. I know all their names.

Still, I want his reassurance.

"And Grandfather will be here, as always."

Oh. *As always.*

Thank god his parents aren't coming.

"No Rodion?" I ask. I was kind of looking forward to watching Matvei with his best friend.

He shakes his head. "Not today."

The door is opened before we reach it, a uniformed attendant nodding and smiling graciously before she looks at me. "Welcome."

Her smile falters, her eyes widening.

"My god," she whispers. "The resemblance is uncanny."

"I know," Matvei says quietly. Me. They're talking about me. I swallow hard.

With a sharp tilt of his chin, he dismisses her.

"Why are they staring?" I whisper, uncomfortably aware of everyone's eyes on me.

"You'll understand in a minute," he murmurs back.

His hand finds the small of my back again. This time, I don't mind.

I'm breathing rapidly, my pulse fluttering. He turns and looks at me, almost curious.

"You ran—repeatedly—from one of the Kopolov family's most dangerous men," he muses. "And you expect me to believe you're afraid of a little dinner?"

We both know it's more than that. I'm about to face the man that has every right, in the eyes of the Bratva, to slit my throat and bury my body. I'm about to face the sister I never knew I had, the one who ended up married to the man I ran from.

I've never wanted to run so badly in my life.

But I smile at him anyway.

"I'm not afraid," I lie.

CHAPTER 17

ANISSA

"Hmm."

Inside, the large formal dining room hums with quiet conversation. Crystal glasses catch the chandelier's light, throwing sharp reflections against the walls. I know who everyone in this room is.

Everyone except the woman who looks like my *mirror image*.

I barely register Semyon, his sisters Yana and Zoya, or even the man who was supposed to be my husband.

My gaze locks on the blonde. A hush falls over the room. Someone drops a glass. It shatters, sharp and brittle in the quiet. No one moves.

"Son of a bitch," Vadka mutters into his drink. "Who knew?"

Matvei exhales a sharp, amused breath. "Gleb, that's who."

I stare, unblinking, at the beautiful woman standing before me now. Willowy where I'm curvy, but the same white-blonde hair, the same blue eyes, the same upturned nose.

I'm dressed in dark-colored jeans and a black top with shiny, high-heeled boots, and she wears a simple pale-pink peasant dress tied at the waist paired with ivory flats.

"It's good to finally meet you," she says. It's so bizarre hearing a voice so much like my own.

Polina.

I stare at her. Her hair is long like mine, falling down her back like silk sheets—pale, blonde, straighter. Mine's wavy. But we have the same eyes, and where I know I'm jaded, her face is soft. Trusting.

God, I miss being able to trust someone.

She wears tiny gold hoops and no other jewelry, except for a gold band on her wedding finger, and I have a line of earrings that go all the way up my ear, gold bangled bracelets, and rings on several fingers.

She extends her hand to me.

"Polina Kopolova. You must be Anissa."

"Yes."

I'm usually bolder than this. Braver. But right now, I feel like a child.

"It's nice to meet you too—except, please understand, I just found out about you. I didn't even know I had a sister."

"I know," she whispers. Something unexpected that I can't quite name passes between us.

And then we're hugging.

I never hug strangers. But this... this feels right.

This woman is my sister.

And I am completely unprepared for the way I react. My eyes sting with tears, my throat tightens, and I can barely swallow past the lump rising in my throat...

Until a deep voice clears his throat beside Polina, and I jump back as if waking from a dream.

Right. Her husband, Rafail Kopolov himself. *Fuck.*

Is this where he puts me in stocks or lines me up in front of a firing squad?

One of Moscow's most feared. Tenacious. Ruthless.

His reputation precedes him—a hardened criminal who shows no mercy.

I let her go as if she's hot to the touch and force myself to meet his gaze without flinching despite the cold, merciless ice in his eyes.

Should I say... I'm sorry?

He is the only one here I have a history with. And none of it is good.

"Anissa," he greets, his voice even, unreadable. "I have to say, I'm surprised."

"Life is full of surprises," I answer, unsure of what, exactly, he's surprised about.

Why did I say that?

"I didn't expect you'd look like my wife's double in an alternate universe." Someone barks out a cough, but no one talks as Rafail's gaze narrows on me, assessing. Cold. Unforgiving.

And then Matvei is beside me, between me and Rafail.

He's bigger than Rafail. And though he is outranked, there's a steadiness to his presence that makes it easier to breathe. Wordlessly, he presses his hand to the small of my back. "Remember your promise to me, cousin," he says in a low, quiet voice.

Not for the first time, I'm grateful he's so possessive.

Rafail's eyes narrow just slightly. There's a tick in his jaw.

Finally, after a long pause, he nods. "I never go back on my promises."

They don't need to say it out loud. *He's promised Matvei that I'm his.*

Matvei told me as much.

And by giving me to Matvei, I assume any retribution Rafail would seek is now void, but... it's an assumption, and those are dangerous.

"Well, well, well," an older, raspy voice says behind me. "We have mirror images here. In all my years, son..."

I turn. Matvei shadows me like he's my bodyguard. I guess here... he *is*. His hand rests possessively on the small of my back.

The elderly man who spoke is hunched over, one gnarled hand gripping the curved end of a cane. His clothes are old and faded but neatly pressed, and there's a twinkle in his sharp eyes.

"I was good friends with twins back in the day," he continues, nodding sagely. "But they knew each other. This? This is the kind of thing they do on reality television, don't they?"

He studies me, then Polina, before his gaze flickers back to me.

"Do you know what we say in Russia about twins in the family?" He smiles. "Two pairs of eyes, one soul."

I blink. My throat is tight. Polina gives me a soft smile that almost negates the look of hatred from her husband.

The old man extends his hand. "They all just call me Grandfather," he says. "Welcome, welcome."

Then, his eyes harden as he waves his cane at Rafail and winks at me.

"I'll make sure my grandson behaves himself."

Polina clutches Rafail's arm. "So will I."

I nod to Grandfather. "Something tells me that cane isn't just a prop."

Someone snorts behind me, and another laugh follows. Sometimes, I think before I speak. Most of the time, I *don't*.

A door in the corner of the room bursts open, revealing a bustling kitchen behind it. The air fills with the fragrant scent of garlic and onions, and my stomach twists with hunger.

A tall, fit woman with dark hair pulled into a merciless ponytail strides in, eyes warm as they land on me. *Yana*.

And the youngest Kopolov sister, Zoya, follows close behind.

"You're Yana and Zoya," I say, nodding. "So nice to finally meet you."

Yana smiles, extending her hand.

"That's Semyon and his wife, Anya," Matvei murmurs, nodding to a stern-looking man a bit older than Matvei with dark hair and glasses. He stands by the bar, his expression unreadable as he glances my way. His wife, the beautiful, auburn-haired Anya, stands beside him, murmuring something under her breath—lips barely moving.

Whatever it is, Semyon nods, then gives me a forced smile.

So yeah, these men like to get married.

The table is set beautifully—large platters of fresh bread, dishes of butter, glasses of water and wine beside each plate, and several sets of silverware. Zoya flits about the table, adjusting things.

"We don't always eat this formally," Zoya says, almost apologetically. "Most of the time, we just sit at the kitchen table. But we wanted to put on a good spread for you."

A harsh voice speaks behind us. The shift in Matvei's posture is instantaneous. "Why? For the woman who has Matvei acting like a madman."

I turn, and my stomach drops as he hisses in a breath and curses.

No.

His parents.

"I thought they weren't coming," I whisper to him.

"They weren't supposed to," he whispers back.

His mother stares at me, her beady eyes raking over me in a way that makes me feel like an animal in a cage.

"This," she sneers, "is how you dress for a Kopolov family dinner?"

Matvei goes rigid beside me. Muscles coiled. Barely leashed violence simmering beneath his skin.

I feel like I've been tossed into shark-infested waters, and I'm bleeding. He shifts—now between me and them, shielding me like he did with Rafail.

I swallow hard.

I'm not used to being protected like this.

His mother tilts her head as if waiting for him to agree or to remind me of my place, but he doesn't even look at her.

"She looks *beautiful*." He bends his mouth to mine and kisses me full on the lips, his hands tangled in my hair. It only lasts seconds, but the whole room seems to hold its collective breath. They all saw it.

His mother. Rafail.

Especially his mother and Rafail.

He's already turned his back to her.

My heart beats madly as I feel the weight of everyone's stares even before I sit down. Matvei's bitchy mother is the worst—her eyes sharp as a blade, making no pretense of kindness or even indifference. His father is quieter, but his presence is no less painful, his scornful gaze going from me to Matvei and back again. I wish they wouldn't acknowledge my presence at all rather than treat me like some kind of misfit. I've faced open hostility before, but there's something uniquely irritating about this.

His mother makes a few snide remarks under her breath, and I swear I hear his father say something that sounds like "trash at the dinner table."

Matvei notices immediately and sits up straighter.

"Is there a reason you two are acting like spoiled brats?" His voice is cold and cutting.

Is it too soon to say he's my hero? I'm still sore from where he...

His mother straightens. "How dare you speak to us like that?" She turns to Rafail. "Aren't you going to make him be respectful?"

Rafail's voice is calm but firm. "I make everyone here behave respectfully toward those who deserve it. We have a truce with Anissa. She's paid the consequences for what she did to my family. As she's done nothing to you, so I don't understand the open hostility either."

I stare in surprise. Maybe there's a reason Matvei respects him.

I can't help but stare at his mother. Her lips press into a thin line. Today, instead of her usual ruby red, she's wearing an offensive shade of pink that makes my eyes hurt. "We have every right to be concerned about—"

"You don't," Matvei interrupts, his voice hard and flat. The dismissal in his tone sends a chill through the room. Then, without a word, he places his hand on my thigh and gives me a gentle squeeze. Something in me melts a little.

Matvei's eyes cut to Rafail, who nods, barely perceptible. It's all it takes.

"You two sit here. By me." His voice carries the weight of authority, just as I suspected. The family patriarch, despite his younger years. I know from my recent research—and what I was told—that he became the head of the family at eighteen, after his parents' untimely death. And though he's barely in his early thirties, he carries the responsibility of a much older man.

I watch as Matvei's parents hesitate before quietly moving. His mother's glare still burns into me, but I just smile—sweet and cutting—my fingers deliberately grazing Matvei's bicep possessively. Her lips press even tighter. Perfect.

Matvei smirks, ever perceptive, and drapes an arm around my shoulders, pulling me closer. I don't resist. His mother practically vibrates with fury.

It's not personal, a little voice in the back of my mind whispers.

Matvei doesn't care about me...

Does he?

He's loyal. Loyal to the Bratva, to Rafail, to whatever code he's built his life around. I'm just a puzzle piece in a larger scheme.

The grandfather, thankfully, is much nicer. Unlike some of the others, there's no tension or unspoken threats laced in his words. He and Zoya are warm, even charming, a contrast to the cold brutality of Matvei's parents. Grandfather asks polite questions, engaging in small talk as if we're at afternoon tea instead of sitting in the heart of a criminal empire. His eyes, however, miss nothing.

"I'm told you're quite skilled with disguises," he says, his gaze mildly amused. With a wink, he adds, "A gift like that can be a blessing and a curse, eh?"

My cheeks heat, but he's so friendly I can't take it personally. "I am. Do you need one?"

"Can you make me pass for thirty?" he asks, eyes twinkling.

Everyone laughs, and Zoya looks at me, thoughtful. "What does that mean you're good with disguises? What can you do?"

My voice drops, aware of everyone in the room watching me. Zoya's cheeks flush pink, like she wishes she could take the question back—or at least ask it in private.

Interesting.

Does little Zoya wish to disappear too?

I can imagine it—being under the weight of everyone in this room. Her older, overbearing brothers. Her cousin. Aunt. Uncle. Grandfather.

"I can do anything from subtle changes to a full transformation," I say smoothly. "Hair color, eye color, facial features—anything easily recognizable. I can manipulate all of that." I lean over to her, grateful when others start talking among themselves, and we can talk a bit more freely.

The wine flows, and food is passed on large platters as I talk to her about different disguises. I wonder why I was so nervous. I like being here now that his parents are sitting beside Rafail like they're in the naughty spot.

Vadka excuses himself with a call from home, rising smoothly from the table. At first, I wish *I* had a phone call that could excuse me from the room, but I'm planted right here, glued to Matvei's side.

Then I see the way Vadka looks at his phone, with a shy, unguarded smile. "It's Mariah calling. Be right back."

Now I'm wishing someone would look at their phone like that when *I* called.

He comes back in a few seconds later. "Oh, hey, she's here. I'll let her in."

Zoya leaps to her feet. "Oh my gosh, I almost forgot the cake! Everybody stay right here!" She flees to the kitchen.

"She does a lot of cooking around here," Matvei says. "She likes to."

"Thank fuck *Matvei* doesn't," a woman's voice cuts in from the doorway. "We'd all be eating chocolate-covered ants."

I look up to see a tall woman with wide brown eyes and soft, wavy brown hair that hits her shoulders, standing beside Vadka. He places his hand on the small of her back as she smiles at me. "Anissa? Welcome. I'm Mariah."

I give her a shy little wave back but feel a little more at ease in her presence.

"Oh my god." Matvei groans, rolling his eyes. "Seriously, we did that *one* time. Wasn't even my idea."

I've never seen Matvei's eyes twinkle like that. He looks almost casual. I hardly knew the man had a sense of humor, but here, among friends and his Bratva brothers, I'm seeing another side of him.

Semyon laughs for the first time. I get the feeling he doesn't laugh very often. "You always try to blame Rodion, especially when he isn't here." He shakes his head. "As if Rafail and I didn't practically raise you two and know exactly how you work in league."

His mother clears her throat. "*Excuse* me?"

To my surprise, this time, it's Semyon who levels her with a look. "You two traveled a lot. They practically lived with us every summer. Did you forget?"

She rolls her eyes heavenward, looking personally offended.

So Rafail and Semyon had firsthand experience raising Matvei and his brother. Maybe that's why Matvei is more tolerable than his parents.

I want to see him around Rodion.

Semyon grins. "Then there was that debacle at the nightclub."

Vadka pulls out a chair for Mariah, bending to kiss the top of her head before she sits. My heart turns over.

"You mean *strip club*, don't you?"

Vadka pulls out a chair and slouches into it, stretching his legs out like he's settling in for a show. He tips his whiskey toward Semyon in a salute. I notice the thick gold band glinting on his hand, the same one that matches his wife's.

Wordlessly, he pours her a glass of white wine. "Oh, don't stop now," he drawls, his deep voice laced with amusement. "I *love* this story. The one where those two idiots tried to scam their way into the most expensive strip club in St. Petersburg."

Matvei shakes his head. "Of course you guys have to bring this up when it's just me on the execution block, and Rodion's free and clear."

"I didn't hear about this one," Matvei's father cuts in, taking another sip of wine.

"I handled it," Rafail says simply.

"There were a lot of things you didn't hear about," Matvei mutters. He drags a hand over his face and groans. "Hell, Semyon, why'd you have to bring that up?"

"Excuse me, the *what*?" His mother's shooting daggers at me with her eyes, so of course I need to hear every detail.

Matvei smirks into his drink. Goddamn... it's *adorable*. I lean in and whisper to him, "Are you *blushing*?"

Semyon's eyes twinkle at Vadka, who leans forward, grinning wide, all charm and amusement.

"It was beautiful. Matvei walks in like he owns the place, claims he's an inspector sent to check their business permits." Vadka chuckles, shaking his head. "Rodion, meanwhile, is in the VIP section, helping himself to free drinks like a fucking king."

A buzzing sounds at the end of the table. Rafail glances at his watch with a scowl but nods to Vadka to keep going.

"We were young and stupid," Matvei says, rolling his eyes.

Semyon snorts. "As if you're both too mature to pull that shit now."

Matvei shrugs and deadpans, "We'd just get away with it now."

I laugh into my hand. Matvei pours me another drink. It feels... *right*.

"And the two of you were absolutely *fucked* the second you saw Rafail walk in."

Matvei winces as if remembering it all in vivid detail. Hooo, boy. I get the feeling Rafail wasn't the type to fuck around.

"Caught red-handed?"

Matvei smirks and shakes his head. "I can still remember what Rafail said."

Everyone quiets as he grins, with straight white teeth and perfect charm. My heart turns in my chest. I swallow. It has to be the wine.

"What'd he say?"

"*If you two assholes are going to run a scam, at least make it a profitable one.*" He shakes his head. "Then he hauled us out of there by our collars." He turns to Vadka. "*You* were there. You could've helped a brother out."

Vadka takes a slow sip of his drink, unbothered. "And interrupt that level of stupidity? Nah. I was way too busy enjoying the show. If I remember correctly, you did get some time with a pretty little redhead before you were caught."

"*Vadka*," Mariah says, elbowing him.

My fingers tighten around my wine glass. I'm not super into hearing about him with another woman. Matvei grunts and shakes his head but leans in and whispers in my ear, "Jealous, *solnyshka*?"

I give him a too-sweet smile and shrug. "Not at all," I whisper back. "I'm just wondering if the girls gave you a refund."

His grip on my thigh tightens.

Excellent.

I note how Rafail excuses himself from the table. Polina looks after him with interest.

The conversation moves on, but I watch Matvei carefully. He isn't just an enforcer, a soldier for the Bratva.

This is a man who grew up in a tangled web of loyalty, family, and control.

And somehow, despite it all, he makes me feel like I belong.

Rafail returns to the room, his gaze sharp on mine. "Matvei. A word."

CHAPTER 18

MATVEI

I don't like being apart from Anissa. But when Rafail tells me to do something, I fucking do it. That's part of the problem, really.

"She's fine," he says, casting a narrow glance at Anissa, who's talking to Zoya.

Should we be worried about that?

"I remember what you told me before I got her," I say, meeting his eyes as we walk side by side to his study, a private place where he sometimes holds meetings, but typically only between those closest to him.

"Is she pregnant yet?" Rafail asks. I want to deck him, but I don't have a death wish.

I shake my head. It's only been a matter of weeks, but it definitely wouldn't be for lack of trying. "No."

"Has she tried to run?" he asks, half rolling his eyes as he adds, "again?"

Fire burns in my veins. I love Rafail like my goddamn brother, but I do not like where these questions are going.

"No. Why?" I narrow my eyes at him. "Don't you trust me to take care of her and make sure she does what she's supposed to?"

He sits in his chair and looks at me thoughtfully before answering. Leaning back, dressed as he often is in a charcoal-gray bespoke suit, not a hair out of place, he looks older than he really is. It's the weight of responsibility; I know it is. Still, he's loyal and protective, but he does not fuck around.

"She's your wife's sister," I remind him.

He blows out a breath and sighs. "I know."

I know he knows, but obviously, I felt like he needed a reminder. If he tried to harm her in any way, I wouldn't stand for it. But I don't want him to even entertain the thought, so it seemed advisable to remind him who she is.

"The Irish are asking questions. They may be jealous."

I shrug. Makes sense. Their agreement with her is up, and I swooped right in. I was well within my rights, but it's their loss. "They'd have done the same."

"Doesn't matter."

I grunt. "What do they wanna fucking know?" I ask, but he doesn't answer right away.

"They're up our ass. Seems she got them in trouble."

Whatever.

"She was a contractor for them. She laid out what they needed to do. It's on them if they got in fucking trouble."

He doesn't speak for long seconds, as if weighing his words. He tips his head to the side. "You have feelings for her."

I look away, not wanting to admit it out loud. I've had feelings for her since the first time I looked at her. The first time I watched her. I saw how vulnerable she was, alone. And then, when I found out how much we had in common...

I decided long ago, before I knew Anissa, that I'd be alone. After Gleb was gone, after my parents hated me, after I knew what love was capable of doing—I *wanted* to be alone. I told myself that she was just a job, but now I know how I feel about her. And I don't even like that. She's in the other room right now.

"Be careful," Rafail says. "Allowing yourself to have feelings for somebody will fuck up your judgment."

I bite my tongue to hold back a retort until I taste copper. Reminding him that *he should fucking talk* isn't gonna go over well. He may be my cousin, but he's my *pakhan*.

"What do you want from me?"

"A reminder of what you promised. And keep her here. If she runs, she's a fucking liability. You know that."

"Of course I do."

He nods. "You do that, and I'll make sure your fucking grown-ass parents stay out of your hair."

"How do you propose to do that?" I ask him.

"Sending them away," he says with a smile that doesn't reach his eyes. "Polina's brother has a place in South Africa. Turns out, he needs someone to house-sit. Free vacation."

The trace of humor on his face vanishes. "While they're gone, you change the locks on your house. Trust me when I tell you, you don't need your parents walking in when you're trying to knock up your wife."

No fucking shit. "Yeah. I'll do that."

He stands, dusts imaginary lint from his clothes, and nods.

I stare at him. "And the Irish?"

He blows out a breath and squares his shoulders. "I'll deal with the Irish."

HER HANDS MOVE with a terrifying kind of precision. Not delicate. Not hesitant. *Expert.*

Like she's done this a thousand times. I watch the flex of her fingers as she loads a clip, her gaze focused on the task at hand.

"You're more comfortable around guns than I thought."

She doesn't look up. "That's rich," she says, her eyes finally twinkling at me. "Coming from *you.*"

The table between us is a graveyard of stripped-down weapons and scattered docs. Forged passports. Burner phones. She crafts identities so easily it's almost disconcerting.

I don't like it. It's a not-so-subtle reminder that she can disappear again at any time. *If* I let her.

I won't. I fucking *won't*.

I sit back, my arms crossed, studying her. "You know," she says, in that voice that weaves around me like magic, "If you keep staring at me like that you'll burn a hole through my skull."

I snort. "Maybe I'm trying to make you stay put."

Maybe I'm not lying.

Her lips twitch in an almost-smile. That damned mouth of hers. Always ready to fire back, sharp and dangerous.

"Afraid I'll run?" she taunts, her eyes sharp.

"No," I lie, my voice cold and flat. "I know you'll *try*."

I know it.

A comfortable silence stretches between us. She flips a passport closed and slides it across the table to me.

"Paris exit route. Clean as it gets."

"Excellent. Rafail will appreciate this."

Her eyes flash hard for a second before she can help herself. She still doesn't like doing what Rafail asks.

She moves to the next document without waiting, like it's the normal state of affairs to move from one person's escape to the next.

"So does...does Polina ever see her mother?" She doesn't meet my eyes when she asks, but I note the way her voice wobbles and she swallows hard, as if nervous.

"Yeah, Ekaterina Romanova owns a place in Moscow, though their family is firmly established in The States, too." I pause. It isn't just *her* mother. She's *their* mother.

"Oh." She continues to arrange paperwork without saying much else. But I know this bothers her.

"Do you want to meet her?"

She looks up at me, her eyes wide in surprise. "Me? Meet her?" Her cheeks flush pink.

"Well, she's your mother. I think it'd be natural for you to want to meet her."

She blinks, her eyes wide, and swallows hard again. "Right. Yeah, I—well it makes me nervous, you know? But I—yes." She lifts her chin up. "Yes, of course I want to meet her."

Standing, she walks across from me, sashaying her sexy hips from side to side. I can't help it. I land my hand across her ass, the noise going off like a gunshot.

"Hey!" but the flush in her cheeks speaks more than her objection.

My phone rings with a call from Rafail. "Gonna fill him here on what we found, okay?"

Nodding, she bites her lip. "Please do."

"And I'll see what I can do about you meeting your mother."

It's funny how she can face the most dangerous mobsters in Europe, yet blanch at the thought of meeting her own mother. I lean in and give her hand a squeeze. "I promise," I tell her, my voice low and warm. "You'll like her."

She blows out a shaky breath. "It's not *me* liking *her* that I'm worried about."

CHAPTER 19

ANISSA

I SLEEP in his bed that night.

And the next.

And the next.

Matvei's hunger for me is endless, a craving that seems to border on madness. He doesn't ask but takes, rolling over in the dead of night, his body heavy on mine, possessive, claiming. A hand on my hip, a rough, sleep-sexy murmur, and then he's inside me, stretching me open, filling me like I was made for this.

I am.

I mold around him, slick and ready at a moment's notice, like a fucking law of nature.

I love it. The way he touches me when the world is silent... when it's just *us*. The way his cock slides in me, thick, deep, owning me. The way we move together.

He's insatiable, and I am *not* complaining.

He's mentioned a baby, and if that is his plan, he wins a gold medal for effort.

We fuck in the shower, in bed, cowgirl style, missionary. I sit on his face. He goes down on me until I'm so wet, then glides into me with perfection. We fuck in every room in his house—the guest rooms, every shower, the dining room table, the kitchen.

He fucks me like I'm his full-time job, and the man is looking for overtime.

I've never been with anyone who could meet my needs the way he does. He takes immense pleasure in watching me come. I didn't know giving a woman an orgasm could be a kink, but it is for him. The way his eyes light up when I moan, the way he groans every time I come, the way he won't come when he's inside me until *I* do.

We're messy and loud and unabashed in our lovemaking, and every single time, I swear I let a little bit of my guard down.

But... my period is a few days late. And I know it's not for the reason he suspects or hopes for.

One night, we share a joint together. I sit in his lap, and he blows smoke in my mouth. I take the joint from his fingers and take a tentative hit. I love the way I get lightheaded, and the pressure on my chest loosens.

But that night, I fall asleep high. I dream. I dream so hard. I'm pinned down and screaming for mercy, but no one comes.

I wake up in a sweat.

I should know it was just a dream. I try to tell myself that it is, that I'm not awake, that I'm with Matvei now, not in my father's house, which isn't even there anymore. But it's so vivid, so real. Especially the fear.

It claws at my chest like a parasite, as if trying to get out of my skin. It shakes me to my core. I can still see my abuser—his thick face and jowls, his oily hair and thick fingers. The way he glared at me when I wouldn't submit. I can still feel the pain.

The kicks to my rib cage. A kick to my stomach. The way he ordered his men to beat me and watched, the fucking bastard. The pain. The helplessness. The blood.

I roll over to find Matvei hard and ready for me. I don't want to tell him no.

I want to forget. He slides into me mirthlessly, fucks me until I scream his name, and falls asleep, still inside me.

But I don't forget.

I remember lying in my room, eating saltine crackers and hot tea, the only thing I could keep down in the aftermath of that brutal beating. My father, not to my surprise, took his friend's side.

"You should've gone with him," he said. "How could you do this to me?"

He looked at the broken, beaten body of his daughter and actually said to me, "You should've thanked me for this. He would've taken care of you."

As if he knew anything about taking care of me.

"He won't take you now," he said, but he never mentioned what happened to me when he arranged my marriage to Rafail. I decided then that I would not be used as their property. I wouldn't be taken.

And a part of me, even now, feels that.

I fall back asleep, almost instantly back in the room at my father's house. I want to wake up again. I know this isn't real —I know this is the past, and I have to wake up.

I thrash in the sheets. They're tangled around my legs, and the pain is too much. I'm still half in the dream, still clutched in his grip, the pain of that night etched in my memory as if carved into stone.

I've never felt so helpless in my life, and I told myself then it was the last time.

No one can hurt you if they can't find you.

There's a wetness between my legs. Strong arms wrap around me.

I scream, thrashing, biting at air.

"Anissa, Jesus, it's me."

I'm pinned to the bed, and Matvei's eyes are above mine, boring into me with concern.

"You're dreaming. You're just dreaming. Are you okay?"

I blink, and his face is in front of me. But I can still see my abuser. I can still hear his oily voice, see the yellow of his eyes, and still feel his grip on my arms as he held me and assaulted me.

It flashes in my mind like a bad movie.

I close my eyes, and this time, the memories don't go away like I've trained them to.

I clear my throat.

I try to speak, but I'm in actual pain. It takes a minute to realize it's not just from the memory.

I shake my head.

"I'm okay," I rasp.

But I'm not.

I'm fucking not.

I want him to toss me in that cage, lock me in, and throw away the key.

Because when I'm behind those metal bars, *no one can get me*.

And I can't run anymore.

The pain radiates across my back and spasms in my abdomen. It feels as if someone's wrapped a vise around it and is pulling.

I try to curl my legs up to my chest, but Matvei is on me.

"Get off," I croak.

Reluctantly, he slides off me as if he somehow wanted to make sure I stayed.

Maybe he did.

"What's going on?" he asks. "Are you sick?"

I lift my knees to my chest and rock, and it does a little bit to ease the discomfort.

"I have my period."

He blinks, and something like pain flashes across his face.

"Your period," he repeats, staring at me.

I nod.

"They're really bad when I get them. I have a... condition."

I shake my head.

It hurts too much to explain about scar tissue, illness, and the fucking plague of my life.

Now I know why I'm wet between my legs. And I want to get to the bathroom to clean myself off, but I'm in so much pain. I don't trust myself to move. The doctor I saw in Paris told me the pain level mimics active labor.

I'll never know.

"You're in pain because of your period?" he asks. Is it my imagination, or is his voice wobbling? This big, strong, fearless psychopath. Why does he sound unsteady?

I nod and squeeze my eyes shut as a spasm of pain takes over again.

There are meds that I can take, but I don't have them. I've tried a few different things, but I've been on the run for too long to gather an arsenal of necessities—things like hot water bottles and the right supplements. Those are the types of things you have when you have a... home.

I haven't had a home in over a decade.

I squeeze my eyes shut when the pain wraps around my midsection, stabbing between my legs, my back aching like it's being pulled apart. I try to breathe through it, pressing my lips together and inhaling through my nose, but this is the worst I've ever experienced. I whimper, hot tears splashing onto my cheeks.

He's standing, wringing his hands, looking at me in helpless confusion.

"What can I do?"

I kick off the blanket when the pain hits me again. To my shame and embarrassment, blood smears my legs.

"Oh god," he says, shaking his head as if reliving his own trauma. Maybe he is.

"I don't know." It hurts too much to think right now. "Give me something to clean myself up. Please," I tack on like an afterthought. It's hard to talk.

One spasm builds on another, then another. I hear his heavy footsteps retreat, then return. The bed sinks down when he sits next to me.

"Let me," he says softly.

I shake my head and reach for the washcloth in his hand while he stands there helplessly.

"Leave me alone," I tell him, riddled with shame and pain.

"This doesn't bother me," he starts.

"It bothers *me*! Leave me alone, please."

I get a momentary break from the pain. I breathe through my nose, clumsily clean the blood, dab my wet legs with the towel, and toss everything in the general direction of the laundry hamper.

I curl up on the bed, and I hear him talking on the phone.

I'm afraid he's going to call an ambulance and have me taken to the hospital, but when I breathe hard and try to listen, I'm hit with another spasm of brutal, blinding pain. And I can't think anymore.

The memory of the night of my assault flashes in front of me every time I close my eyes, but when I open them, the pain seems even harder to bear.

I try everything.

I roll onto my side and bring my knees to my chest, a move that sometimes brings temporary comfort. It doesn't.

I get on my hands and knees and rock back and forth—a move an OB in London once taught me—and it has worked before.

Not this time.

I stretch my arms and legs on the bed like a starfish, and it hurts so badly I immediately crawl back into a fetal position, grit my teeth, and bear it.

Just like I did that night. When fighting didn't work, and I couldn't escape, I bore it and reminded myself that I wasn't going to die, that this wasn't the end, and that, eventually, I would get my vengeance.

But there is no getting vengeance when my own body is assaulting me.

God.

I've ruined his sheets.

I bleed heavily because of scar tissue, and I've never found anything that helped with that either.

I need feminine supplies. Privacy. A shower.

But I can't.

I'll get new sheets. I just don't want him near me right now.

There's silence.

Just me.

And my pain.

My memories.

My shame.

And then I hear two voices. A female one and a male one, followed by another male one. But then one leaves, and it's only Matvei and a woman.

And the voice, it... sounds just like my own.

No—

The door opens, and Polina comes in.

She's wearing slouchy sweats, her hair in a haphazard bun, and thin little glasses on the tip of her nose as if she's just woken from sleep and hasn't put her contacts in yet.

"Anissa, tell me what's going on."

She sits on the edge of the bed next to me and reaches for me, then stops herself midair and places her small hand on the bed beside me instead.

My cheeks flame with embarrassment.

I've only just met my sister.

I don't know her at all.

And yet—here I am.

Bleeding through sheets. Crying from pain.

Holding onto the memory of a past I wish I could carve out of my brain forever.

I don't want to see her right now.

Matvei is behind her, pacing on the phone.

She gentles her voice.

"I went to midwifery school," she says softly. "I know a little bit about these things. I'm not an expert, but I might be able to help. At the very least, I might know people who can."

And right in that moment, I look into the eyes of a woman I just met but have somehow known *forever*.

And now, I'm crying for an entirely different reason.

I swipe at my eyes and nod.

"He needs to leave," I whisper.

She looks over her shoulder and holds her head high like the queen that she is, then jerks her chin toward the door.

"Leave us alone."

"I'm not—"

"Go," she snaps at him.

Even from here, in my daze of confusion, I see the way his

eyes narrow, his shoulders snap straight, and then he turns and walks away.

She's the wife of the *pakhan*.

He can't disobey her.

"There," she says with a smile that somehow makes the pain seem a little more bearable.

And then she says something else, but I don't hear her.

The roaring in my ears drowns out everything as another spasm of pain hits.

I rock. I cry out. I grip the sheets so hard my knuckles turn white.

And it doesn't stop.

I can't breathe.

I can't think.

"Is it endometriosis?" she asks, running through a few other conditions I've heard mentioned before, but I don't know for sure.

Because then, I don't hear her voice anymore.

The wave of pain assaults me like the lash of a whip on flesh.

Raw.

Brutal.

Unforgiving.

My breath catches, and I try to hold onto the sheets, move

into a fetal position, and rock back and forth, but it doesn't work.

Polina climbs onto the bed next to me, places both hands on the small of my back, and puts firm, steady pressure.

"My god, you poor girl. I can feel the spasms in your back. Breathe, Anissa. In through your nose, out through your mouth," she says, adjusting her hands on my back in just the right way, and then she presses.

Relief.

Blissful, glorious relief.

Like my body was caught in a vise, and she just pulled the release button.

"Oh my god," I gasp. "Whatever you're doing, that feels better. It feels so much better."

My voice is wobbly and shaky, and I'm still blinking back tears.

But at least now, I can breathe.

"Good," she says in a gentle voice that makes me want to weep.

I'm a fucking mess.

Then she raises her voice. "Matvei!"

The door immediately opens, and he stares, his eyes wide, as she rattles off a list of things that he needs to fetch for her. She tells him exactly where to get them.

"Make it fast! If I think of anything else, I'll call you!" she yells, applying pressure to the spasm in my back.

She presses her thumbs in circular motions—one clockwise, one counterclockwise.

It feels so good.

I breathe, clutching the pillow as another spasm comes. My cheeks heat with embarrassment. I need to get cleaned up.

"We'll get you what you need," Polina says quietly. "Let your body do what it's meant to. This will bring relief from the pain. Just let yourself go through it. We'll draw a bath when this subsides. I promise, it will get better. You'll be okay. I'm so sorry."

She says it so softly.

She doesn't ask questions.

She doesn't pry.

And in that moment, she's doing something that brings tears to my eyes for an entirely different reason.

She's humming something—soft and pretty and soothing—in Russian.

Something I've never heard before.

Between the waves of pain, she runs her fingers through my hair, smoothing the damp strands from my forehead. She rubs my back, brings ice water to my lips, and every time the spasms start up again, she does that miraculous pressure-point massage that makes it bearable.

And she's right.

I'm a mess, but the pain is gradually easing.

"Have you always had this intensity around your cycles?" she asks.

I shake my head. "Only recent years." And I know exactly why but don't want to tell her. If I tell her, and she tells Matvei...

"It's often genetic," she says.

And before I can stop myself, I shake my head again.

No.

That's not why.

"Surgery?"

I shake my head again. Too late, I realize I may have told her more than I meant to by default.

She's quiet for long minutes, massaging my tense muscles.

"Someone did this to you," she says in a low voice.

And I realize, when I shake my head to deny it, it's too late.

She knows.

When I don't deny it, maybe it's confirmation.

But thankfully, Polina doesn't ask any more questions.

A heavy knock sounds on the door.

"My god," she says with a laugh. "Matvei does nothing half-assed, huh? He's always been that way, from what I've heard."

"Open up!"

"You can come in."

Matvei walks in, carrying so many bags it looks like it's Christmas morning.

I smile, shaking my head.

"Did you buy out the store?"

He scowls. "It's Sunday. They weren't open. Stupid fucking laws."

I bite back a smile, even as the pain lingers.

"Do I want to ask how you got everything?" Polina asks, her eyes twinkling.

He smirks at her. "You told me to get this shit, and I got it. So, no."

"Come here, Matvei. Your hands are bigger than mine, so you'll probably do a better job than I will. When the contractions happen, you need to put counterpressure right here."

She takes his hands, placing his fingers exactly where they need to go.

"Pressing here will help alleviate some of the pain while I get what she needs, okay?"

When his large hands take the place of hers, she's right.

His hands *are* stronger.

At first, he's tentative, as if he doesn't want to hurt me.

"It's okay," I whisper. "You can press harder. It feels good."

Polina is rifling through the bags, making sounds of approval.

"Oh my god. You even got the prescription meds already. Did you wake the doctor for this?"

He scowls at her. "Of course I did."

I almost smile even through my pain. I can imagine his heavy fist pounding on a door, a gun at a hapless doctor's head.

"Of course you did," she repeats. "Just like any of you guys would have."

"You bought steak and chocolate? How many places did you go?"

"As many as I had to."

"All the years that I've known you, I never actually thought I'd say this—but you're sweet. This is sweet."

I smile when he grunts.

They keep talking, but I don't hear because the pain is rising again. I try to stifle a whimper.

It starts slow, creeping over me in waves, then—

The band around my middle tightens.

Harder.

Excruciating.

My back spasms.

I clench my teeth together.

"Breathe," Polina says, her hand in mine. "*Matvei.*"

His huge hands span my back, pressing against the spasms.

Relief.

Blessed relief.

Polina tears through the bags, shakes pills into her hand, and presses them to my lips.

There are more than I expected.

At least four. Maybe six. I lose track.

She presses a straw to my mouth.

"Swallow. This will help."

Then something large and warm presses across my back, replacing his hands.

I miss his hands. They're comforting.

I shiver as he lays his hands on top of it, his fingers wrapping around where the material ends and my bare skin begins.

That's better.

"This is a heating pad. It's going to help. Just let the heat do its magic. This will make you feel a lot better soon."

"Physical touch helps. It soothes," she says softly.

At first, he touches me as if I'm about to break—as if even the slightest contact will send me spiraling into more pain.

But it doesn't.

It feels good.

The way he's touching me now...

His hand on my neck, soothing, his rough fingers grazing

over tender skin. He pushes damp hair off my forehead, off my neck, the same way Polina did.

But gentler.

Because it's *him*.

His hands move lower, massaging the tight knots in my shoulders, the tension in my back, my arms, and the tops of my legs.

I'm no longer embarrassed by the mess I've made now.

The relief feels too good, and neither of them cares. So I don't either.

"Good. Doing so good. Just like that. Just like that."

She's talking to me in that soft, soothing voice, the kind that makes me want to weep.

She tells me about the medicine she gave me—something over the counter that actually helps staunch the flow of blood. Pain relievers.

"Water therapy will help too," she says. "Let's get you through this next spasm. By then, the meds should start to kick in, and you'll want to take a bath. I'll start it."

Matvei sits with me, and we don't speak.

I'm glad.

He wouldn't know the questions to ask me like she does, but I'm afraid that if I speak right now, I'll say too much.

And not just about my past.

It feels good.

I feel safe.

I love you.

No.

I can't talk right now.

There's something about being vulnerable—compromised—about bearing the weight of something all on your own for so long and then having someone else come in and take the other end of the yoke from your shoulders that makes a person feel even more exposed.

And I don't do vulnerable.

"How are you doing?" Polina asks. "Scale of one to ten, where's the pain at now?"

"Seven," I whisper.

"Good. That's good. We'll get you down to at least a two or three by the end of the afternoon."

"Two or three?" Matvei growls as if personally offended. "How about zero?"

"I'm not a magician," she says with a smirk. "Just a dropout midwifery student."

I smile. "You did good for a dropout."

"Thanks, sis," she says, smiling back at me. "Don't ask me to deliver your baby."

I look away. I'm crying over everything these days.

"Okay, let's get you to the bath," Polina says.

My cheeks flush with embarrassment.

I'm a sticky mess, but Matvei doesn't care.

He bends down, lifts me into his arms, sheets tangled all around me, and carries me to the bathroom.

He jerks his head at the door, and Polina leaves.

"I can stay a little longer if you need me," she says.

"Thank you."

He stands me in front of the tub, and the sheets fall to the floor. I'm naked beneath it.

Wordlessly, he lifts me, gently settling me into the warm water.

It feels good.

I lay my head back and close my eyes.

A few seconds later, there's the sound of a splash.

I look up and see him, naked, climbing into the tub with me.

I open my mouth, but before I can speak…

"Little witch, for fuck's sake, let me take care of you."

He holds me in his arms, on his lap.

And for some reason, it's okay.

I'm still bleeding, but if he doesn't care, neither do I.

He grins at me, his eyes warm and affectionate. "Listen," he murmurs, "if you think a man like me is afraid of a little blood, it's like you don't know me at all."

My cheeks flush in embarrassment.

I note the way he tips a cup of warm water over my head, little droplets trickling down my face.

I sigh contentedly, and when I do, he keeps going.

"Feels good," I whisper.

He runs a soft washcloth over my shoulders, my neck, and under the water, over the curves of my body.

Between my legs.

Over my tender breasts.

Across my back and up again.

He rinses and repeats.

Rinses and repeats.

And when the waves of pain come again, he shifts me, turning me over so I'm held in his left arm, resting across his shoulder.

His other hand spans my back again, pressing steady and firm until the pain passes.

And I think I might love this man.

We stay in the tub until the water grows cold.

I shiver.

"Do you want more hot water?" he asks quietly.

I shake my head. "No. I wanna go back to bed. Please."

"You don't have to be polite," he says with a smirk. "Just bark out orders. This is the one time you're the one in charge."

"You might regret that," I say teasingly.

I earn a rare smile and flash of white teeth. "That's my girl," he says quietly. "There she is. You must be feeling better."

That's my girl.

I never knew how much those words could mean to me.

He pulls the plug on the drain, and I watch the water swirl down, shivering.

Then he wraps a towel around his waist, then one around me, and carries me to the bedroom.

The bed is freshly made.

Polina sits in a chair by the little desk in the corner, tapping something out on her phone.

"Better? The meds should've kicked in by now."

I nod. "Thank you so much."

"Of course," she says, getting to her feet. "We're sisters. I do have to go, but I'm going to leave very specific instructions for him."

My heart sinks.

I don't want her to go.

I like her here.

She sees the look on my face and smiles.

"I promise you, he's got this. And I'm giving you my phone number so you can text me. I happen to have an in with his boss."

She's teasing, but there's a serious edge to it, I know.

"Thank you."

It seems like too little, and yet something passes between us.

"And you owe me nothing. Just keep coming to the family dinners. As I keep telling the other girls, we need more women in this family."

She pauses, tilting her head. "Oh, and don't be afraid of my husband." She stands and smiles. "He really is a bit of a softy."

She leaves, and as the door clicks shut behind her, Matvei looks at me. "That's actually not true."

That makes me smile.

"I'll be right back. I have to talk to her. Here. "I downloaded some games and shows for you. You're staying in bed today. Polina says it'll help. And there's a book too."

He hands me a ridiculously large tablet and a book.

I stare. It's *The Best of Poe*.

My throat tightens.

I raise an eyebrow. "I don't stay in bed all day."

A look crosses his face, and his voice drops. "You do if I tell you that you are."

I smirk. "If you start bossing me around, I'm gonna text Polina. She said she has an in with your boss."

His eyes darken, amused. "Go ahead. Text her. And if you get out of this bed, I'll spank your ass. Not now. But I have an excellent memory."

I stick my tongue out at him like a child.

He smiles, shaking his head. "That's one. Keep it up."

The door shuts behind him.

It still hurts, but not as much.

It's better than it has been in a long time.

I wonder what medicine she gave me.

I hear them talking on the other side of the door, and a part of me wonders—if I hadn't run... none of this would've happened. I would've been forced to marry Rafail.

I can't imagine being with anyone but... Matvei.

And I know I'm not feeling well, that I'm compromised, and I... He's the one who gets me. There's something about his irreverence and hard edges that makes me crave more of him.

No, this isn't how I planned *anything*.

And I do worry about what he'll do when he finds out the truth about me.

Especially because I know what he wants from me.

But right now, I'm doing what I always do.

Get through today.

Survive.

I've never thought about a future.

And I can't think about one now.

CHAPTER 20

MATVEI

I stare at Polina.

"What the fuck are you telling me?"

When her eyes grow hard, I have to remind myself—I'm talking to the wife of my boss. He'll fucking cut my tongue out if I disrespect her.

I blow out a breath. "Sorry. It's not you I'm mad at."

Rafail stands behind her, watching me. Tense.

He'll kick my ass if I disrespect her, and I'll have no choice but to let him.

"Listen, I'm not a medical professional," she says, "but I know them. And we *are* going to get her in with someone."

I nod tightly. "I know. We're going to find someone we can trust."

"Absolutely," she says. "But I'm telling you this because I know how you operate, and I know if that were me in that bed, Rafail would want to know the truth."

My jaw tightens. "What truth? I want you to spell it out for me."

Rafail growls behind her. "Say please."

Jesus fucking Christ. Am I eighteen again?

I grit my teeth. "Please."

Polina doesn't flinch.

"What she's experiencing right now is sometimes related to a genetic condition, like endometriosis or something similar," she says. "But she told me she has scar tissue. Do you know where scar tissue comes from?"

Of course I fucking do. I grunt. "Surgery. Injuries"

"Sometimes, yes. People do have scar tissue from surgery." She levels her gaze at me. "But you also get scar tissue from an injury that hasn't healed."

I frown.

Why would Anissa have scar tissue that would cause her to bleed heavily during her period?

How would someone get scar tissue that—

And then it hits me.

Like a freight train.

Like a gunshot to the fucking chest.

I go momentarily blind with the realization.

"You mean—" My voice is barely a rasp. "Someone fucking did this to her?"

She takes a step toward me.

"Lower your voice."

I inhale sharply, struggling for control.

"I don't know for a fact," she says. "But it's a definite possibility. It's something you need to look into."

My hands curl into fists.

"Don't ask her now," she warns. "Help her through this. And—"

"Okay." Rafail steps forward, voice like steel. "Before you do fucking anything, you talk to me."

His eyes are sharp, unyielding. "We're not in a position to start another war, Matvei." A beat passes. Then softer, "Not yet."

No, we're not, but that doesn't mean that I can't seek vengeance anonymously. They don't need to know who I fucking am. But I need a lot more details before I do anything.

"I thought you'd wanna know," Polina says quietly. "Be gentle with her. That's excruciating pain."

I don't tell Polina that I already know this because I put my little witch through pain with my own damn hands. She fucking revels in it. Now she's *crying*. I shake my head, wishing that I could find whoever did this to her and end it right now.

Rafail announces, "We'll talk later."

They leave, and before I go inside to Anissa, I need a fucking minute.

She's not pregnant.

There's no baby. Not this time, anyway.

I wait until I'm alone to brace my arm against the wall. I press my forehead to my arm and let out a ragged breath.

She's not pregnant.

God.

I told myself from the very beginning that I had to make her stay, that I had to ensure she could never escape me. If she carried my child, even if she ran, she'd never truly be free—she'd have a part of me inside her.

But now I know the truth. It was never just about that. The need to keep her goes deeper, far beyond blood, far beyond possession. With or without her, she belongs to me. And I won't ever let her go.

She's my responsibility now.

It killed me to see her face contorted in pain.

And I need to make it better.

Then I'll find out who did this to her.

CHAPTER 21

ANISSA

I drift off to sleep, and this time, I don't dream. Thank god.

If I have to relive that night one more fucking time...

I wake to hear Matvei on the phone. I don't know what he's talking about, but I can tell he's asking questions, and he keeps saying things like, "Okay, that's good to know. Perfect. Yeah, of course I can do that. Thank you."

When he comes to me a few minutes later, he's holding a tray in his hands.

"What is this?"

I sit up in bed, the pain still there but not as excruciating as before. The medication Polina gave me helped, and so did the heating pad.

"These are the foods you need right now," he says, his brows knit in consternation.

Why is this so adorable? He's never done anything that actually made me think, *that's adorable*, but this?

"This is a bowl of berries with antioxidants, and there are walnuts and eggs. And some beef sausage." He looks up at me, serious and stern. "There's, like, iron and stuff."

"Did you make this for me?"

"Of course I did. Why do you look so surprised?"

"Because you're the same man who caged me," I say, tilting my head to the side. I wink.

"And I'll cage you still if you don't eat your fucking breakfast," he says.

Aww. On brand for being an asshole.

"There's spinach in the eggs. You need your leafy greens. And this is sourdough bread, toasted with butter. It's for digestion."

"Oh my god, you sound like some kind of fitness influencer."

"A what?"

I shake my head and smile. "Never mind. This looks delicious. Thank you."

"How's your pain level right now?"

"Tolerable."

"Scale of one to ten?" he snaps sternly.

I shrug. "I mean, like... six, seven."

"Holy shit! A six? Are you serious right now?"

He sets the food down and picks up his phone, checking something. "You can't have any more meds for another couple of hours..."

"I can deal with a six. I'm starving. Just let me eat. Maybe it'll bring it down or something."

Eating is not gonna bring my pain level down, but he's freaking out.

My appetite is ravenous. I eat one bite after the other, and I smile at him over a mouthful of food.

"You did good. Thank you. Did you eat too?"

He shrugs. "I'm fine."

"Yeah, no, that's not an answer. Sit down and eat."

"That's for *you*."

"Matvei, you made enough food to feed a football team." I stare at the mountain of eggs and toast in front of me.

He scowls. "You need to eat."

"I *am* eating. But seriously, how many eggs is this?"

"Four." He folds his arms. "You need protein."

I point at the ridiculous pile of toast. "And what's with six slices of toast? Worried I'd run out mid-bite?"

He shrugs. "The first two didn't toast right, so I just... kept going."

Despite everything, I feel a small smile tug at my lips. "I think you accidentally made an entire loaf."

"Maybe." He gives me a look. "Are you gonna eat or just keep running your mouth?"

To appease him, I take a few more bites. It's actually really good. I pick up the water he gave me, pausing when I notice the pink tint. I narrow my eyes. "What'd you do to the water?"

"Electrolytes." He says it like it's the most obvious thing in the world. I take a sip, shaking my head. "You really *don't* half-ass anything, do you?"

He smirks. "Not when it comes to you."

"And the bathroom is filled with... supplies and stuff." The tips of his ears turn pink.

If I wasn't already falling for this man before, this might have done me in.

"I just got off the phone with Rafail and then Zoya."

That catches my attention. "Zoya? What's going on?"

"Oh, she was the one who helped me decide what you needed. Polina had to go somewhere with Rafail, but Zoya told me what food to cook and what supplies to get."

I nod. "I'd really like to get to know Zoya better. Seriously, can you please eat some of this food with me?"

He sits down, dutifully picks up a slice of toast, and takes a bite, locking eyes with me like it's some kind of serious business negotiation.

"O'Rourke warned us about Interpol," he says between bites. "They're breathing down our necks. They're working with the Russian authorities, and they're looking for you."

I shrug, rolling my eyes. "I figured they would eventually."

He gives me a sharp look. "Oh shit. Seriously?"

I nod. "Of course. It was only a matter of time."

His jaw tightens. "Yeah, and the Irish won't cover for you. The only reason they're not cooperating with Interpol is because they fucking hate them and formed an alliance with us."

That part surprises me.

"So I take it you and Rafail aren't too keen on the idea of me running again?"

I can't quite keep the petulance out of my voice.

I don't like feeling like a caged bird.

But I'm so damn tired of running.

"Do you and Rafail have a plan?" I ask curiously.

I take another bite of fruit, then more eggs, chasing it down with the pink electrolyte drink. It's actually pretty good.

My plan has always been to run.

Run from my father.

Run from Rafail.

Run from Matvei when I was being chased.

But what other options do I have if running isn't one of them?

Matvei watches me carefully. "For now, Interpol believes you're still in London. They have no idea that you're here with me."

"And the only one who does—the only wildcard—is O'Rourke," I finish for him.

His gaze darkens.

"Tell me one more time," he says, voice low. "Were you or were you not involved with O'Rourke?"

I shake my head, answering honestly. "Of course not. I told you—the Irish wanted nothing to do with me. They used me as a contractor, but I was always kept at arm's length." I give him a serious look. "And even if I were, you and I both know you'd risk the entire *alliance* if you did anything about that."

His eyes narrow. "Worth it."

I shake my head. "Matvei, you know The Undertaker's reputation as well as I do."

He blows out a breath, shaking his head. "Like fuck I do. Doesn't mean O'Rourke isn't fucking obsessed with you."

I give him an incredulous look. "*O'Rourke?* I don't think so."

He stares and mutters to himself, "She has no fucking idea..."

"What? How dangerous he is? Of course I do. I was there for years while—"

"*No,*" he says, shaking his head. "How fucking gorgeous *you* are. How any man gets one look at you and needs to have you."

I stare at him, and just because I don't know what to say, I reach for a ripe strawberry, but before I can take a bite—

A spasm of pain shoots across my back, wrapping around my abdomen like barbed wire.

The fork clatters to the plate.

Matvei pales. "Are you okay?"

I grit my teeth, shaking my head, trying to push the tray off my lap.

I need to curl up again.

I need to—

Matvei moves fast.

In one swift motion, he grabs the tray, sets it aside, and eases me onto my side.

His huge hand spans my abdomen, pressing flat across my belly. With his other hand, he massages my lower back, strong and firm, working over the knots of tension with slow, practiced strokes.

It feels so good.

So fucking good, as if his hands were meant to do this.

I breathe through it, feeling the contracting pain lessen little by little.

Over and over, he massages my back, whispering something soft in Russian, but I don't quite catch it.

"There you go. Breathe," he murmurs.

I feel like I'm in labor, and he's my doula.

And for the first time, a pang of grief hits me so hard I'm not prepared for it.

It slams into my chest, twisting something deep inside me, aching so fiercely that I struggle to breathe.

My throat tightens.

I shake my head, so fucking sad.

And I know when I tell him the truth, he won't have any use for me anymore.

All this time, I've been wondering how to get away.

And now, my greatest fear is that he'll *want* to get rid of me.

I'm so fucked up.

The pain subsides enough that I can think again, and when I do, I force myself to speak.

"I need to use the bathroom," I whisper.

My body is tight, aching from holding onto the pain.

Matvei helps me sit up.

"Of course," he says gently. "Let me know if you need anything."

I hesitate.

Then, "Thank you."

When I open the bathroom door, I draw in a short breath.

He's got all my supplies in a little basket, neatly arranged next to Epsom salts, scented bath oils, and lotions. High-end, luxury items I wouldn't buy before now because it always seemed like such a waste. He has half a dozen hot water bottles on a shelf, numerous vials of pain meds, and other supplements too—iron, pain relievers, homeopathic remedies I've never seen before. Essential oils, roller balls, everything.

I come back to the room a few minutes later, shaking my head. "Did you go on a little shopping spree?"

"I picked up a few things," he says with a shrug. "We're having steak for dinner too. Supposedly, liver is really good for you, but that sounds disgusting."

I nod in agreement. "I'd rather be in pain than eat that. But I don't want to stay in bed all day."

"Just for today," he says softly but firmly. "After today, I'll consider letting you out of bed again. But for now, you stay here."

Frustration wells in my chest, and I cross my arms, staring him down.

"But I don't want to."

I barely refrain from stomping my foot like a damn brat. "What if I get out of bed anyway?"

He gives me a look and quirks an eyebrow.

"Do you know exactly what will happen if you get your little ass out of bed?"

"Don't *patronize* me."

"Don't *disobey* me."

I throw my hands up in the air. "I don't need to stay in bed all day!"

"And if you step foot out of bed, you won't sit for a fucking week. So maybe make a choice."

A little thrill runs through me.

Why do I like this?

I'm not going to unpack that right now. I'm still trying to sort out the whole cage thing.

"Bed," he says sternly.

"Fine, *Daddy*," I throw back at him.

Oh fuck. I'm not prepared for that feral look in his eyes.

My heart sings. *This, this, HIM.*

He picks me up and gives my ass a—kind of—gentle smack. For him.

He doesn't want to hurt me because I'm already in pain. Oh my god, he's so cute. Bossy prick.

"You are so fucking lucky that you're not feeling well right now," he mutters as he carries me back to bed. "I swear to god, I would redden that pretty ass of yours so damn fast."

"Is that a promise?" I tease, trying to sound sultry, which only earns me an adorable growl.

He lays me back down, and I'm very reluctant to admit that it actually feels really good. Fresh sheets, clean linens, and a thick duvet still warm from the hot water bottle he tucked inside.

I sigh contentedly.

"See? It's not that bad. And I have a couple of other things to keep you busy too. First, Rafail has a job for you."

He grabs the huge tablet, rifles through a couple of apps, and taps one.

"See this? You can help. Yana is going to walk straight into Interpol and erase every shred of evidence they have on us."

I blink. "I'm sorry, she's doing *what*?"

Matvei doesn't even look up. "You heard me. They've got files—names, locations, transactions. Your picture. It's bad. Yana is the only one who can get inside without raising alarms, with your help."

I stare at the screen, the official database pulled up in front of me. "And how does she plan on doing this?"

"That's where *you* come in, of course. She needs an airtight cover—new credentials, backstory, access to codes. You're going to make her disappear into the system."

I exhale, already calculating the layers of forgery I'll need to pull this off. "And if she gets caught?"

His expression darkens, and my heart thumps. "She won't."

Okay, alright.

I rub my hands together with glee.

I didn't want to lie in bed all day because all I'd do is think about how uncomfortable I am. But now that I have a job to do? That's so much better.

"But she doesn't need that until tonight, so you can take your time. However, after that..." He smirks. "I downloaded a few things."

I flip through, my eyes widening at the details.

Wow, I love this.

"There are three different streaming apps for you. Zoya and Ember did give me a whole list of books for you to read, but I don't trust them. They read mafia romance. Who the fuck does that?"

"Um, me? Starting today?"

He shakes his head, smirking at me.

"I downloaded a couple of games too. No idea what they are. They were highly rated."

I narrow my eyes suspiciously. "Why did you do all this?"

"Because I'm trying to make sure that I don't have to tie you to the bed," he says with practiced patience. Then he lowers his voice, and his eyes darken, half-lidded.

"Believe me, I have every *intention* of tying you to this bed. But not until you're better."

A shiver runs through me, heat pooling in my stomach.

"Wait. Did you buy me...a *teddy bear*?"

A caramel brown teddy sits at the foot of the bed.

He shrugs. "So what if I did?"

Then his phone rings.

"Under the covers," he orders. "I have to take this."

I curl up, flipping through the tablet with glee. It's *slick*. And I love this next job.

Yana is intelligent and capable. I know precisely what kind of disguise I'm going to put her in.

And she's going to love it.

UNHINGED

I'm flipping through my contacts, creating the document she needs, and making really good progress when I hear Matvei on the other line.

"No. Yeah, I know. Not this time."

But when I go to check through the apps here, I see a file folder. I click it out of curiosity and freeze when I see a familiar name on one of them.

Gleb.

My eyes dart to the door.

He's still talking, his voice rising and falling, deep in conversation.

I keep two browsers open, ready to shut one down the second I need to.

But I can't help myself.

My fingers tremble as I click on the file.

I turn the sound lower and stare at the footage in front of me.

My heart is in my throat.

On the screen, a man who looks exactly like Matvei—but younger, angrier—hangs by shackled wrists, his body bloodied and bruised.

Oh my god.

I don't want to watch… but I can't look away.

It's a window into Matvei's past. A glimpse of who I'm really dealing with.

I need to watch.

I need to see what happens.

I can't make out who stands in front of him, but the deep voice from beneath a hood sounds like Rafail.

"Confess what you did to all of us. Details."

"I tricked you," the man says, voice shaking, equal parts angry and repentant. "I made you believe you were trapped in this, but the entire time, I knew it was a different woman. I knew they were identical. I knew you'd fall for it, that I could trick you into it."

"You conspired to make us enemies of the Romanovs."

They go on and on, discussing details I don't fully understand. But every word that comes out of the man's mouth convicts him further.

I know they're going to kill him. I'm watching brutal history unfold while keeping an eye on the door because if he sees me watching this...

They fire off question after question, one after the other, until finally, Matvei steps forward.

"Recite the *Vorovskoy Mir*."

The prisoner's face crumples.

"Matvei, please. You're my brother. We grew up together. You can't do this."

"*Recite it*."

Matvei doesn't shout.

He doesn't have to.

He strikes the man with something I can't see, and the scream that follows makes me flinch.

Matvei's voice is merciless. "You know the penalty for betrayal. But I want you to know exactly what you did that brought us here."

The door handle turns.

My breath catches.

I rush to click the X button, my hands shaking, and quickly move to the other browser window.

Matvei steps inside, looking down at his phone as he does.

"Making any progress?"

My heart aches.

He's a monster.

But he's my monster.

Maybe this is why he loves Edgar Allan Poe—the macabre, the dance with death, the horrible longing for peace that never comes.

Desperation.

Because sometimes, staring into darkness with your own two eyes makes the one you dwell in that much easier to handle.

I manage to speak. "Yeah, I'm making progress. I'll have it done by the end of the day."

"All right," he says. "Take a break."

He winks at me, and my heart turns over in my chest.

"I don't want Rafail to think you'll do exactly what he says the moment he asks."

A smirk.

"I'm the only one who gets that privilege."

I scoff. "That's what you think."

CHAPTER 22

MATVEI

Anissa is almost better.

She's managed to pull herself out of bed, and I've allowed it.

She did such an impressive job with the task Rafail gave her that he wants to assign her another. But I tell him she needs a break because she's been sick.

The truth is—I don't want her working.

I miss her.

I've done everything I can to baby her. And while she protests and insists she can handle herself, she likes it.

I know she does.

And goddamn, I love having someone to take care of.

She praises my cooking and sighs contentedly when I rub her back. We take every bath or shower together now. I love the way she lets me massage her skin and wash her hair.

I even painted her nails. *It was harder than it looked.*

But it hasn't been easy not fucking her through all of this.

I've banged a few off in the shower, but it does nothing to satisfy my appetite.

I want her hot, tight cunt wrapped around my cock.

Her nails clawing at my back.

Her over my knee because she's earned a good fucking spanking with her sass.

I want *her*.

But I don't want to hurt her.

Rafail gives me a laundry list of tasks, and when I finally go looking for her, she's nowhere to be found.

"Anissa!" I yell, fearing the worst. My heartbeat thunders.

"Over here!"

I follow her voice and find her standing in the center of the room, surrounded by a ridiculous amount of shopping bags.

The glint in her eyes is wicked.

I take one look at the mess she's made and groan. "Oh my god."

She grins. "Nah," she says, shaking her head. "He's not gonna save you tonight."

"Woman," I growl. "Please."

"It's been days," she purrs, stepping closer. "I'm fine now. Really. I *want* you."

My jaw tightens. "I don't want to hurt you."

She tilts her head. "What if I *want* you to hurt me?"

I shake my head. "I won't do it that way."

But that doesn't mean I can't touch her.

That doesn't mean I can't make her come.

I strip her slowly, deliberately, kissing the slope of her shoulder, the curve of her cheek.

With a sigh that makes my dick hard, she whispers, "I've missed this."

"So have I."

I bury my face in her hair and inhale.

I remember the way I used to ache for her scent when I was stalking her.

I wanted her so fucking bad.

And now...

Now, she's in my arms.

And she's so much more than I ever imagined she would be.

I nuzzle the swell of her breast, flick my tongue over her nipple, and lay her on the bed. I'm dizzy with need, I want her so damn bad.

"I want you inside me," she whispers. "Please."

I shake my head. "Not yet. I want to make sure you're better."

She moans, arching against me, and whines when I pull away.

I smirk. "Behave yourself."

She smirks right back and spreads her legs.

Fuck.

Her pussy is glistening, her thighs slick with arousal, driving me out of my fucking mind.

"Maybe you can fuck me in the shower," she suggests, her voice low, teasing. "Maybe you'd feel better about that."

"*No.*"

Her lips part in protest, and she lets out a whine. "Why do I have to *beg*?"

I've had enough.

I flip her over my lap, press my palm to her lower back, and cup her ass.

She gasps.

But *of course*, she only squirms and spreads her legs wider, offering herself to me.

I groan, sliding my fingers through her wet heat, teasing her and circling her aching clit.

"I do owe you a spanking, don't I?" I murmur.

A wicked little smirk. A slow, deliberate nod. "I think you do... *Daddy.*"

Oh, I like the brat.

I like the brat *a lot*.

I spank her, my palm curving as it slaps across her ass perfectly.

Jesus, that feels good.

"Say it again."

"Say what, *Daddy*?" Her voice is all tease, all temptation. "Is that what you want? Is that why you fed me in bed and took care of me?"

I spank her again, harder this time, my handprint marking her perfect ass. "You kinky little witch."

She moans and writhes, grinding against my fingers.

"Fuck me, Daddy. Please."

"I told you. Not yet." I rub slow, teasing circles over her clit. "That doesn't mean you can't come, baby. Here. Open up for Daddy."

Jesus *fuck*, I can't believe I just said that. I can't believe how fucking hard it made me.

I stroke her, sliding my fingers deep inside her, and she moans, her hips rocking desperately against my hand.

Fuck a week, might as well be an eternity.

I squeeze her nipples, circling her clit as she takes all of it, her body trembling beneath me.

"I'm so turned on," she gasps. "I can't let go. I can't... I'm all tense."

I spank her again.

"Are you trying to rush me?" My voice drops, turning lethal. "Who said we're on a timeframe?"

I lean down, pressing a slow, open-mouthed kiss to the red handprint on her ass. She shivers.

I love that reaction.

She moans and rides my fingers, but I slow down, taking my time because I know what she needs.

I lay her on her back, and her eyes go wide as I wrap my hand around her throat. I flex just enough for her to gasp while I pump my fingers inside her.

Her hips lift off the bed, begging.

I press my fingertips into her neck, her pulse racing under my hand.

I stroke her clit, bend down, and bite her nipple.

With a strangled cry, she comes. *Hard.*

Her back arches off the bed, and I don't stop. I keep stroking, teasing, watching the way she writhes beneath me, lost in pleasure.

Jesus, she's beautiful when she comes like this.

And I am hard as fuck.

"Oh my god," she pants out, coming back down from her high.

She reaches for my belt buckle, her hands shaking.

"I'm not going to—"

"I know, I know." She pouts. "But if I don't get your cock in me right now... Promise me I will soon," she demands, her lower lip jutting out petulantly.

It's adorable.

Her little pout.

Her need.

"Oh, I promise," I murmur darkly. "I'll fucking rail you. Harder than you've ever had it before. Every. Fucking. Day."

I lean down, my lips grazing her ear.

"There won't be another cycle, Anissa."

She stills.

"I'll put my baby inside you."

Her breath hitches, but she doesn't pull away. Instead, she strokes my cock, her gaze darting to the side as if trying to process it.

Then she bends, licks the head, and moans.

That's all the encouragement I need.

I brace myself over her and fuck her mouth.

She moans, swallowing me whole, sucking, licking the tip, her eyes rolling back as if I'm the most delicious thing she's ever tasted.

"Yes," she groans around my cock. "Fuck my mouth."

I fuck her hard—until her eyes water and she cries out. But she's into this.

She cups my balls, her head moving in rhythm, tugging me back and forth, taking me.

"You take me so fucking good, beautiful," I growl. "Such a good girl, taking my cock. That's right, baby. That's exactly what Daddy wants."

I fist her hair, guiding her, my cock hitting the back of her throat, and she swallows perfectly.

Jesus.

She strokes the base of my cock, licking and sucking my balls until I feel it—until I know I'm about to come.

She nods, encouraging me, eyes burning with hunger.

"You gonna take it?"

She grins around my cock. "Yes. Give it to me. I want to taste you."

That's it.

I come so hard I see stars, spilling into her mouth, and she swallows every fucking drop.

Her tongue circles me, teasing, stroking, milking me for everything I have.

Fucking perfect.

I needed this.

I missed this.

We collapse onto the bed, the smell of sex thick in the air.

She grins up at me. "I'm game for doing that again."

I chuckle, pinching her ass.

She squeals. "That hurts! You spanked the shit out of me."

"Didn't give you half of what you deserved," I grumble.

She tilts her head, hopeful. "Is that a rain check?"

I shake my head. "Yeah, baby. It's a rain check."

We lie in the quiet, my fingers threading through her hair.

I cradle the back of her head, pressing her to my shoulder.

It feels right.

Too fucking right.

"You're better," I murmur. "But we need to talk."

She freezes, but before she can say anything, I continue.

"Listen. I talked with Polina."

She stiffens.

I nod, my throat tightening. "Remember, Polina is loyal to Rafail. She has to report anything that could be... concerning. Anything that could impact our Bratva. Potential blowback."

Her brows knit, her lips pressing into a thin line. "Yeah. I won't forget that."

I swallow, then go for it.

"Polina told me that the condition you have right now can be genetic." I pause, watching her face. "But that it's likely from scar tissue."

Her expression doesn't change, but she goes completely still.

"Anissa. Is that true?"

She's silent for a long moment before she whispers, "I don't want to talk about it."

I tighten my grip, my fingers pressing into her skin. I'm careful not to hurt her. "You have to."

"Why?" Her voice is raw. "It's in the past."

I lift her hair, twisting gently, just enough to tilt her chin and force her to meet my eyes. Her gaze is wide. Unblinking. But she doesn't look away. And the raw pain in her eyes makes me vow to kill whoever hurt her.

I'd do anything for her. *Anything.*

"Because I need to know," I say, intentionally gentling my voice. I lean in, my lips grazing her ear, my breath hot against her skin. "If there's someone in your past who hurt you—someone still *breathing*—tell me now."

My fingers curl tighter. "Because if there is, I'll make sure they don't for much longer."

I let the words sink in.

She swallows, and for the first time, I see it.

Not fear. Not horror.

Hope.

I press on. "Scar tissue comes from two things, Anissa." I pause. "Surgery or injury." I wait. "Did you have surgery?"

She exhales, then shakes her head. "No. But I won't be the only one spilling secrets, Matvei. I'll tell you what happened to me"—she tilts her head, studying me—"if you answer a question of *mine*."

I nod.

I have nothing to hide.

"I want you to tell me all about the night you had to kill your brother."

Her voice is steady, but her eyes... her eyes hold something deeper.

"I know you want to understand me," she continues, "but I need to understand *you*."

I wasn't expecting that.

Wasn't expecting that at all.

"Fine." My voice is rough. "I'll tell you anything."

She tilts her head, considering. "I'll even go first if you want me to," I add.

She nods. "I'm going to take you up on that."

I draw in a breath.

I've never told anybody what happened.

The only people who needed to know... were there with me.

If my parents knew, they would hate me even more than they already do—if that's even possible.

They know he died.

They know he was punished.

They know I was there.

They don't know why I was the one who pulled the trigger.

"My brother betrayed the Bratva." My voice is steady, cold. Detached. "We have a code. A sacred code. He broke it. And because of that, he faced the ultimate consequence. *Vorovskoy Mir*, the Thieves' Code."

The Bratva comes before all else.

Never cooperate with the authorities.

Never, ever betray your brothers.

She exhales softly, her voice barely above a whisper.

"Et tu, Brute?"

I swallow.

"He was my little brother," I say, my chest tightening. "I protected him. I loved him. When we were younger, I held him accountable for things, but I never imagined I'd have to hold him accountable for this."

She doesn't flinch.

She doesn't recoil.

She just absorbs it.

And the pain in my chest loosens just a little.

"I can see that," she murmurs. "What happens when someone betrays the Bratva?" she asks. "I know what the Irish do—something tells me the Bratva is even worse."

I let out a humorless laugh.

"I don't know," I admit. "The Irish are pretty fucking brutal. We lose the privilege of our tattoos."

She cringes.

Her eyes widen. "Oh my god. So you... you *remove* them? I'm guessing that doesn't involve a laser."

"Yeah."

I don't tell her how.

I don't tell her that, in my brother's case, it involved a blowtorch.

The smell of burnt flesh still makes me retch if I think about it too long. I can't even grill anymore.

I force a smile. She looks at me like she understands exactly what I mean.

"Oh, Jesus, Matvei."

"Yeah." My throat tightens. "That was just the beginning."

I drag a hand through my hair. "I made him state the code while he was dying. Semyon had already beaten the shit out of him. He was conscious when I finally got to him." I swallow. "I told him I loved him. But I was loyal to the process. And I was the one who pulled the trigger."

She doesn't speak for a long moment.

"You shot him?" she finally asks.

I nod.

Rafail didn't make me dispose of the body.

I was a fucking wreck after that.

I couldn't sleep.

Couldn't eat.

My mother tried to have me committed, but Rafail intervened. She didn't know the half of it.

I shake my head, laughing bitterly. "Started smoking then."

"Did it help?" she asks quietly.

I look in her eyes. "Took the edge off."

A flicker of something like understanding passes through her expression.

"Took years to find you," I continue. "You know that."

She swallows. "I know."

"And it wasn't until Semyon needed help and I went through Anya's brother's computer that I finally did."

Her lips part slightly. "Because of the Irish."

"Yeah." My jaw tightens. "The Irish."

I thought telling her this would be brutal. And it is. But somehow, saying it out loud makes it a little easier to bear.

I exhale. "Your turn."

The memory of what I had to do has me fired up.

I need another target—one that ends in victory instead of crushing devastation.

For a moment, she doesn't speak. Then she lets out a slow breath like she's bracing for impact. "I think I need a shot. Or drugs."

I smirk. "I can arrange that."

"That... would actually be really good," she says.

I nod, walk over to my desk, and pull out one of the joints I keep for special occasions. I don't smoke often, but sometimes, it helps. I like sharing one with her.

I light up, take a slow drag, and bring it over to her.

I pass it to her, watching as she presses it to her lips. She inhales deeply, holds it for a moment, then exhales slowly.

Tendrils of smoke curl through the air. The sweet, smoky smell is the only one I can handle.

We pass it back and forth in silence.

The flicker of fire.

The ring of smoke.

The sweet, earthy scent.

The pressure in my chest eases just a little.

I lean back in bed.

"That'll make me horny," she murmurs.

I smirk. "Is that supposed to be a warning?"

She exhales another slow drag.

"Rafail wasn't the first person I was promised to," she says suddenly.

I blink.

That is not where I expected this conversation to go. I'm already ready to murder someone, and I don't even know the story yet.

"My father had a friend," she says, her voice quiet. Controlled. Too controlled. "He was old and gross. He had a reputation for hurting women. Easily twenty years older than me. And when I found out my father promised me to him, I ran." She swallows hard. "That was the first time."

She stops and closes her eyes for a second. I hold her hand, pushing beyond the need to hear everything now. "He caught me."

Her voice is flat. Devoid of emotion. That makes it so much worse.

"He said he wouldn't have an ungrateful brat for a wife. So he had his men... beat me."

My hands clench into fists. The room feels too small, the air too thick. "They laid me down. Kicked me. Broke my ribs. Stomped on my abdomen." She exhales shakily. I blink to clear the red in my vision. "Two black eyes. A busted lip. Four broken ribs." A pause. "I didn't know I sustained those until my father brought me to a doctor a month later because he was sick of waking up to the sound of my coughing."

I can't fucking breathe.

This is the only time in my life I remember wishing that someone was still alive only so that I could have the privilege of killing them all over again.

She doesn't react, just stares past me as if she's still locked in that room. "My father said I was an ungrateful little bitch, and I deserved what I got."

Something inside me *snaps*. My vision tunnels. The entire world narrows to her.

"So after I healed," she says bitterly, "he arranged to give me to someone else."

I force the words through gritted teeth. "Rafail. Who was the man who hurt you?"

She looks away.

"Who was it?" I growl.

"I don't remember."

She's lying.

Why the fuck is she covering for them?

I lean closer, my voice a razor's edge. "You know I'll find out. There's no point in lying to me."

She still won't look at me.

"Anissa."

Nothing.

Then finally, so quietly, it almost doesn't reach me, "I'm not worth starting a battle over, Matvei."

The laugh that escapes me is dark and vicious.

I kneel on the bed beside her, grip her chin, and force her to look at me.

"That's where you're wrong," I murmur. "You're worth the fucking war."

Her eyes fill with tears, and she tries to blink them away.

She fails.

"Why me?" she whispers.

I give her the simplest answer because I don't want to tell her how much she means to me.

"Because you're mine."

I pause.

"You know I'll find out who it was, and easily."

If it was someone in our alliance, I'll fucking—

She exhales. "I really don't know. But I could find out." Her lips twitch. "Forgery is my specialty, after all."

Again, she doesn't meet my eyes. "What if I'm not who you think I am? What if—"

"I told you. You're mine. I'm not under any delusion that I know you perfectly or that we'll never have struggles, nothing to figure out. But what do I know about you?" I tilt her chin up, forcing her to look at me. "You're fearless. Brilliant." I smirk. "Kinky as hell. And you were meant for me." My voice drops, dark and certain. "I know that. You're my woman. And anybody who laid a fucking finger on you is dead."

Her breath catches.

"I've killed for a fuck of a lot less than this, woman."

Her eyes light up, and that wicked little smirk curves her lips.

My little witch.

Casting her spell on me, magic sparking in her gaze.

"Come here."

She fists my shirt and yanks me toward her.

I shake my head. "I want you to get some sleep. I have work to do."

She props herself up on her elbows, watching me thoughtfully. "I'll try..." She pauses. "Back in my apartment—did you fuck around with my sleep meds?"

I meet her gaze head-on. "I did. I gave you something that would make you think you were hallucinating."

She shakes her head, muttering, "You're one psycho fucker, you know that?"

I smirk. "I know."

Her eyes narrow. "What else did you do?"

"I'm not telling you."

"You've already admitted to writing on my walls." She glares. "Did you fuck around with my playlist? Did you put a Russian lullaby on it?"

I shrug. "Maybe."

She scoffs. "You rearranged my clothes, didn't you?"

I shrug again.

She shakes her head but is already scrolling through her phone. I watch as her fingers fly over the screen.

She's searching for someone.

Aria.

It's six hours earlier in America—she should be able to get her attention at this time of day.

"You took my blonde wig," she says suddenly, her eyes locked on mine.

I exhale sharply. "Do we really need to go through all this? Can't we just let bygones be bygones?"

She crosses her arms. "Fucking around with my bank account was a low blow, Matvei."

I arch a brow, already opening the door. "I never fucked with your bank account."

She stares at me, brow furrowing.

Who the *fuck* touched her money? Was someone else fucking around with her?

Fucking *who?*

And then my phone pings.

Goddamn, I have to take this call.

Aria.

CHAPTER 23

ANISSA

I WAKE from my dream with a start.

This time, I don't remember what happened. I just know I was running; someone was chasing me, and it wasn't Matvei this time.

Who was it?

I blink, trying to clear the fog from my mind.

Instinctively, I pat the bed next to me to feel his reassuring warmth and heat.

He's not there.

I sit up, glancing at the corner of the room, where fairy lights glow softly against the walls.

My cage.

I wonder if it can be repurposed into a daybed.

Nah.

I keep looking, hoping—because I need to see him.

But he's not here.

Instead, he's left me a tray of snacks, and there's a mini-fridge stocked full.

I quickly make myself a plate of cheese and crackers, grab a drink, pop the top off some seltzer, and settle into bed with the tablet.

But as I scroll mindlessly through a show, my mind keeps circling back to his words.

"I never messed around with your bank account."

A chill runs down my spine.

If he didn't... then who did?

I stand and cross the room, moving to the large window that overlooks the grounds.

I think about the look in his eyes tonight when I told him about what happened to me.

About the assault.

I didn't tell him the repercussions of that assault.

I can't.

If he finds out the truth... will he still want me?

The thought of losing Matvei fills me with a strange kind of grief.

The kind that should only come with death.

For the first time in my life, I feel wanted.

Seen.

Understood.

I never could've imagined this chain of events.

I exhale and follow the sound of his voice, but... it isn't just his voice now.

Is he talking on speakerphone?

When I walk down the stairs, I realize Matvei isn't alone. There's a younger guy with him. A younger, very *attractive* guy with an athletic build, strong jawline, piercing gaze, and what looks like a perpetual smirk. The ink that scrolls over his shoulders and up his neck marks him as Kopolov family Bratva.

Rodion?

"Hi," I say tentatively from the doorway.

The stranger flashes me a grin. "You're up? Feeling okay?" His brows knit together slightly, studying me.

Just a moment ago, they were both talking about very violent, very mafia things.

But Matvei's demeanor shifts the moment he sees me.

The tension in his jaw releases. His eyes, normally storm clouds and razor-sharp, soften in a way that makes my breath catch. He shouldn't be looking at me that way. I might do whatever he tells me. I might follow him to the ends of the earth.

Without a word, he lifts his arm—an invitation, silent but sure. Like I belong there and he was waiting for me.

A lump rises in my throat. Maybe it's because he's the last person I expected to feel *safe* with.

I step closer. Slowly. Warily. I'm still unsure of my footing in this family. Maybe I'm afraid it's only temporary.

He doesn't rush me but waits, steady as stone, until I'm within reach.

"Rodion, this is Anissa," he says with unmistakable pride. "Anissa, Rodion."

Rodion eyes me with undisguised curiosity. "Ah, the little witch," he says, lifting his glass in mock salute. I see the thick band of gold that glints in the overhead light on his ring finger.

"Ah, the partner in crime," I reply, lips curling into a smirk. "Nice to finally meet *you*. I've heard plenty of stories about you and Matvei."

Rodion groans. "Whatever he told you, it's slander. I'm innocent."

"Back when we were younger..." Matvei begins.

"We got into *way* more trouble than we do now," Rodion finishes with a wolfish grin. I half expect him to swallow me whole.

"I'd argue the stakes have gotten higher," Matvei murmurs dryly, pulling me into his lap as if it's the most natural thing in the world.

His arm settles around me. His fingers brush mine, grounding me. My head finds his shoulder—when did that become the place I want to be?

"Did we wake you?" he asks softly, his voice quieter now, just for me.

There's something about this dangerous man going soft for me that melts me into a puddle.

"You okay?" he asks softly, a murmur in my ear. Rodion's brows lift, and he looks at his friend in mild surprise.

I shake my head. "Yeah. I was starving. I had a weird dream and... I don't know. I couldn't sleep."

Matvei's gaze sharpens.

"Was it another nightmare?"

I shake my head again, but it's a lie. I don't want to divulge anything personal in front of Rodion. Matvei might trust him, but I don't.

"I don't want to talk about it right now," I whisper. Rodion politely scrolls on his phone as if giving us some privacy.

"You need something to eat?"

"No, I'm fine. You left me with enough snacks to fatten me up like a pig being led to slaughter."

Rodion groans. "Of course he did. Asshole needs to feed his junk food addiction. Always gets the munchies with those goddamn joints. That's how Rafail caught on we were smoking in high school." He shakes his head as if still pissed at Matvei. "He'd fucking eat pickled *everything*. Dill pickles, tomatoes, straight out of the jar like a psycho. Platters of dumplings. Sleeves of crackers. Piles of chocolate bars or anything battered and fried."

"I had help," Matvei says, his eyes twinkling.

"I bet."

"I can still see Rafail staring at the empty packages in the kitchen and shaking us down for our stash." Rodion shakes his head. "Hey, so I came here to tell Matvei the good news," Rodion says with a smile. He pulls out a pink stick. I blink. "Ember's pregnant."

I don't expect it. The stab hits my chest. The second I look at him—when I look at Matvei's face—the pain is there, hidden behind a fake smile.

"Congratulations," I say, but my congrats sound watery even to my own ears.

Matvei's thumb brushes over the top of my hand—soothing, gentle. A shared moment of grief I wasn't prepared for, for entirely different reasons.

His wife peed on a stick, and he jumped in his car and drove here to tell Matvei in person.

That's so adorable. And it makes me so fucking sad.

Rodion stands. "It's late. I'm sorry to keep you guys up. Just wanted to tell you the good news. Tomorrow, we ride, brother," he says with a smile.

Brother. I bet that hits him harder than Rodion thinks. He has two other brothers at home. Matvei buried his.

And what are they doing tomorrow?

Matvei gets up to see Rodion out. I barely notice. I'm so caught up in my thoughts, trying to decide what to do, what to say.

Matvei comes back to me. He has that look that I've come to crave.

Possessive. Haunted.

"Come here," he says, crooking a finger at me.

He sits in the overstuffed chair and spreads his knees wide. Jesus, he's so fucking sexy. There's a glint in his eyes. It smells like trouble, and it makes my heart sing.

This room is all dark wood, gleaming hardwood, laced with the smell of old books. They're stacked on tables and shelves. The furniture is minimalist, leather. It's like an old-fashioned study, and it surprises me that this is Matvei's.

Matvei sprawls on the leather chair, his knees apart, resting on his forearms. He has on a T-shirt that he wears to bed, the fabric stretched thin across the large expanse of his chest.

He snaps his fingers and points to the floor. His eyes go dark when I don't come to him right away. "So that's how we're playing this?"

My heart thumps in my chest when his voice drops to a low register.

"Crawl to me."

I'm instantly wet.

"Take off your shirt," I counter. I want to see his tattoos, his scars. Everything.

"This isn't a negotiation," he says, but his eyes twinkle with something like mischief.

His voice drops to a lower register, and I want this. I want this so fucking bad.

When he hurts me, when he stares at me, when he touches me, when he makes me come—he makes me feel wanted in the best possible ways, and everything else fades to vapor.

"Are you testing me? You do not want to test me."

Oh, but I do. I so fucking do.

"I'm not gonna warn you again."

Excitement bubbles in my chest. I throw him a look of challenge.

"Yeah? Fucking make me."

With slow deliberation, his hands go to his waist, his eyes meeting mine.

At the sound of his belt unbuckling, my stomach clenches. My mouth is dry, and a quick panic sets in.

Did I push too far?

He's a dangerous man.

He's *my* dangerous man.

"I warned you," he says.

At the same time, he stands and pulls the leather belt out in one swift move, folding it so the buckle rests in his palm, forming a loop.

I look around the room because now seems like a really good time to run.

But it's small in here. Kind of cramped. And even if I did...

I turn.

Too late.

I scream out loud when his hand grabs the back of my head, yanking my hair so hard it hurts. My pulse spikes. My clit throbs.

He pulls me forward and bends me over his desk.

Books fall. Pencils clatter. Trinkets click to the floor.

My hands scramble to find purchase on the gleaming top of the desk, and it reminds me of that first night at the bar.

Only this time, he has a belt.

No pool stick.

Lucky me.

He shoves my face down on the desk, and with the same hand holding the belt, he strips me, the leather teasing my naked skin.

He has an easy job of it with my loose leggings.

"Don't—"

The leather cracks across my ass—hard—taking my breath away, but not so hard that I don't know he's modulating himself.

A man like him could do serious damage taking his belt to

me, and the fact that he knows this and is so damn careful with me makes my pulse race with excitement.

I try to push against him. I writhe. But he holds me down so easily.

I love the feeling of being overpowered.

The way he presses his hand to the back of my neck. The way his other hand lifts the belt back.

"What do you need, little witch?" he says in a low drawl before snapping the belt across my ass again.

And again.

The next time, the leather hits the crease of my thighs, and it feels like fucking fire.

I howl. Squirm. Writhe. But it doesn't matter.

He just holds me down and strikes me again.

"I asked you a question," he growls.

My eyes fly open and land on a quote pinned to his wall.

"Deep into that darkness peering, long I stood there—"

He chuckles, shaking his head, and finishes the line for me in his deep voice, "Wondering, *fearing...*"

The next lash strikes harder. I clench my teeth.

I'm leaning into this now, relishing the stripe of leather against my skin.

The pain that blooms into heat.

The arousal between my legs.

My racing heartbeat.

The feeling of being overpowered. Dominated.

Free.

My mind is a blank slate as it continues, his mouth in my ear.

"Cast your spell, little witch. Cast your fucking spell. You know I love it. You know I'm here for it. Spread those fucking legs and cast your spell on me."

The belt drops to the floor, and his hand comes to my ass, scouring, massaging the skin, and I love this. I love it so much, his rough palm and the erotic pain.

His fingers are at my pussy, sliding through my wet heat, in and out, just like that time at the bar, and I want more.

"I've missed you," I say because he hasn't been *in me* since before my period, and I want him so badly.

"Say it again," he growls.

"I missed you, Matvei."

"Beg for my cock."

"I want you inside me. I want you to fill me. I want you to make me come." My voice is shaky, trembling—I want him so badly.

Break me. Ruin me. Put me all back together again. Make me whole.

Then the blessed relief of the sound of his zipper. His hot cock at my entrance. I whimper in need, unashamed, holding my breath. A gasp of relief as he pushes in.

He slams into me hard, and I take him. He stretches me, fills me. My need climbs higher and higher. His mouth is at my ear, his body pressing down on mine, skin to skin. I feel his heartbeat against my back, and I've never felt more powerful in my life.

He whispers filthy, sweet nothings in my ear. "You're so fucking wet. Give me that cunt. Give me that dirty little cunt. I wanna fill you. I want you dripping with my cum. I want you to know this is you and me. This is me making you have my baby."

I whimper, my body arching, opening for him, my nails digging into the wood beneath me.

"Is this what you wanted? Did you want my cock?"

"Yes," I breathe out.

He pulls almost all the way out of me.

I sob with need. "Matvei!"

I want him in me so badly.

Then he slides back in slowly, stretching me, filling me. I'm so full, and my pussy clenches around his cock. It feels so right, pressed up against the desk, and my ass is on fire. My pussy clenches as he slams in and out, the rhythm and tempo of his thrusts harder than ever before.

As if, somehow, he's trying to brand me. To make me never forget him.

As if ramping this up—pushing deeper, fucking me harder—will make me his forever.

It's wrong and primal, and I'm so fucking here for it.

My orgasm takes me by surprise with its intensity. I cry out.

"Are you coming without permission?" he says in a deadly voice.

I couldn't stop myself now if I tried. My words tumble over each other.

"Please. Please, can I come?"

"Come, my sweet little witch. Come on my dick. Take me. All of me," he growls in my ear.

I start to come, and then, his hand, tangled in my hair, finds the back of my neck.

He squeezes, and I cry out.

His thumb circles my throbbing clit, and I come so hard I scream. I'm blinded, breathless, as he pulses inside me.

In that moment, when we're unraveling together, pleasure consuming us, a little part of me thinks—*I love you.*

He's ruined me for any other. He's my one and only.

I slump against the desk, boneless. We breathe in the quiet for long minutes. He gently tucks my hair behind my ear and kisses the side of my temple. I melt.

I sigh when he slides out of me. He turns me and picks me up. His hot cum trails down my thighs, and I don't care. I'm a dirty mess, but I'm happy.

For the first time in my life... *I'm happy.*

I'm aching, so fucking fulfilled. My mind is blissfully blank.

He carries me to bed, lays me down, cleans and dries me.

I roll over, my eyes heavy with sleep, when I feel him lower himself onto the bed at my feet.

"I need to taste you," he growls. "God, I've missed your fucking cunt so bad. I've dreamed of this. Let me eat you out."

I'm half-asleep, still boneless from the last orgasm he gave me, when he spreads my legs, drapes my thighs over his shoulders, and buries his face in my pussy.

The first lick makes my hips arch—it feels like heaven. I'm so sensitive but already so turned on.

He suckles my clit, then licks me again, all the way down the length of my slit. I cry out. He lashes my clit with his tongue, groaning like a man possessed, like he's starving, dying of thirst, and I'm his only salvation.

He licks and sucks and groans—greedy, devouring me.

I'm already tensing up, already ready to come again.

He flicks the tip of his tongue against my clit again, and I shatter into bliss.

He eats me out until I'm coming down from the first one, then pushes through.

"I can't," I say. "It's too much, Matvei."

"Relax into it. You can come again. It's not too much, baby. I'm greedy for your cunt. So fucking greedy for your cunt."

Slowly, with just the barest touch of his tongue, he eases me gently, and I'm almost there again.

He lightly teases me, like a promise, like a kiss. His tongue plays and taunts until I want more.

Then his tempo increases. He lashes my clit again, sucking me greedily until I come again so hard my hips fly off the bed.

He grips me, anchoring me. As I'm coming, he slaps my inner thigh hard, and I spiral into ecstasy. *Oblivion.*

I'm floating, weightless.

He spanks my thigh again. Bites my flesh. Soothes it with the flat of his tongue.

I'm screaming his name, my fingers stabbing into his hair. I'm pulling, yanking, hard enough to rip it from the fucking roots.

He only laughs a dark, low growl.

"That's my good girl. Such a good girl, taking Daddy's mouth. Stretching your pretty pussy for me. That's my girl."

"You are *so dirty*," I say, and I can feel the grin stretching across my face.

"God," he growls, giving my pussy an appreciative kiss. "You make me mad."

I melt even more.

He kisses me *right there*, right on my throbbing pussy, and it feels like worship.

This big, strong, dangerous man is on his knees, worshiping me.

"You were meant for me," he says with a crooked grin. "You're in my blood, woman."

He kisses my thigh. My hip. The softness of my belly. My navel. The underside of each breast. My collarbone. My neck. My chin. My cheek.

And then, he finishes it off with a kiss to my forehead.

A forehead kiss.

That's what I've needed all this time—his lips on my forehead.

"I want you to trust me. So when you wake up tomorrow and I'm not there, I want you to trust me."

I know. I've known it all along. But I like hearing him acknowledge it—this is what it's all about. The cage. His belt. Kidnapping me and making me his. The times in bed. The way he's massaged me, taken care of me, kissed me. The way he makes me come and the way he listens. All of it.

Matvei does nothing half-assed. He is all in... *for me.*

Maybe *I am* a witch. Maybe I *have* cast a spell.

But what if I don't know the next incantation?

So I swallow the lump in my throat and pretend that I'm okay. I pretend that I believe I'm worthy of a man like him—or anybody at all.

And I lie.

"I trust you."

But even as I say the words, even as I feel how they taste on my tongue, I know at the heart of it all...

It's me I don't trust.

UNHINGED

CHAPTER 24

MATVEI

I sit beside her for way too long, watching her sleep.

There's a certain magic in it.

I have loved and lost in my life. My sister, eighteen years old—an accident that forced me from childhood into adulthood.

But I've never loved a woman.

Until now.

And it scares the ever-loving shit out of me.

I sit beside her, watching her sleep like a fucking creep. I push her hair out of her eyes. I lean in and smell her, needing a hit. I watch the rise and fall of her chest until Rodion calls.

He's found the location of the man I'm going to fucking destroy.

I leave her with reluctance, pack my bag, and slide my phone into my back pocket.

He comes tearing up in front of the house on two wheels, and I shake my head with a grin.

God, I missed the douchebag.

He screeches to a halt and jerks his head toward the door, rolling down the window.

"You think I'm gonna open the door for you, princess? Get in the fucking car." He grins and holds up a paper cup. "Got your coffee."

I open the door and toss my black duffel onto the floor of the car. The metal inside it clicks, and he raises an eyebrow at me.

He's drumming his fingers on the dashboard, sipping his fancy little coffee, probably laced with cream and sugar and whatever other bullshit he puts in it.

"How can you drink that shit?" he asks, giving me a side-eye glance at my black coffee.

"I take it like a fucking man," I snap back at him.

He cackles, and I grin.

This is how it always is—the two of us, taking on the fucking world together. And when Rafail finds out what we did, we'll stand side by side while he absolutely destroys us.

Just like in high school.

Only this time, Rafail will probably just lecture us. We're both bigger than him now.

We ride at dawn because this motherfucker who's about to meet his maker is a one-hour drive away.

"He's not close," Rodion says. "We have some catching up to do, honey."

"Oh, shut the fuck up." I groan, looking out the window. "You wanna tell me again all about how your wife's gonna have a fucking baby?"

"You know you're happy, Uncle Matvei."

"I think, technically, I'm a cousin."

He furrows his brows and tips his head to the side. "How the fuck does that work?"

"Well, I'm not really your brother," I tell him, shaking my head. "I'm your cousin, which means your baby is like—I don't know—second cousin? Once removed? Or whatever the fuck."

He frowns. "Let's go with uncle. We don't have to get caught up in fucking technicalities."

True, true.

"You get any sleep yet?" he asks.

God, they love giving me shit.

I blow out a breath. "What do you think?"

"I think you're a filthy asshole who had to bang his woman to get fired up for the kill."

He cackles and slugs his milkshake of a coffee. Then he tells me about his trip with Ember, about the work she's doing, and he says it with so much pride. He talks on and on about shit he didn't care about before he met her.

"You really love her."

He shakes his head, and for once in his life, he's sober. "You have no fucking idea."

He exhales hard. "Did I picture her having my kid? A little piece of the two of us—an actual human? I fucking *cried*."

I roll my eyes. "People have babies all the time. It's the circle of life and all that shit."

He looks out the window and shrugs. "But I wonder if they appreciate what that means sometimes, you know? You and I... we've seen a lot. We've lost a lot."

We don't speak for long minutes, just looking ahead. I've buried my sister and brother. He's buried his parents.

We talk about old times. He tells me about the latest fucking indie album he downloaded that Ember got him into, and I give him shit about it.

Who the fuck listens to that shit?

Then he puts it on, and I have to admit—damn, it's good.

He tells me about Semyon and how funny it is to see his cold, ice-hearted brother actually fall in love.

I bitch to him about my parents, about how I changed the locks and haven't told them yet.

I want them to just show up and try the lock.

Feels like poetic justice.

"Tell me about her," he says quietly. "I know why you got her. How do you feel now? She still got you under her spell?"

I shake my head. "She is my little witch," I say affectionately, looking out the window.

But I'm not really joking.

I mean it.

She *has* cast her spell on me.

He smiles at me and nods. "Brother, I understand."

And I know he does.

I saw the way he talked about his wife last night.

This is the man who tracked down the bastard who hurt his wife, beat the shit out of him, duct-taped him to a tree, and made him watch while he fucked his wife before he killed him.

Yeah. He knows.

He shakes his head and smiles, but it's a little self-deprecating. "Like, you're just walking around, you know? Living life. Same shit. And then she just—" His voice drops. "She just comes into your life and turns everything on its head. And nothing's the same. Nothing ever goes back to the way it was. And you can't imagine... you can't imagine going back to the way things were before her. You can't imagine life before her. Or after her."

He glances at me.

"That's exactly what it is."

"Good. I got you all sentimental and fired up, just like I wanted. Takes a lot of energy to kick the shit out of somebody. But if you do it for a reason? Totally different. This woman deserves your protection, doesn't she, brother?"

I swallow hard again.

"She fucking does."

"Tell me what she's like."

I know he doesn't really care.

But he cares about me.

So I tell him everything.

"She's the smartest person I've ever met. Not in some show-off way. She's just like... always ten steps ahead." I lean back against the seat and pause. "She's obviously gorgeous, but even like... when she's sleeping. When she wakes up. When she's sitting in my T-shirt drinking coffee and giving me shit for taking it black."

He chuckles. "I get you. So you're saying... you *like* her."

I ignore him. My voice goes harder. "She looks at me like she's trying to decide if she wants to kiss me or kill me. And the fucked-up thing? Sometimes I think I'd be fine with either."

Rodion whistles. "So you met someone who actually *gets* you. Psycho you. And doesn't judge."

I don't answer right away, just stare as Rodion drives like a bat out of hell, and we eat up the pavement, trees whipping past our windows.

"Nah, man. It's worse."

"Worse?"

"She sees *through* me. Like every part of me, even the shit I don't let myself think about."

Rodion's smile falters. "Damn."

"She knows I'm dangerous. Fucked up. And doesn't even try to fix me. She doesn't *want* to. She just... matches it."

"Sounds *romantic*. What the *fuck*, dude?"

I smirk and sip my coffee. "You're just jealous I found someone who could stab me or love me in the same breath."

Rodion snorts. "That's some real soulmate shit. The greeting card companies should hire you." He pauses. "You gonna wife her up?"

But he gets it. He knows.

"Of course."

"And *that's* why we're on our little errand. No one fucks up your wife and lives to tell about it."

I nod. "And that's why this motherfucker's a dead man walking."

CHAPTER 25

ANISSA

I WAKE UP, and even though he told me he wouldn't be here, I still feel for him.

I like the reassuring weight of him next to me in bed.

I don't know where he's gone; all I know is that he asked me to trust him.

So I push myself up, blanket sliding off my shoulders, scanning the room...

And that's when I see it. A small, pale-blue crystal sitting on the nightstand. It's smooth, set carefully next to a scrap of paper. I unfold the note.

> *Supposedly this one wards off nightmares or bad vibes or whatever the fuck. The internet said it was calming. Don't laugh. It's pretty, like you.*

My phone buzzes with a text, and my heart thumps in my chest. Oh my god, I've got it bad. I think I might love the man.

Love. Well, fucking hell.

I really do think I love him.

But when I look at my phone, there's nothing from Matvei. Just Polina.

> **Polina**
> Hey, just checking in. How are you feeling today?

I smile and text her back.

> Much better, thanks.

> **Polina**
> Oh good. I know that Matvei is out today, and I also know that he's put heavy security at the gates for you. Didn't want to wake you, but he was chatting with Rafail early this morning.

> Maybe Anya and I can come by later tonight? After we're done with errands with Stefan, we'll bring food from her bakery.

Wait. What?

> Anya has a bakery?

> **Polina**
> Anya just happens to own the most delicious bakery this side of Moscow.

> Oh my god, I love that. Wait—does she really? Does she have sharlotka cake?

My mouth is already watering at the thought of the layers of flaky pastry and apples.

> **Polina**
> It's her specialty, and those are my number one favorite.

> Me too.

> **Polina**
> 😊

> Maybe that weird stuff they say about twins being separated is actually true.

> **Polina**
> Maybe it is. And… Do you also drink ice-cold diet soda for breakfast?

> Nope. I'm a coffee girl.

> **Polina**
> Ugh, betrayal.

Minutes pass, no message. Am I being too weird, too forward, too—

> Sorry, Rafail was talking to me, and he gets really impatient.

You don't say.

> **Polina**
> Stay busy and try to get some movement in —it'll help with the whole recovery thing. We'll be by later this afternoon

> Okay, sounds good.

Matvei has a home gym, of course, fully decked out. I get a good sweat on, and damn, it does feel good. I walk on the treadmill and do some body-weight movements, nothing too intense.

And yet, as I move about his house, making food, doing laundry, something feels off. I know I have to trust him, and I do... to an extent. But I have the nagging feeling that his mission today had something to do with what I told him.

I know that he's got an intense job description, so it isn't outside the realm of possibility that he's doing anything from going to pick up more ammo, overseeing a gun trade, or kicking the teeth in of someone who betrayed them. I have no idea what the fuck he's doing, but I can't shake this eerie feeling. Something isn't right.

My phone buzzes with a text, and I look to see if it's Matvei or Polina, but instead, it's an unknown number. I stare at the screen, and before I click the button, I look out the window just to remind myself that there are armed guards at every entrance of this place.

Why do I feel... scared? I'm not usually afraid, but I am now. It feels like the stakes are higher. For the first time in my life, I don't want to run. I don't want to leave. I found a home, a place where I want to be.

I click, surprised to see it's actually... Cillian O'Rourke.

> **Cillian**
> You need to leave, Anissa. Now. You're in danger.

I hesitate. *What?* He doesn't send warnings without reason.

> Who? What are you talking about? Is it Interpol?

> **Cillian**
> No, thought it was, but they've got bigger fish to fry. Looks like it's someone within

What the fuck is he talking about? The Irish aren't the ones coming for me, the law isn't—

> **Cillian**
> You need to leave

I check my surroundings again. Matvei isn't here, and I know he's getting revenge. For me. He doesn't need me to approve it; he's doing it because that's who he is.

I dial his number, and to my surprise, he answers right away. He's breathing heavily into the phone.

"Are you all right?"

"Yeah, but I got—I got a text from O'Rourke," I tell him.

"What's he saying?" He grunts into the phone.

"He told me that I'm in trouble and that I have to run. He says there's someone in the family, Matvei."

"That's impossible. Fucking O'Rourke. We've all taken

oaths to each other. It couldn't be. Stay there. I'm coming back for you soon."

"Are you sure?" I ask, feeling strangely uneasy.

"I'm sure. I want you to go to our bedroom and lock it from the inside. Do you understand me?"

I nod, even though he can't see me. "Yeah. You said you have guards here, that it's safe."

"It is. My house is a fortress. But I want to be able to find you right away when I get back, alright?"

"Okay."

Matvei exhales sharply. "Stay strong, love.."

My heart thumps in my chest.

I want to tell him I love him. I want to tell him that I will be here when he comes back, but the urge to run is so damn strong...

I pace his room and try to occupy myself. His tablet. I'll work on the disguise that I promised I'd get Rafail. I grab the tablet to work on it when I remember—I never finished watching that video of him with his brother.

Do I really need to see that?

I know he was the one who took his brother's life in the end, that he was forced to. I know all that, but I wonder now... Why do I have to watch it? Why can't I get it out of my mind?

I need to know. I need to know what forged him into the man he is today.

Now is as good a time as any. He's not here.

So I climb into the bed with my back against the wall. I turn on the tablet, my hands shaking. I hit play and fast-forward halfway to where I left off before.

My hands are clammy. I feel nauseous. I don't want to see this; I really don't.

But I have to look at the raw brutality that knit the fabric of the man I love.

So, with all the strength I have, I hit the arrow to make it play.

Just as before, it's dark and hard to see.

Matvei is asking questions now, pacing, and I've never seen him look like this before. He's sweating bullets, his hands in his hair, he curses, and he—

Oh my god.

This is going to *kill* me.

I can't. I can't look away.

Matvei's crying. My heart feels as if it's breaking into tiny pieces to see my big, strong bear of a man with tears streaming down his face.

"How could you do this?" he says, his voice shaking. "How could you? You took vows. I did everything I could to teach you to be loyal to our family."

His brother looks him in the eye and says something strange —something almost unthinkable.

"I *was* loyal to our family, Matvei."

That's enough for him.

Rafail's voice snaps like a whip. "You took the vow of *Vorovskoy Mir*. And it's your brother's duty to do what has to happen next." He jerks his head to Matvei.

A click of a gun.

"Please." Gleb's voice shakes. "Don't—I promise. I'll never do it again. Don't, Matvei. I love you. Matvei, I'm your brother—"

Bang.

The boom echoes through the cold room, and his body slumps in the chains.

I'm crying freely now, swiping at my eyes, but it's useless. The betrayal digs deep into my soul, carving something jagged inside me. Matvei falls to his knees in front of his brother's lifeless form, cradling him in his arms—the very brother he just killed.

He'll never forgive himself for this.

And I am broken.

Sobbing harder than I have ever cried in my entire life.

It wasn't until I saw him fall to his knees, rocking his brother's body to his chest, that I knew.

I know.

I love him.

Matvei is shattered—broken like me. And somehow... somehow, he's still standing, still breathing, still bearing the weight of it all. And now, I understand why he's so fiercely loyal. He's told me, but there's something about witnessing the way he holds his brother, the way his hands tremble as he presses his forehead to the bloodied skin.

I'm sobbing so hard I almost don't see Rafail behind him. The video continues. Rafail places a firm hand on Matvei's shoulder.

"I'm so sorry, brother," Rafail whispers, voice rough, broken.

They're both crying.

Oh my god, this is the worst day of my life.

I go to shut it off but see the video isn't done yet. I sniff, watching, unable to look away.

Matvei's face is pale, his shoulders slumped. Rafail falls to his knees beside him, and I force myself to understand. To truly *know* what he has lived through, what he has done. The weight of it settles over me like chains.

The video fades, but then I hear Rafail's voice, steady.

"You know the law," he says like it's gospel. "You took the life of a brother out of duty. A family member. The blood debt must be balanced."

The blood debt.

Matvei doesn't flinch or look away but lifts his head, his voice quiet but firm. Reciting the words like a vow.

"A life taken, a life given. I took blood from the family. Now I give it back."

A pause. A breath.

"It is my duty to bring new life into this world."

Rafail nods once. Solemn. And just like that, the sentence is passed.

A shiver of cold fear traces down my spine.

No.

No.

I stare at the screen, the words echoing in my skull.

The blood debt must be balanced.

This isn't about revenge.

This isn't just about ownership.

This is about legacy.

This is about continuation.

I am his future.

And I can't bear children.

CHAPTER 26

MATVEI

We walk into the smoky, dimly lit pool hall like we own the place.

Because we fucking do.

The moment I step inside, a ripple of awareness spreads through the room. Men like me don't walk into places like this. I don't belong here. At least, that's what they think.

Conversations die. Cues hesitate mid-shot. The air is thick with the stench of stale beer and cigarette smoke, but beneath it is something far sweeter.

Fear.

Rodion winks at me, and I nod.

For once, he doesn't bother with theatrics. Good. I want to get this over with. He steps up to the bartender, leans in, and wordlessly rips up his short sleeve, exposing the unmistakable mark of the Kopolov Bratva.

The bartender doesn't hesitate.

His eyes go wide—*too* wide. His hands tremble as he looks at me.

I nod and roll up my own sleeve.

"Jesus Christ," he mutters, making the sign of the cross.

Then he slams his towel onto the counter and nods once.

"Clear the room."

It reminds me of the time I cleared the bar for Anissa, only this won't be as sexy.

Men abandon their games. Drinks are left untouched. Laughter dies in their throats. The smarter ones don't look back as they hurry for the exit.

The dumber ones hesitate.

They want to see if it's worth finishing their drink.

Rodion sighs and winks at me before drawing his gun. He cocks it, aims at the ceiling, and fires.

Bang.

The last stragglers run, pushing and shoving like rats in a flooding tunnel.

I narrow my eyes at Anissa's attacker. "Not. You."

Within seconds, only one man remains.

Yaroslav Solov.

The fucker barely looks up from his drink.

He's about fifty years old. His bald head gleams under the single beer-stained overhead light. So heavy he has no neck, his beady eyes set deep in his thick, doughy face.

This is the bastard who hurt my woman.

And this is the fucker whose life is going to end tonight.

"What the fuck is this?" he sneers, rolling his shoulders, affecting an air of authority he doesn't have. "Do you know who I am?"

I approach slowly, rolling my wrists and stretching my fingers. A man about to get to work.

"I know exactly who you are."

He scowls. "Then you know you just made a fucking mistake."

I grin, laughing darkly. "That's what you think."

I tilt my head, my voice quiet and deadly.

"Anissa Laurent."

He freezes.

A beat of silence.

Somewhere behind the walls, I hear mice slithering and squeaking.

"What about her?"

"Funny thing," I murmur, stepping closer. "She's mine now. And I know what you fucking did to her."

He blinks. His confidence wavers.

"I don't know what the fuck—"

"And you," I say, my voice low and cruel, my vision blurring with hatred, "are the motherfucker who hurt her."

He stands too fast. "I don't know what you're talking about."

Rodion snorts, pulling out his phone and flipping the screen toward him. It shows his three guards, knocked out cold and locked out of the bar.

Yaroslav's face pales. "What the fuck?"

I grab a pool cue off the table and smash it across his face.

The crack of wood against bone is deafening.

But no. That's not enough.

I toss the broken cue aside and reach for a glass bottle instead. He tries to deflect, but it's useless. With a swift, brutal motion, I bring it crashing down onto his skull.

Blood sprays.

He stumbles back, clutching his jaw.

I sigh, shaking my head, almost disappointed.

"You'd think they'd learn by now," I murmur to Rodion. "Just shut the fuck up."

But they never do.

They always have to say the same fucking thing.

And I always get to break them for it.

Yaroslav spits blood on the floor. His chest heaving, he tries to reach for me. "You fucking—"

I don't let him finish. I grab his collar and slam his face into the table. Once. Twice. Three times. And still, my need for blood is barely sated.

He fucking hurt her.

I can almost hear her crying, screaming, begging for forgiveness. This motherfucker is gonna hurt.

The wooden table is slick with blood when I finally let him go, letting him crumble to the floor, groaning and disoriented.

Round one. I win.

I kneel beside him, my voice smooth and calm. "Did you hit her first? Did you have one of your men do it? Or did you just grab her by the throat like a fucking coward?"

He moans something incoherent, blood bubbling at his lips.

Rodion doesn't wait. He walks over and gleefully kicks him in the ribs. Hard.

This isn't the first time we've beaten the shit out of somebody together. Somebody who deserved it.

Yaroslav chokes on a scream.

"I asked you a question," I snap in a too-calm voice.

He curls in on himself, must've already figured out he's a dead man. But still, he has the fucking audacity to say what he says next, a dying man's last words. "She was a whore—"

Rodion doesn't let him finish. He delivers another brutal kick, this one to the spine. Yaroslav's body jerks violently, and he screams.

I exhale through my nose, shaking my head, then press my heel to his chest, crushing him to the ground.

My hand moves to my belt, where the weight of my knife rests.

My phone buzzes.

Rodion's foot pauses mid-strike.

I glance at the screen. *Anissa.*

Rodion smirks. "Perfect timing."

I get off Yaroslav. Rodion takes my place, kneeling on the son of a bitch, a knife to his throat.

"Move, and I'm gonna slice you right here," he says, tapping the tip of the blade right over the man's heart. "That way, you bleed. Maybe even get to see a little of your own blood before I leave you for him. Unfortunately, this isn't my kill to make."

When I answer, my voice shifts—gentle, something softer.

"Everything alright?"

On the floor, Yaroslav whimpers.

Rodion sighs and stomps on his ribs to shut him the fuck up.

Anissa's voice is trembling. "Hey. Everything's fine. Cillian's crazy."

I lean against the table, eyes never leaving the battered form of the man who abused her. "What's up, love?"

"I just... I need to talk to you when you get back," she says softly. "I wanted to hear your voice."

There's something in her tone... hesitant. Fearful.

I don't like it.

"I'll be there soon, baby," I say, my voice smooth, as if I'm not currently standing over the beaten body of the man who hurt her.

Rodion kicks Yaroslav again, and he hisses out a breath.

I press a finger to my lips, signaling for silence.

Anissa exhales. "All right. Just... be careful."

I smile, warmth creeping into my tone. It's for her that I'm here.

"Always, little witch. I'll be home soon."

Rodion looks over at me and shakes his head. "Wow."

I end the call and don't ask him to elaborate as I slip the phone back into my pocket.

A switch flips.

All softness is gone.

The predator is back.

Rodion cracks his knuckles. "Back to business?"

"We can't prolong this. I need to get back to her." I crouch beside Yaroslav, grab him by the throat, and squeeze just enough for panic to set in.

"Look at me."

His swollen eyes flicker open, dazed.

I lean in, my voice low, deadly. "You put your hands on her. That was your *first* mistake."

I pull my knife free, running the tip along Yaroslav's jaw, not slicing through flesh. Yet.

"Your second..." I drag the blade lower, pressing it just under his sternum.

"Thinking you'd fucking get away with it, you son of a bitch."

Yaroslav sobs, blood and snot running down his face.

"Please—"

I drive the knife into his gut. He howls.

I twist the blade. Slow. Precise.

I hurt him. I'll kill him now. I'll own this.

I watch the light start to fade from his eyes.

In a whisper, I deliver the final words he'll ever hear.

"She's mine now, you son of a bitch. Go to hell knowing that I don't ever share."

I twist the knife again.

"This is your payment for what you did to her. No one will ever hurt her again. Especially you."

I pull the blade free, and Yaroslav chokes and gurgles. Blood splashes on my hands before I go still.

I wipe my knife on his shirt and stand.

Rodion exhales, cracking his neck.

"Well, that was satisfying. I think we were too easy on him."

"Definitely. But I need to get home to her."

I slip the knife back into place and pull out my phone.

Anissa is waiting. I left her safe, but I want to see her with my own eyes.

"I'll call for cleanup. Let's get you home to her," Rodion says.

I nod and dial her number.

This time, she doesn't answer.

The phone rings. And rings.

Why the fuck isn't she answering? I just talked to her.

I pull up the security footage of my estate on my phone.

Everything looks normal.

I'm just about to shut it off when I see a car in the driveway.

Not mine.

I zoom in.

"Rodion, who the fuck is this?"

I call my head of security. He answers on the first ring.

"Sir?"

"I just tried to reach Anissa, and she didn't answer. Is everything all right?"

"Yes, sir. Your mother is here for a visit. She said she couldn't get the door to work, so I let her in."

A chill skates down my spine.

I meet Rodion's eyes.

He looks at me and stands up straight.

"The fuck?" he asks.

I changed the locks on my door so my parents wouldn't get in but failed to tell security.

Shit.

As far as they know, my parents are allowed on my property.

And Anissa isn't answering the phone.

Rodion shakes his head, and every piece of the fucking puzzle clicks into place.

Like a gun cocking.

My brother betrayed us.

But what if—

What if he wasn't the one behind it?

We have to get back.

Fuck.

I'm an hour out.

Fuck.

CHAPTER 27

ANISSA

I PACKED A VERY SMALL BAG.

One shirt. A knife. My skincare products, the crystal he bought me. No matter how much the need to leave feels urgent, I can't seem to rush the packing because I don't *want* to go.

None of this belongs to me. Not the house, not the man, not even the silence. *I* don't belong here. I can't stay, knowing that the only thing he needs to make his world right is the one thing *I can't give him*.

My hands tremble as I pack the very few things I own and zip the bag halfway. The book of poems lies on top. My throat gets tight.

And all I loved—I loved alone.

My stupid tears don't ask permission; they just come of their own accord.

I go downstairs and walk to the pantry. And for some reason, I can't do it. I can't think of what I need, what I have to say, where I could go.

We're not married. I'm not his wife.

All the other women of the Bratva, they're married. And that means something to these men.

I'm just... me.

I can't bear him a child. I have nothing to bring to the table.

And he says he owns me.

But what does that mean in the greater scheme of things?

Nothing.

Nothing.

The thought of leaving him feels like I'm breaking my own heart. I've never felt understood like I do with him. I've never wanted someone the way I want him. My life went on before him, but now... for the first time ever, I had begun to hope.

And hope is a beautiful thing.

But when I go downstairs, I'm *not* alone.

The kitchen lights are dim. I can still smell the lingering scent of the citrus cleaner I used to wipe down the bathroom. The back window is cracked open, and a draft makes the kitchen curtain flutter.

I shiver, then freeze. My heart kicks into my throat.

I can feel the presence of someone else. It can't be someone who shouldn't be here; the doors are locked, and security's here. I didn't hear anyone breaking in.

"M-Matvei?" I call out, but it's impossible. He can't be home yet unless he teleported. I just spoke with him on the phone—he said he was still an hour away.

There's no way—

Oh, shit.

No.

Not this again.

I slowly turn.

"Irma?"

Irma stands near the pantry, arms crossed, eyes gleaming like she's been waiting for this. She wears one of her signature too-tight sweaters and blinding lipstick.

I smile sweetly. "Did you run out of grocery money again? Looking for a free meal? Sorry to tell you that the only thing Matvei and I cooked last night was meth, and there's none left."

She glares.

"Ha-ha. Just kidding. It was weed."

His mother narrows her eyes at me.

"Why do you hate me?" she asks.

My need to run is quickly forgotten. I'm not leaving her in this house unsupervised.

"I never did anything to you," his mother says, obviously still trying to keep my attention on her. And then she keeps talking—blah, blah, blah—but I tune her out.

And then I realize something that sends a chill down my spine.

His parents don't have keys to this house anymore.

Matvei changed the locks.

"How did you get in here?"

"I have a key," his mother says.

"No, you don't. He changed those locks."

"Why?" his mother snaps. "I've had a key to his house since he bought it... until *you* came on the scene." Her voice rises in pitch, in volume.

"Because he didn't want you walking in while he was fucking me in the living room. Does that make you feel better?"

"Honey, you're just someone he's wasting his time on."

"It's kinda gross how jealous you are."

Her voice is so smug, so sure. "He doesn't want you. Don't you think if he wanted you, he would've *married* you, like the rest of them? Done this the right way instead of bringing you back here like you were some kind of cheap whore?"

It stings.

I tell myself not to listen, not to pay attention.

I'm stronger than this.

But I already feel so low, so useless.

I can't be anything for him.

"You should run," she says coldly, cruelly. "You should get out of here while you still can."

"You hate me because he picked me over you," I say, my voice low.

"He didn't pick you," she snarls. "You're just the body he's fucking while he waits for someone better."

My heart lurches, but I push through. She's trying to hurt me, trying to cause me pain.

"You hate him for what he did to your son, but don't you know how he's gone out of his way to be loyal to you? Even after everything you've done to him?"

I hate them.

I hate them so much.

"You stupid little whore," his mother hisses, real hatred gleaming in her eyes. "All of them... they stole it. It should've been ours."

"What are you talking about? Stole what?" Is she delusional?

I shake my head.

"I have no idea what you're talking about," I snap.

"Of course you don't," she sneers. "You're just a stupid little bitch who thinks she knows better."

The way she says it—so dismissive, so cold—something clicks in my mind.

I stare. *No.*

"You put him up to it," I whisper.

It wasn't just his brother going behind his back.

She let her own son bear the brunt of it.

And she let her other son pull the trigger.

Fury rises in my chest.

His mother shakes her head, her eyes cold and calculating.

"Matvei loved those cousins of his way more than his own brother. Just the way he treated him after he betrayed them was enough to show it. We all knew it."

I'm struck by how horrible she is.

She was complicit in all of it.

It's because of her.

"Run, you stupid little bitch. I'm glad you're not having his baby. We don't need your kind around here. Pack your bag and fucking run. He'll find somebody else. Somebody better. Somebody who can have his babies."

I stare at her.

"What do you think you know about me?"

"I know everything. I was there the day Gleb supposedly betrayed everybody. I know exactly why he sent them after Polina instead of you. I knew the Irish were going to take you in. You young kids think you know everything, but some of us have been here for decades, way longer, before you were born, and we have connections." She points a long, pointy nail at me. "Some of us have alliances in places you haven't even thought of. So take your bag, and I'm going to make this very easy for you. It was too much for you. You needed to run. You had nowhere to go, but this was no place for you. So you left. You're going to write him a note and make sure he never finds you again."

I shake my head. "*No.*"

"Yes," she says, her voice like steel. "I want you out of my son's life. You don't deserve a penny of his money or a second in this town. You're nobody. You're nothing."

Every word falls like a sledgehammer. And in the weight of realizing I can't give him the one thing he needs, I *feel* like nothing. Like nobody. My throat tightens.

But I will not be *bullied* by the woman behind this, especially not before I tell him everything.

She raises her hand as if to slap me when someone grabs me from behind and pulls me back.

I scream.

"Hey. It's me."

I look over my shoulder to see Yana holding a gun. She speaks into her phone. "Please tell him we've detained Irma."

I can leave now before there's no turning back. Before he's married to me. Before he actually cares. This is it. This is the time.

I pick up my bag, my hand shaking. It's time for me to do what I do best—become invisible. Disappear. Just like the little ghost he says I am.

"I don't think so."

Vadka stands in the doorway, tall and strong, the square cut of his jaw firm, glaring at Irma.

"When Rafail finds out what you're complicit in..." he begins, and Irma's eyes go wide.

"I don't take orders from him."

I move to the side. They won't see me, maybe they'll be distracted.

"No," Yana says smoothly. "We're well aware. But your husband does, doesn't he? I was under the impression that my brother pays your credit card bills, your rent, and the stipend you both receive since Gleb was killed. No?"

"I'm not giving any of that up. It's my right!"

Keep them talking. Keep them talking.

I could take my bag and slip out the back door. I don't want any of them to see me.

Yana looks at me. "The decision to stay or go is up to you." Her voice drops, softer, almost pleading. "Please don't go."

She turns back to Irma.

"And I'm going to tell him what you did," Yana says.

"Bitch," she snaps.

Yana laughs, a pretty, tinkling little sound, and Vadka growls. "For fuck's sake, don't make me shoot a woman, Yana."

I stand at the door.

If I don't go now, I never will. One look at him—one word—and I'll fold. He'll ask me to stay. And then I'll be trapped in this house forever.

It's not just that I won't get another shot at this. It's that if I see Matvei, if I take one look into his eyes, I won't be able to walk away.

I have to go.

I stare at my bag. I stare at the exit. Vadka and Yana hold my space, letting me go, knowing that Matvei will lose his mind. When he gets here, he's going to be distracted. I could—

Tires squeal outside, and Irma's eyes go wide.

Oh no. It's too late. Rodion and Matvei are back.

It's too late.

Matvei and Rodion are running toward us.

The moment his eyes land on me, I feel it... like gravity just doubled. His gaze drops to the bag. The energy between us tightens like a wire about to snap. His jaw clenches. His shoulders square. We both know exactly what this is.

There's a shriek behind us.

His mother is running.

"Matvei! They're trying to kill me!" He freezes, shocked.

A gun goes off, and Irma falls to the ground.

He doesn't look at her. He looks at *me*.

Not my face—my hands.

The bag.

His breath catches.

"Anissa."

Just my name.

Matvei comes straight to me. "Are you okay? Did she hurt you?"

A second vehicle screeches to a stop.

His father steps out.

"What is the meaning of this?" his father screams, taking in the sight of his wife on the ground, covered in blood. "Who shot her?"

Yana rolls her eyes. "I clipped her shoulder. It's a superficial wound. You'll be able to wipe it with a piece of gauze." But then her voice lowers, ice-cold, her ruthless gaze settling on him like a blade. "But when you find out the truth of what happened, you're going to wish I did more than that."

CHAPTER 28

MATVEI

I can't fucking think straight. My mother's bleeding, shot by my cousin, who's implying that my mother's done something. She came here, onto my property, without permission, bypassing my guards, so I can't imagine her intentions were any good.

And Anissa... Anissa's carrying a bag. A fucking bag.

My ears ring. Not from the gunshot, no, from the pressure building behind my temples like something's going to snap.

The house is a cacophony of voices, the screech of tires, phone calls made, and harsh commands. Vadka meets me on the front lawn, takes one look at me, and nods to Rodion. "Irma's going into our custody." He looks at me apologetically. "I witnessed everything, brother."

Rodion steps forward, composed. His look is deadly. Certain. "We'll get her patched up. Then Rafail needs to hear it from us."

"Rafail," my mother spits. "The fucking usurper. The—"

Yana is already moving. She grabs my mother by the hair and yanks her up like a rag doll. My father lunges, but I intercept him, slamming a hand into his chest. He fights me, but he's weak, and I could snap him in half. I fucking want to.

"Those that speak of my brother with disrespect lose their tongue, Irma," Yana says with cold derision. "Please. Give me a reason to never have to listen to you speak again. Say one more word." With a flourish, she brandishes a slick knife.

My father growls and fights. "How dare you talk to her like that?" The guards step in. It's all noise, the sounds of prey in their dying moments, caught in the grip of a hungry predator.

Rodion's hand is on my shoulder. Heavy. Grounding.

"We'll deal with this, brother." He lowers his voice. "We can't prove anything without the council's collaboration, but the evidence is clear. Rafail won't order the execution yet. But it'll be permanent exile. And if she returns... it's a kill order."

That breaks something in me.

Then I see her... gripping the handle of the bag.

I walk to her—calm, controlled—as if I move too fast, she'll run like a scared mouse.

She flinches when I reach her. I wrap an arm around her waist. "Are you alright?"

She nods, obviously shaken. "Yeah. I'm okay." She reaches a hand to my cheek and searches my eyes. "Are *you*?"

I feel like I'm not here, like I'm floating outside myself, watching the scene play out from a distance. My skin feels too tight. My breath too shallow. Everything inside me is splintering.

"Why do you have a bag packed like you're leaving?"

She looks away from me and bites her lip.

"*Anissa.*"

"Don't," she whispers.

"Don't what?"

"Don't tell me to stay."

I step in closer, crowding her space. I hold her chin and tilt her gaze to mine so she has to look up. My world is crumbling around me, and she's the one certainty. "*Why?*"

She swallows hard, her eyes locked on mine. "Because I won't be able to tell you no, Matvei. Because I'm weak. Because I—"

I kiss her. I lean in and wrap my hand around the back of her neck, holding her to me. She whimpers, crying into my mouth. I swallow her moan. My tongue meets hers. She bites my lip, and I groan, our breaths mingled.

"Inside," I growl into her ear. Rafail will want to talk to me, and my brothers will need to meet. We'll need to ask questions, and I'll have to give him answers. What I know about my parents. What we do next. How complicit were they in my brother's betrayal? Why the broken, lifeless body of the man who hurt my woman is buried in a shallow grave. Why Anissa needs to pause all her work for my Bratva so she can erase his name from the face of the earth.

But right now, I want her.

I need her.

I grab her bag out of her hands and throw it into the open door of my house. It slams against the wall and slides to the floor.

I'll chain her to my fucking bed before I let her run.

CHAPTER 29

ANISSA

MATVEI LEANS IN, cups the back of my head, and whispers low and dangerous, "Unpack your fucking bag."

Something inside me snaps. I don't move right away, just stare at him. His chest is rising and falling, and it looks like he's barely keeping himself in check. I'm the spark to his tinder; one false move, and he'll ignite.

"*Anissa.*" My name sounds like a warning.

And god help me—just as before, I don't *want* to run. Not from here. Not from his family. Not from *him*.

"Matvei." My voice is choked from barely held emotion. What could have happened just now—what *did*.

He narrows his eyes at me.

"Go ahead. Run, little witch. I'll give you a head start. Mount your broom and fly far, far away from here. I'll drag you back by your hair, put you back in your cage, and throw away the key."

"You don't understand, Matvei." My voice shakes. "Your mother was right. I'm not—"

"*Don't.*" His voice is deadly calm. "Don't quote that fucking woman to me. She's nothing. She's *done*. And what she said about you, about us, means *nothing*."

My lip trembles, but I won't cry, not now.

"Look at you, being all brave," he says with pride. "So brilliant. So perfect. A little ghost until I dragged you out of hiding." He leans in, his voice brooking no argument, the wall to my dam. I'm shaking as he enunciates each syllable. "Un. Pack. Your. Bag. *Now*."

I draw in a quick breath. Unpacking that bag will be a concession.

I glance up at him. He's watching me as if he already knows I'm going to do exactly what he says.

I kneel. The zipper's broken, the contents spilling on the floor.

One by one, I start pulling things out.

I'm a failure. I've escaped warlords, Bratva, entire syndicates. I've walked through fire and emerged unscathed.

I can't escape one man?

Sweatshirt, passport. Toothbrush, cards. The backup IDs I forged weeks ago.

My hands tremble. My chest is too tight. My heart aches.

Every time I set something on the floor, it feels like I'm removing a strip of armor.

I feel him behind me. Watching. Waiting. Simmering.

When I'm done, I rise slowly. I don't turn to face him yet; I can't.

"Done?" His voice is raw and possessive, calm water to mask the churning anger.

I nod. "For now."

He's behind me in seconds, his hands curling around my waist. His chest presses to my back before he spins me around to look at him. He tilts my chin up, searching my face, as if demanding the truth from my gaze before my words.

"Say it, Anissa. Tell me that you're mine."

He wants the words, but if I say them, I can't take them back. If I say them, I belong to him—no more escape plans. No more exits.

Just him. Just us. Just *this*.

So I don't give him what he wants right away. How can it be true? *How?*

I've never belonged to anyone before. I never believed I could. He's not just asking for possession. He's offering *everything*.

And it terrifies me.

I should tell him no one gets to claim me. That if I want to walk away...

"I can't be yours, Matvei." I hang my head. This is where it ends. This is where he sees it, what I've always feared—I'm not enough.

With a brutal tug, he spins me around to look at him, his hand beneath my chin. "Like fuck, you can't." His eyes gleam with possession, his grip immovable.

I press my forehead to his chest, letting myself breathe in his scent.

I stumble over my words. I need to say it out loud.

"I can't give you children, Matvei. I know. I-I watched the video."

"What video?" he asks, deadly quiet, the kind that makes my heart thump harder.

"The-the promise you made. About your vow to uphold. To Rafail—"

He doesn't let me finish but grabs my jaw gently but firmly and makes me look at him.

"You watched it," he says slowly. "And then you decided, on your own, without a single fucking word to me, that we were done? That you were going to run?"

I blink. A tear rolls down my cheek.

I try to pull back, but he holds me there, fierce and immovable.

"Do you think I would've walked away?" His voice breaks. "That I would've just *let* you go? That I'm that fucking shallow?" His hand tightens on me to the point of hurting. I want him to hold me even harder.

"I—" My voice trembles. I can't finish the sentence. He's right. I *did* decide I was going to run.

"You assumed. You decided. You came up with this world in your head where I didn't *want* you if you couldn't have children?"

When he says it like that, my heart thuds. My throat tightens.

Maybe I didn't want to face rejection again. Maybe I don't know what it means to be safe. Maybe I *want* something real.

I don't want to run anymore.

I want to be caught.

"Yeah," I whisper. "I... didn't want to hurt you."

He quirks a brow, stern and unyielding, and I can hardly bear to look at him. "You thought running from me would be better than telling me the truth?"

I sigh and nod. Yeah. Yeah, that's exactly what I thought.

He shakes his head. "You think I only want what you could give me?"

He pulls me closer, his forehead pressed to mine. My heart aches. His eyes are pure fire.

"*Fuck*, woman."

Tears roll down my cheeks. "I thought—" I shake my head. "All this time, you've talked about getting me pregnant, having a baby. And then I saw *why*. I felt that."

His face twists with anguish and anger. My heart aches. He's lost a sister and a brother and just found out his own mother betrayed him. And I... decided to run.

His breath catches. "This is my fault. I own this. I haven't shown you enough how much you mean to me." He shakes his head. "I'm sorry. You mean fucking *everything* to me. I heard what that bastard did to you, and I had to avenge you, *now*. I should've been more patient. I should have stayed." He shakes his head. "I never should've left you to be assaulted by my asshole of a mother. Never. I'm sorry, Anissa. Forgive me."

I nod, swimming in a well of emotion that hits me in waves. His eyes meet mine, unrelenting. On fire.

"I choose *you*. Not what you can give me. You're *mine*."

He holds me and lets me cry. Cradles the back of my neck with a gentleness I didn't know he could give and I didn't know I needed. He wraps his hand around my waist as if trying to fuse the two of us together.

I try to speak, but the words are stuck in my throat. My vision's blurred. I taste salt and shame as a half sob breaks from me. I try to hold it in and fail.

"I want *you*. Not some fucking fantasy. Not some goddamn bloodline. Me, of all people, should know how fucked up that shit is. If I ever have a family, it'll be with you. Even if it's just *us*. We'll figure it out. But you, Anissa? I choose you."

I can hardly think straight when he says in a low, dangerous growl, "If you ever think of leaving again, I'll chain you to the bed and make you take your meals in your fucking cage."

He leans in. "And I am *definitely* branding you."

I shiver. The word makes my stomach clench. I shouldn't want something so brutal, so vicious, but the craving inside says otherwise.

Still, I cling to him, my heart pounding. "You're *crazy*."

"As if *you're* perfectly sane."

Right now, I'm still broken, still raw.

"God, Matvei," I say. I drop my head to his shoulder. I try fruitlessly to ignore the way this feels like blessed relief. "Do you guys ever do anything normal and boring?"

He kisses my forehead and pulls me to his chest. "Semyon plays chess…"

"And you and Rodion probably drag race high."

"Don't knock it til you try it."

We're trying and testing—my snark and his sarcasm—but it feels tired and heavy. Uncertain.

I sigh. "If I try to leave again, will you really chase me?"

"Chase you?" His voice drops, low and calm. "I'd burn the fucking world to the ground to find you."

My chest aches, my eyes sting, and my nose tingles.

I *believe* him. That's the problem. And worse? I want him to mean it.

I should walk away. I should fight him again, tell him no one gets to chain me. But instead, I lean in.

I press my forehead to his chest, letting myself breathe in his scent. "This is complicated," I whisper.

His arms tighten like steel bands. "Doesn't have to be."

For a moment, the world stops spinning, and it's just... *us*. No Bratva. No Irish. No escape routes and betrayal, no demand to be any more than we are.

His hand slides beneath the hem of my shirt, resting on bare skin. The rough, warm feel of his palm sends a calm through me.

Maybe he's right.

Maybe it doesn't have to be complicated.

"I'm sorry," I whisper. He doesn't ask me for what.

I'm sorry your family sucks.

I'm sorry mine does too.

I'm sorry I'm broken.

I'm sorry you are too.

"Me too," he finally whispers back. His hand isn't gentle or cruel, just certain, branded heat, his words against my ear. "You can't run, Anissa. Because I will *always* fucking find you."

I close my eyes because I realize then—I *want* him to.

"Our families are fucked up."

"Yeah." The sun has set, but we haven't turned any lights on. Sometimes, it's easier to face the truth in the dark. "We'll make our own family. We can, you know."

I swallow hard, still leaning against him, still relishing the certain feel of his palm against my back.

"We can... *what*?"

"Do better. Break the chain."

I can't help but smile. "Break the cycle of generational trauma with therapy and positive life choices?"

"Jesus," he says with a grimace. "I wouldn't go *that* far. You do know who I am, don't you?"

I'm deflecting, as usual, joking even though I know there's an undercurrent of truth.

Break the chain.

Yeah. I like that.

I nod, a smile emerging through the tears. "You're the man I ran from." I press my palm to his chest. "And the only one I ever wanted to catch me."

He leans in and kisses my forehead. The brush of his warm lips makes the ache in my chest ease a little. "Inside, little ghost. We need a quiet evening at home."

I tip my head up. "Does a quiet evening at home involve—"

"Whatever you want it to?" he interrupts. "Absolutely."

JANE HENRY

CHAPTER 30

ANISSA

I ALWAYS THOUGHT the Kopolov estate looked imposing and majestic, but tonight, it almost looks... cheerful. My sister lives here. My newfound family.

When Matvei opens the door, the smell of Zoya's cooking wafts through the air, and my stomach growls.

His parents have been detained, and if I know anything about the Kopolov family and loyalty, they'll wish Yana's shot wasn't only a warning. I'm not sure what part his father plays in any of this, but my gut feeling is that they were both complicit.

Rafail has had an office set up for me, just past the dining room, all souped up with every electronic I could possibly need. I can't get used to this feeling of being *wanted*. Useful. Not some tacked-on contractor who's disposable and invisible but someone who's an actual asset.

Matvei's here to talk to Rafail about what happened. I feel for him after everything he's been through, but he doesn't seem as bothered as I'd expect.

"Anissa," he says with a sigh. "I hated my parents. I did my best to do what was right, but they made their bed."

Yeah. And now they'll sleep in it.

It's a small gathering after dinner. A quiet night, but the air still feels charged from what happened the day before. The Kopolovs are scattered throughout the estate—some in a lounge nursing drinks, Polina looking after her children.

Vadka prowls, restless and irritable, but he doesn't say much. He scowls out the window, his eyes tracking every shadow and car that passes. I get the feeling he doesn't stay here very often in the evening. Matvei's mentioned he has a wife and son and doesn't socialize with the rest of them like he used to, but it seems the latest events have shifted everyone's focus.

"Where's Zoya?" Yana asks curiously, but she's nowhere to be found after dinner. I feel for her. In a way, her problem is the opposite of mine. I always *felt* invisible. She probably wishes she could be sometimes.

"How are you?" Yana's look of concern takes me by surprise. She seems so serious, borderline ruthless, but there's an underlying layer of concern that makes me feel appreciated and wanted.

"I'm good," I tell her honestly. Now that I've decided to stay, now that I feel like I belong, the constant need to move, to run again, isn't harping at the back of my mind. I'm relieved, honestly. I didn't know how much that restless energy drained me.

I excuse myself, trying to temper the pride I feel. I have an *office*. I have a list of *work* they need me to do, so when I go to the office they have prepared for me, no one asks any questions. I *love* that.

The space Rafail's set aside for me is ridiculous—sprawling desk, dual monitors, encrypted terminals, and fingerprint scanners. State-of-the-art equipment and a setup people kill for. *It's mine.*

For a second, I let myself breathe, settling into familiarity. I can hear Matvei's voice on the other side of the door, sarcastic and rough. The familiar huff of a laugh and clink of glass. My chest warms as my fingers hover over the keyboard. The blue light of the screen casts a shadow over my hands as I log in.

Then I hear it. The soft click of a door opening, but not behind me where the entrance is. I freeze.

"There y'are."

My stomach drops. My pulse races. I scream internally and know if I had the wherewithal to scream for help, I'd be instantly flanked, but when I turn, I see the entrance to the office is already barricaded. And Cillian O'Rourke leans against the wall like he owns the place.

I stand. "What the fuck are you doing in here?" My chair scrapes against the floor, my heart racing. I should scream for help. I should—

"Go ahead. Yell for help. I've got explosives prepared to detonate with the click of a button." He holds up his phone.

It glints in the overhead light. "Modern technology. Don't even need a fancy detonator anymore. The apps do it all, hmm?"

Explosives. He's got this place hot-wired. If I scream... I shake my head, my mind racing. Matvei's mother and father were in league with the Irish. Of fucking *course* they were. How else would their son have gotten in so deep? They played the long game, biding their time, and all the while, Rafail *trusted* them.

He walks in a slow path around the room. "I like what they've done with the place. You were always better working with the right toys, weren't you, lass?"

"What are you doing here?" I ask in a low whisper. If the others hear, and Cillian pulls that trigger...

He doesn't answer right away. Just walks a slow, circling path around the room.

"You... you were plotting this. *You* were the one who fucked with my accounts. *You* were the one who fucked with my flight when I tried to leave—"

"For a clever lass, it sometimes takes you a minute, doesn't it?" He smiles faintly. "You *were* losing it, and that sick boyfriend of yours was having his fun, eh? I just nudged things along."

I want to throw something. My chair, my laptop. But I don't. Just on the other side of the door, I have a goddamn cavalcade ready to come in, but who knows how many others he's planted? I could take his phone...

"You were working with his parents," I say, my voice flat. "All this time."

I try to keep calm, my palms planted on my desk. I don't know where this is going, but I know one thing for sure—I'll need to record what he says if we're to keep peace with the Irish. I click a mouse on my computer and begin recording.

"Don't move," he snaps in a low whisper.

Cillian's eyes flicker, a glint of crazy behind the charm. "He and I had an understanding. You weren't *meant* to go off-leash like this. You weren't supposed to *belong* to him," he murmurs. "You were meant for something bigger." He steps closer. "For *me*."

Rage rises in my chest. I glare at him. "And yet you never made a move. You kept your distance, didn't you? None of you cared two shits about me."

"That's where you're wrong, lass," he says, low and quiet. "It's complicated with us."

He laughs softly, but there's a sick sort of tone to it. "I watched you. You think I didn't want to come for you? But in my world, women are owned. I wanted you to think I didn't want you and knew if I made my move too soon, you wouldn't have *felt* it. I knew if you felt you didn't have a place with us, you'd appreciate it when you did."

What kind of fucked-up narcissistic bullshit is *that*? He's batshit crazy.

"Matvei was a tool. A weapon." His eyes narrow dangerously. "But he doesn't own you. You know how the Kopolovs work. Has he married you, lass? Even fucking proposed?" He shakes his head. "No. You're his kept woman." He leans in. "Disposable. His little ghost, who can vanish into vapor."

Oh god. He's sliced me open and rubbed salt in the wound.

"So this is what you're going to do," he says, leaning in, the bright red button right under his finger. "Unless you want me to press *detonate*."

CHAPTER 31

MATVEI

I NURSE my drink just in time for a pause in my conversation with Rafail. There are voices in the room where Anissa's supposed to be—low, muffled. And then...

Silence.

The kind that crawls up your spine and makes you *listen*.

At first, I figure she's doing what she always does—taking voice notes, maybe making a call. She's obsessive like that. Precise. Controlled.

But there's nothing now. Not even the rustle of movement.

Rafail notices me staring at the door.

"Relax," Rafail tells me. "You have to let go of some control, Matvei."

Well that's rich, coming from him. Still, he has a point.

My attention gets pulled away when Polina comes down the stairs, having finally put the kids to bed. She looks around, her expression pinched.

"Where's Anissa? Yana? Zoya? Where is everybody?" she asks.

Rafail opens his arm in a lazy gesture and smirks. "Matvei and I are nobody?"

"I mean the girls," she says, rolling her eyes.

"We haven't seen Zoya," Rafail replies. "No clue where she ran off to. Yana went to FaceTime her husband, and Anissa's in the other room doing some work. She asked not to be disturbed."

"It's just... eerily quiet," Polina says,shaking her head. "I don't like it. I have this weird feeling. And didn't we have guards posted at the main gate?"

Rafail flicks on his phone and pulls up the security app, eyes scanning the feed. "They're right there," he says, turning the screen so she can see. Polina studies it but still looks unconvinced.

"They weren't there a minute ago. I *swear*. It's strange."

"Mrs. Kopolov," Rafail says, amused, "Have I finally corrupted you? Seeing enemies in every corner?"

"I guess so," she mutters with a forced smile, but her brow stays furrowed. "I dunno. I mean, I think twin intuition's a real thing..."

I nod and pour myself another drink. I don't like that Anissa isn't here. I hate when she's not close enough to touch. After everything that's happened? I want her within reach. Always.

And if Polina says *her* intuition is on alert…

"What's the latest on my parents?" I ask, pouring another drink.

Rafail sighs, shaking his head. "Unlike Gleb, we can't prove they've been working with anyone. But chances are? Your mother, at least, knew exactly what he was doing."

My hands curl into fists. "Her *own* son…"

Rafail drags his finger along the rim of his glass with a grim nod. "She always favored your younger brother. You *know* that. And your father? He hated that *I* became the *pakhan*. Of course their behavior tracks, brother."

It does. It fucking does.

"None of us would blame you for being loyal to them," Rafail says. "If anything, it's a point in your favor. You're a lot of things, Matvei, but disloyal? Never."

Polina's staring into her glass now, silent.

And everything's still quiet in the other room.

Too quiet.

I don't like it.

I don't *trust* it.

I need to see Anissa. I need to see her with my own eyes.

Polina meets my eyes. "Check on her," she says, her brow furrowed. I'm already on my feet.

"She should've come out by now." I'm already moving.

I stalk to the room she was in—no laptop hum. No scribbled notes. No *Anissa*.

My pulse slams into overdrive. "Anissa?" I call out as if she's just around the corner. Maybe she went to use the bathroom or get a snack. I can still smell the faintest whiff of the body spray she uses clinging to the air. My little ghost. "Anissa!"

Something flashes in the corner of my eye just as a bloodcurdling scream comes from outside. Polina races to the window. "It's Zoya. Oh my god, it's Zoya. She's at the gates, Rafail. She's—what is she doing?"

Rafail opens the window, the fastest way to get to his sister. "Zoya!" he yells into the darkened night. Floodlights beam on Zoya as she falls to her knees in front of the guards, who haven't moved position since Rafail showed us the footage.

Oh god.

Oh god, no.

"What's happening?" Polina asks, her hand covering her mouth.

"Yana!" Rafail screams behind him. "*Yana!*"

The sound of footsteps echoes on the stairs. I'm at the monitor, my hands shaking. The red light means something's recording—the screen's recording, like a video on a phone. It's *still* recording. With trembling hands, my vision blurred in fury, I hit the stop and rewind buttons until I see movement on the screen.

Five minutes ago.

She was here five minutes ago.

And she's not alone.

Cillian fucking O'Rourke.

And Anissa... walking beside him. She's not restrained or drugged. Her expression is unreadable. Too calm.

Like she *planned* this.

I asked her if they were a fucking couple. I *asked* her. He was too close, too out of place, I didn't trust the fucking...

Behind me, Yana and Rafail are having a rapid discussion. Yana hands Polina a gun while Rafail calls the lockdown order for the estate. Yana goes to retrieve Zoya. Voices shout, and footsteps run through the house as security snaps into place. Windows and doors are locked. I'm dimly aware of it all happening behind me as I force myself to watch the video.

Don't react.

Stay calm.

I'll fucking kill him.

My vision tunnels. He didn't take her. She went with him.

My hand shakes as I rewind the video, forcing myself to watch every frame. My stomach turns, my heartbeat racing in my ears.

"What the fuck are you doing?" Rafail snarls.

"She recorded it. She fucking recorded it." I shake my head. "O'Rourke was here, Rafail. Don't lock us down. For all you know, you're locking the goddamn Irish in here with us."

"We're in an alliance. A truce," Rafail grinds out. He's in denial.

"Not anymore."

I turn. *Vadka*. He leans against the doorway, calm as ever, his arms crossed. The room stills.

"You gonna stand there and whine about O'Rourke giving fuck all about our goddamn alliance, or are you gonna do something about it?"

I want to rip his fucking head off.

Anissa is gone.

"What did you just say?" I growl at him.

"You fucking heard me."

"*Hey.*" Polina glares.

Vadka ignores her. "You're watching the fucking video like she left you a love letter. If it were me, I'd be on that fucking road already."

"Shut the fuck up."

"I'm just saying"—he pushes off the frame—"maybe she was in league with him. Maybe she was a fucking spy. Maybe—"

I lunge.

Rafail shouts, but I've already got Vadka by the collar, slammed up against the door.

"Say another word. One more goddamn word and I'll put you through that fucking window."

He stares me dead in the eyes. "You think this is about her running? That the Irish fucker means something? That's not what this is about."

"What the hell are you talking about?"

"You're talking about a woman who worked firsthand with our enemies. And her top skill? *Erasing*. If she wanted to be found, you'd already have her."

"Enough! God, you stupid idiots. The video is right here. Listen!" Polina plays it for us, the whole damn thing.

"But he doesn't own you. You know how the Kopolovs work. Has he married you, lass? Even fucking proposed? No. You're his kept woman. Disposable. His little ghost, who can vanish into vapor."

"He threatened her with *bombs*. *Here*! Right on our *estate*," Polina says. Rafail goes still.

Vadka shakes his head. I let him go with a parting glare. "We need to find those before we do *anything*."

"I have to find *her*."

"You've got a tracker on her?" Vadka asks. He narrows his eyes on me.

I nod, watching Polina, and whip out my phone.

"Not on her, but her phone's location tracking. She probably shut it off."

But when I pull up the app and watch her location, it's right there. A blinking light.

"She's headed southwest."

Yana storms back in. "Zoya's alright. Shaken but okay. They're dead, Rafail. Bullets straight through the temples, propped up to look like they're still there, guarding. Freaked her the fuck out."

"Motherfucker."

Vadka meets my stare. "Maybe she wanted to see what you'd do. Left the record button on. Tracker still active."

"Or maybe it's a trap," Rafail says.

I drag my eyes back to the monitor and watch the last frame again—Cillian's hand on her shoulder. *Familiar*.

I will find her.

And when I do?

She's not fucking walking away again.

Vadka stares at the tracker. "Wait. I know exactly where they are."

CHAPTER 32

ANISSA

"Son of a bitch," Cillian growls, slamming his phone down hard.

I flinch. I need that phone. It's the only thing keeping his leverage alive, the one threat he's still clutching to use against the Kopolovs. And if he touches that fucking detonate button...

His jaw tightens, teeth grinding like he's chewing through bone. Hands strangle the steering wheel.

I wonder if Matvei's noticed I'm gone yet. I saw the guards' bodies—slumped and still at the gates—and I wondered how long it would take before someone realized they were dead. Until they realize I'm not where I'm supposed to be.

As I stare at Cillian, I can't help but wonder... What would've happened if I'd stayed with the Irish?

There was a time I would've gladly become his. Molded myself into his perfect weapon. But back then, I didn't know what I needed. Didn't know who I was. Back then, I just wanted someone to care... to choose me.

My heart aches.

Cillian doesn't care about me. He never did. He just wants what he was denied.

But I'm going to play along. The more he thinks I'm his soft, compliant little puppet, the easier it'll be to make him drop his guard.

"What's the matter?" I ask lightly, all sweet curiosity.

He eyes me sideways, suspicious, and doesn't answer. But I know exactly what that call was. One of his men inside the Irish ranks. Something went wrong. I just need to guess the right pressure point and twist.

"Something go sideways?" I ask casually. "Wasn't this supposed to be seamless?"

"You don't know fuck all about my plan."

I shrug, feigning indifference. "I knew it had something to do with fucking over the Kopolovs. And I figure you're trying to find a place where you can stash me without anyone finding us."

Still nothing, but the silence is telling.

I look out the window, trying to track landmarks. I don't know this area well, but some of it is vaguely familiar. We haven't driven far. We're still within Bratva reach.

That means I have time. That means I have hope.

"Give me a weapon," I lie smoothly. "I know how to use one."

He snorts, eyes still on the road, and doesn't respond.

"This rope's tight," I add, wriggling my wrists a little. "Starting to cut circulation."

His jaw twitches, but still—nothing. Just that brooding silence.

"If you let me—"

"I'll fucking gag you if you don't shut up."

I blink at him, all mock-hurt and wounded pride. "Cillian." I pout. "I thought you liked me. Wanted me."

"Watch your fucking tongue, woman."

He pulls into a dark parking lot. Industrial. Quiet. No cameras that I can see.

"We're staying here for now," he says, throwing the car into park. "Don't do anything fucking stupid. You know what I'll do."

I drop my eyes and lower my voice. Soften everything about myself.

Then I look up through my lashes and say in a slow, husky purr, "Yes, sir. I understand."

His eyes flare, just for a split second.

Bingo.

If he tries to kiss me, I'll bite him.

His hand grips the back of my neck, not possessive like Matvei, not grounding. No. It's rough. Cold. Controlling. It doesn't make me feel wanted. It makes me feel *used*.

He hauls me out of the car and shoves open a side door.

The place smells like aged wood and old whiskey. Voices murmur beyond a closed door. A bar. It's crowded, familiar, but not enough for me to know where we are.

My eyes lock on Cillian's phone tucked tight in his back pocket.

I need him to pull it out, just for a second. And then I need to take it. Everything depends on that.

He mutters something under his breath, then yanks open a back room and pushes me inside.

His movements are tighter now, jittery and desperate.

This didn't go the way he planned. Good.

He faces me, his voice low and clipped. "This is what you're gonna do. You're gonna act like everything is fine. Like you're with me willingly. You understand?"

I nod slowly. "Of course. I want to go with you. I've always wanted to be with you, Cillian."

There's just enough truth in that—just enough of the past—to make me nauseous. I'm disgusted with the girl I used to be, the one who wanted someone like him.

"Good," he says, his mouth twisting into something like a smile as he unbinds my wrists. "That's a good girl."

When Matvei says that, it burns through me in a way that makes me ache. When Cillian says it? I feel like I'm going to throw up.

But I keep my expression soft. Keep the lie alive.

He pulls out his phone.

My heart starts to pound. Not yet, but close.

So fucking close.

"If my suspicions are right," he says, "he won't even notice you're gone."

Snort.

That's where he's wrong. So, so wrong.

"We're going to have to go out there," he says, eyes narrowing. "No funny business. I'll press that fucking button—you know I will."

Something about the way he talks—he's unraveling. Like he's losing his mind, losing his footing. Unsteady. Dangerous.

He's always had a temper, a vicious one. And when his plans don't work out exactly the way he envisioned? He doesn't pivot but explodes. I need to use that against him, need to needle him, make him slip, then take control.

"What's the matter?" I ask softly, feigning innocence. "Something go wrong?"

He growls, "You don't need to know the details."

"Of course not," I say sweetly. "I trust you."

I'm definitely going to throw up.

He brushes his hand over the back of my head in this awkward, almost-too-familiar way. "That's a good lass. Sit at the bar and have a drink. Behave yourself."

I have to stroke his ego. The narcissist's poison.

"You're so strong-willed. It's what I've always loved about you. Especially when you're in charge like this."

He gives me a half smile and winks. My stomach flips. Fucking asshole.

He leads us to the furthest corner of the bar.

"Keep your head down. Look at no one," he murmurs. "I have to take care of this."

"I know. Of course. Yes, sir."

So fucking gross.

From where I sit, I take in every detail I can. He's on his phone again—ten feet away—muttering into the mic like a dumbass. As if Matvei and his entire bloodline aren't coming for me. As if I'd ever go with this asshole willingly.

Fucking idiot.

Someone catches my eye. A woman at the bar. She sees me, and at first, there's recognition in her eyes. She raises a hand, then freezes when she sees who I'm with.

Does she think I'm Polina?

But then something shifts, and her eyes sharpen. She looks at him, then back at me.

Slowly, she turns her palm up in a silent gesture of... help?

Her brows rise in the universal question: Is this your choice? Are you here willingly?

I glance at him. Then back at her.

I shake my head.

Her back straightens, and her expression turns ice cold.

She leans in to whisper to another woman at the bar— someone vaguely familiar, though I can't place her.

They murmur. Point discreetly.

The bartender takes out a phone. Her fingers move fast.

My heart turns in my chest.

Does she know who he is? Does she know *what* he is?

Cillian drops back into the seat next to me just as the waitress arrives.

"Two Guinness," he barks.

I hate beer.

The tray comes, and with it, a sweet smile from the waitress and a napkin she slides across to me.

Cillian's distracted, back on his phone again.

I glance down. <handwritten note>"Are you here against your will?"

One side reads YES, the other NO.

I tear off the NO, smile, and push it back to her. She returns to the bar, where the three women huddle again, whispering.

Cillian's a big man—brutal, tattooed, and armed.

I can't take him on alone.

What's their plan?

What's next?

I fake a sip of the drink—definitely not touching it. It's probably drugged. Wouldn't put it past him.

Another fake sip. Another glance.

The bartender tilts her head toward the bathroom and raises an eyebrow.

Yes. That's the out.

"I need the ladies' room," I say, my voice soft, submissive again.

"Hold it," he snaps through gritted teeth.

"I can't," I say, weaving desperation into every syllable. "Please, Cillian. Just come with me."

I know damn well he won't step foot in a women's restroom.

"For fuck's sake," he growls, firing off another text, making another call.

"I have to go. Just let me out."

I don't sip the drink. Just pretend again.

When he finally rises, the woman from the bar is shadowing us.

I walk. He flanks me.

"No fucking funny business," he growls. "I'll press this fucking button." His phone screen still shows the app, ready to detonate.

"Of course," I say dryly. "Just need to piss."

He growls again, his grip like a vise around my wrist. I wince.

"You're hurting me," I whisper, not loud enough to cause a scene, just enough to bait him.

"Thought you liked pain," he says, his eyes locked on mine.

"I've been dying to have a fucking woman I could hurt. You're the perfect bitch for the job."

I want to fucking kill him.

"Is that your plan? Beat me into obedience?"

"Now, now. Jesus, woman. You're such a fucking liar."

We reach the bathroom.

And then—chaos.

The door slams open.

The entire fucking Kopolov family storms in.

Time stops.

The bartender lunges. She's closer to him than I am.

"Get his phone!" I scream.

She kicks his wrist—his phone flies, skittering across the bathroom tiles.

He roars and grabs her. She slams into the wall.

"Let her go!" someone screams.

It's not Rafail. It's not Rodion.

It's Matvei.

His gun is drawn. His eyes are lethal.

And he's charging...

For me.

It's *chaos*.

I wish I had a weapon.

Then something drops out of Cillian's pocket. A thumb drive?

I snatch it and shove it into my pocket just as he slams me into the wall. My skull cracks against concrete, and stars bloom in my vision.

Matvei's gun is pointed straight at Cillian. His eyes are wild, glass shattering around us, people screaming as they scatter.

"You broke the fucking alliance when you took my woman!" he roars.

Then he pulls the trigger.

The shot jerks Cillian's arm, but he doesn't stop. He whips his arm around again, aims, and fires. Another shot cracks through the air—this one hits him square in the chest.

Cillian's shot goes wide.

I scream as the woman who came to see me crumples to the floor. Another scream tears through the bar, and then there's no more waiting. Just bullets, one after the other. Matvei empties the entire cartridge into Cillian, a single-minded execution.

I hit the floor, crawling toward the fallen woman, trying to lift her, when someone slams into me. My vision skews, colors warping, noise fading. My head... Did I get hit?

Matvei keeps firing. His body is trembling with fury, and his mouth is twisted with something feral. An avenging angel in black emptying hell into Cillian's chest until the man's eyes go vacant, bleeding out onto the floor.

Then Vadka is beside me, gasping, his hands trembling as he lifts the woman's limp body into his arms. And then he breaks. Sobs rip out of him, uncontrollable. Seeing a big, scary, grown man on his knees weeping like a child breaks my heart.

It wasn't supposed to go like this.

The bartender kneels beside them, hands shaking, whispering prayers or curses or both. Tears stream down her cheeks.

But me? I'm stuck. Frozen.

What just happened?

"Come with me," Matvei says, pulling me to my feet, his voice a low growl. "You're safe now. Come with me. I'm not ever letting you go."

I don't even know the woman. But she's dead. She's gone. Just like Cillian. The bartender lets out a keening wail, voice rising over the carnage. I'm crying freely now, barely aware of what he's saying.

Matvei pulls me through the back door fast.

"My brothers will handle it," he says, quieter now. Controlled. "We're going home."

My voice trembles. "His phone... he had an app. It would've triggered a bomb."

"I know," he murmurs. "You got the phone. You did good. You did so good."

No. I didn't.

"Because of me, people are dead. Maybe more than I know."

"It wasn't because of you," he whispers into my ear, arms wrapped around me like steel. "This is war, baby."

Hours later, we're all back at the estate. The air is heavy, the grief thick, and we've gathered.

"I'm sorry," I whisper, shaking my head. "I'm so, so sorry."

Matvei meets my gaze.

"You have nothing to apologize for. Name one thing you could've done differently?" His jaw clenches. "If anything, *I'm* the one who opened fire."

Rafail stands, eyes burning. "The one to blame is dead," he snaps. "Cillian O'Rourke broke the alliance. He was the one who pulled the trigger."

Her. The woman. Vadka's wife.

The bartender's sister.

Vadka isn't here.

Silence swallows us. Zoya sniffles softly, wiping at her eyes.

"You want someone to blame?" Yana speaks up, voice razor-sharp. No tears, just fire. "Blame his parents. They started this."

She turns to me. "I combed through that drive you gave us, Anissa. I know everything now."

Matvei shakes his head, but Rafail cuts him off with a raised hand.

"I swear to god, if you apologize, I'll deck you myself," he growls. "Your parents are the assholes. Not you. Was it your fault they put your brother up to this? No. We know the truth now."

Matvei sinks onto the couch, his head in his hands.

I slide beside him and rest my head on his shoulder. "Rafail is right. It wasn't you," I say softly. "It was your parents. It's time that you let all that go now."

For a long moment, he says nothing. His breath shudders out of him like he's exhaling years of guilt. And maybe he is.

"Yeah," he says, shaking his head. "I'm done carrying that shit. They don't get to own me anymore."

He tightens his grip around my shoulder.

It feels right. I need this. I need him.

Semyon sits across the room, nursing a drink. His white

shirt's unbuttoned at the collar, sleeves rolled. He leans forward, elbows on his knees.

"I went through the thumb drive," he says, voice calm but weighted. "Thank you, Anissa, for having the presence of mind to grab it. It has everything—the Irish's plans, every plot. There never was an alliance."

Yana places a steady hand on his shoulder.

Rafail steps forward, his voice like thunder.

"I want to be clear. No one in this house is to carry guilt." He jabs a finger toward me. "Anissa, you did what you had to do. He would've pulled that trigger. My men confirmed it—there were bombs, and they were wired to his phone. He was not bluffing."

Why me? Why start a war over me?

Matvei speaks quietly, bitterly. "Turns out it wasn't just Cillian. My parents were working with him. They've been playing us. Playing me."

My stomach sinks. I still feel responsible.

Rafail clears his throat. "The Irish will retaliate," he says. "Tonight, we killed one of their own. The Undertaker is going to come for us."

His words land like stones.

"I'm not sure we can stop a war."

Zoya pales. "A war?" she whispers.

Rafail nods, grim.

"This is how it works. We killed one of theirs. Doesn't matter the reason. To them, there is no good reason."

"And they killed one of us," she says, her voice shaking. "Mariah..."

She breaks into a fresh sob. I wrap my arms around her. I'm crying, too, and I didn't even know her. But I saw Vadka kneeling on the floor, holding her shattered body. I heard the sound that left his throat. That kind of grief doesn't need translation. My heart broke right along with his.

"What can stop absolute bloodshed?" Zoya asks. Her eyes are shining, furious and lost.

Rafail shakes his head. "I don't know. I don't fucking know." He pulls out his phone. "I'll call McCarthy myself. They'll know he's gone within the hour."

A throat clears in the corner of the room.

Every head turns toward the shadowed edge of the space where an old hand rests on the cane's handle, gnarled and steady.

"I have a few things to say," Grandfather rasps. His voice is frayed with age, but it carries. "Just a few things."

Rafail stiffens, arms crossed over his chest. Zoya lifts her chin, staring her grandfather down. Matvei's arm wraps around my shoulders.

"Tonight," Grandfather says softly, "we grieve the loss of one of our own. I did not know Mariah, but as the wife of one of my boys, I grieve her with the rest of you."

He pauses and lets the silence settle before continuing.

"And yes, Cillian taking Anissa was an act of war. No one can deny that. The alliance is broken. Or maybe it was never formed to begin with."

He glances at us, eyes sharper than they should be for a man his age. "But there's something you young ones don't understand yet."

He smiles, not unkindly, and taps his temple. "In the old days, before technology did all our thinking for us, we studied the old ways."

He looks to Rafail. "You'd be wise to get on the phone with The Undertaker. Immediately. Calm the storm before it hits. And you'd be wise to recall the ancient rule carved into the McCarthy family tree."

"What rule?" Rafail asks, his voice hoarse.

Grandfather looks at him like he's already disappointed. "Your family took one of theirs. They killed an innocent. With no provocation. Under Irish law, that triggers a six-month moratorium on open war."

He looks at me next, eyes impossibly clear. "If The Undertaker is the man I think he is, he's his father's son. That boy would slit his own wrist before defying Irish law."

Then his eyes flick back to Matvei. "You have six months, son. You know exactly what to do."

And to Rafail: "You do too."

Matvei nods. A six-month truce.

Grandfather looks to Zoya. Something passes between them, silent but heavy. Something I don't understand yet.

Then Matvei turns to me and takes my hands in his.

"In front of my family," he says, voice low but certain. "In front of all of us—while we're grieving, while we're broken—I want to take the first step in something right. You promised me, Anissa, that we'd break the chain. Start fresh."

He swallows. "So I'm asking now. Will you marry me? Help me rebuild my family?"

Truth. Alliance. Hope.

"Atta boy," Grandfather whispers, pumping his fist.

I nod, whispering, I won't give this a second thought. I know my answer. "Of course I will."

Matvei lifts my hand to his lips, his gaze locked on mine, and brushes his lips over my knuckles. Possession disguised as chivalry, and I fucking adore it.

"Oh my god." Yana chokes up, dabbing at her eyes. "You two are killing me."

Matvei pulls me to him and kisses my forehead so fiercely that I feel it in my chest. My eyes flutter closed, and tears fall.

"I love you," he whispers. "I love you so damn much."

Six months.

Maybe Rafail can buy us six months of peace. But what happens after that?

Matvei catches my hand and laces his fingers through mine. His mouth finds my ear.

"A ring's not enough for you, is it, my little witch?" he murmurs.

"No?" I tease. "What do you have in mind? You can't cage me for life."

"But I can," he growls softly. "And I will. Any other motherfucker touches you, I'll skin them alive."

"And if I run?"

Sometimes I like to say shit just to hear him growl.

CHAPTER 33

ANISSA

I GRIT my teeth as the hot weld bites. It's not over, not really. But I breathe through it.

Yana taught me how to breathe through tattoos. Polina explained that in natural childbirth, bracing against the pain makes it worse, so you have to relax and breathe through it. Accept that fear is natural. Pain is only pain. Fear is the killer.

Breathe in. Breathe out.

Matvei watches, curious. "Did you even feel that?" he asks, shaking his head and staring at me in disbelief. "When they branded me, I thought I was going to die."

I blow out a breath and wipe my brow. "It hurt." I laugh under my breath. "Honey, I say this with love, and I hope it doesn't sound condescending, but if men were the ones going through childbirth, the human race would've gone extinct centuries ago."

My back throbs. My skin sears. But I breathe through it.

And I'm here.

I'm fine.

I wink at him. "Try keeping up, big guy."

He doesn't try to hide the way his gaze drops to my raw, red skin seared across my lower back. His breathing shifts. Slower. Heavier.

His voice lowers, intimate and rough. "You let me mark you. I'll never forget this, Anissa. Thank you."

I turn to face him, the heat between us already thick and coiled. He's close enough that I feel his breath on my cheek.

His hand curls around my jaw firmly. Commanding. The kind of touch that doesn't ask but claims. His mouth meets mine, all heat and hunger. I kiss him back, biting, resisting, pulling him in deeper because I love to fight him, and I love when he fights me back.

He groans low in his chest, the sound vibrating against my mouth. His knee slides between my legs and presses my thighs apart. "Show me your ring," he growls. "I want to see it."

I wiggle my fingers, my diamond engagement band glittering in the overhead lighting.

"Fucking gorgeous," he says, gently moving his hands up and down my sides but careful not to touch the throbbing pain in my back. "You're mine."

"You think you own me?" I throw back at him, teasing, defiant, pushing against the wall of resistance I love. "You better fucking earn it."

He does. He *does*.

In one swift motion, he lifts me as if I'm weightless. My legs wrap around his on instinct as he carries me toward the bed. He lays me down and places me headfirst. I grin, already half-naked from the branding. His hands make rapid work of undressing himself. And then he's there.

Skin to skin. Heat to heat.

"I'll stop if you say it, baby," he says, his voice raw and possessive. "I know you're in pain, and if you—"

"Stop it," I say, my words breathy. "Fucking take me. I want you. I need you."

He takes his time, his movements torturously slow and deliberate. Slowly, his grinding thrusts force me to feel as he slides himself into me. His mouth never leaves me for long—on my neck, biting across my shoulder blades, dragging across my spine, but careful to leave the throbbing brand alone.

I dig my fingers into the bed, wishing I were on my back so I could drag my nails along his shoulders and mark his skin.

"I want you like this. Trembling under me. Marked by me. Mine."

He thrusts in and out, perfect pleasure making the pain fade and give way to bliss.

I come apart beneath him, and he follows, moaning my name, buried to the hilt, his body trembling over mine.

His forehead meets my back. His breath kisses my skin in the brutal aftermath of branding and lovemaking.

"I love you," he whispers.

My eyes flutter open, landing on the pressed black clothing that hangs on the back of the door. I let out a sigh.

"And I love you."

"Let's go, baby."

CHAPTER 34

ANISSA

THE FUNERAL is brutal in its simplicity.

No cathedrals or soaring music. Just a stone courtyard behind the estate. Her body is wrapped in white. Mariah—the woman I barely knew and still mourn. They say she liked flowers, had a green thumb, and was the mother to her little boy everyone wished they'd had.

I like that.

Without thinking, my fingers brush along the rough surface of the obsidian stone in my pocket. Protection. Power. I imagine I draw strength from it. Maybe we all could.

Vadka stands tall and silent. Stoic. He hasn't spoken, not one word to anyone since the shooting, as if he's afraid when he opens his mouth, he will fall to pieces. His jaw ticks once, like a pulse, but he's otherwise marble. And it breaks my heart.

He stands beside the grave and doesn't move. His sister-in-law Ruthie holds the tiny hand of a little boy dressed in a black suit who seems blissfully ignorant of the horror before him. I wish he wasn't here, but the Bratva will do what they feel is right. And shielding children from brutality is a luxury they don't seem to afford.

Ruthie sniffs, then breaks into loud, choking sobs. She clutches a scarf to her chest and presses it to her eyes. Silently, Yana comes to her side, wraps an arm around her shoulder, and Ruthie's head falls to Yana's chest. She weeps as Zoya wordlessly kneels in front of the small boy, says something in a soft voice, then lifts him in her arms and takes a little walk.

Vadka doesn't move.

A line of Kopolov men stand shoulder to shoulder, dressed in identical black suits, wearing identical hard expressions and black armbands to signify mourning. Even Rodion is still and solemn as Rafail steps forward and drops a small bouquet of flowers on the grave.

They each follow suit. One by one.

Each steps forward, dropping flowers on the grave and a little token—a picture, a scrap of something personal. Bratva tradition.

Matvei hooks an arm around my waist, grounding us. Silently, his fingers link with mine. Present. Warm. Unshakeable.

We stand in silence as Semyon builds a fire. It starts small, and then each man, in turn, tosses dry wood on top, one stick at a time. We stand in silence, watching the fire grow in strength and heat with each stick, until it's a glowing furnace.

I watch and stare. Proud to be part of this family. Proud to stand shoulder to shoulder.

Yana approaches from behind. Ruthie stands nearby, holding her nephew, Zoya's hand in hers. Yana, unlike the men, is dressed in light gray. A quiet rebellion, maybe.

"You two," she whispers, "belong to each other. Today, we mourn what we lost. And you remind us that we keep living. Stronger together."

I belong now, and that's both beautiful and terrifying. Because this family protects what's theirs and destroys anything that gets in its way.

I blink hard, tears falling. I've never wanted to be *wanted* like this.

I belong.

Yana smiles. "She would've wanted us to plan your wedding."

Matvei tenses but doesn't look at us.

Yana nods. "We lose, and we gain." She eyes me thoughtfully. "I look forward to welcoming you to our family, Anissa."

The fire burns, and the war is coming.

But today?

Today, we remember.

And today, we begin again.

LATER, after the fire dies and the sky goes to pitch, we gather inside. I like that no one wants to go home. The long table is dressed in black with crystal accents. It's an odd blend here today as we gather to eat together. Mourning for a life lost. Celebration for our engagement. Or just... family.

The Kopolovs have a way of rolling with grief, not being brought down by violence and fear. Matvei's hand rests on my thigh, a quiet and immovable weight. I like it.

Across from us, Rafail nurses a drink. He's different than I thought he would be. In my mind, I built him up as a monster to be feared, but I see how he is with his family and Polina. Loyal. Stern, yes, but human. He smiles at me and lifts his drink. I truly think he's forgiven me for running. He lifts his glass with a nod that feels like a benediction and a warning wrapped together. And maybe it is.

"Turns out you were just what the bastard needed, Anissa." He tips his chin toward Matvei.

Polina smirks beside him, tapping her nail lightly on the crystal rim of her glass. "Indeed."

A car pulls up outside the window. Polina's eyes widen. "Oh, I didn't know she meant she was coming *now*."

I open my mouth to ask for details when out steps a regal

woman, older but not frail—silver hair swept into a neat bun, a pale pink sweater softening her sharp profile, slim-fitting jeans.

UNHINGED

I know her.

It hits me like a blow to the chest.

She's Polina's mother. The woman that adopted her. I freeze, when a warm hand moves to the nape of my neck and gives a gentle squeeze. "Relax," Matvei says in my ear. "You'll like her. I promise."

Polina goes to open the door, then gestures. "Mama, there's someone special I want you to meet. Anissa, this is Ekaterina Romanova. My mother."

Ekaterina smiles and extends a hand.

"Anissa. I owe you an apology."

There's a sigh in her chest, as if she's been carrying this moment for too long. Her eyes grow soft—sorrowful—but there's steel beneath the sadness.

"I believe I owe you all an explanation."

The words hang heavy in the air, thick as storm clouds.

The room swells with tension as Zoya, always the gentle soul, attempts to soften the sharp edges. "May I bring some tea and refreshments?" she offers, her voice light but tremulous.

Rafail gives a small nod of permission, and I watch her scurry off like a dove trying to calm a battlefield.

I wish she could.

Zoya lays a tray of tea between us, Ekaterina finally speaks.

Her fingers tremble on the delicate cup as she places it back on its saucer.

Her eyes find mine.

"I've explained to the Kopolovs, but you're owed an explanation as well, love. I fear some of this..." her voice catches, but she pushes through, steadying herself, "...is my fault."

My throat tightens.

She swallows and lifts her chin, choosing bravery over shame. "I wanted a daughter," she confesses. "More than anything. My husband resisted for years. Daughters..." She swallows, her voice brittle with old wounds. "They're not born to rule in our world. Sons secure power. Daughters secure alliances."

Mmm. Indeed. Tell me about it.

Her hands knot together in her lap.

"And then one day, he brought me Polina."

Her gaze softens as it settles on me, a sad smile pulling at her mouth. "A miracle," she whispers. "She was my miracle."

My chest aches.

She presses on. "I didn't know—*I swear to you, I didn't know*—until years later, that she had a sister. That you were separated. No one told me until it was too late."

She blinks back tears, but one escapes, sliding down her cheek.

"The adoption was closed. Sealed. They wanted no contact." Her voice hardens, not with cruelty, but with the pain of helplessness.

Her breath shudders as she releases it.

"I was afraid," she admits, her voice almost too soft to hear. "Afraid of what I would find. Afraid that if I pried too hard, I would lose you both."

For the first time, I see the full measure of her fear.

"I let fear guide my choices," she says, not looking away from me. "And for that, Anissa, I ask your forgiveness."

Ekaterina's voice trembles but does not falter. "I was wrong."

Silence stretches. Every eye in the room is on me.

"You were afraid," I say quietly. "And I wish things hadn't happened the way they did, but I don't believe any of you are the ones to blame, and the ones that *are* to blame aren't here anymore."

I reach for her hand. She clasps mine, her grip tight with unspoken apologies, and something inside me finally, blessedly, begins to ease.

Her voice steadies. "You two are joined now. Sisters. A bond that can't be broken." She stares at me and shakes her head. "The similarities are uncanny."

And in this moment, as I sit between my family and my future, I realize something deeper than bloodlines or vengeance.

We are all just trying to survive.

Matvei isn't smiling right this second, but god, we've been through a lot at this point. His parents, exiled. His brother, gone. Almost losing me. His vow to Rafail...

He looks *at peace*.

The pressure of his hand on my thigh increases slightly. I feel it and lean in closer to him.

Old instincts whisper, *run*.

But I stay.

I stay and choose what I thought I never could.

I meet his gaze, and he surprises me with a soft, shy smile.

My heart tumbles in my chest and my eyes grow misty. Something about his vulnerability in that smile makes everything slide into place like pieces of a puzzle.

The wine suddenly tastes sweeter, his touch heavier, the room warmer. I feel like my heart expands to twice its size, sitting beside my new family...and the man I love.

EPILOGUE

ANISSA

MATVEI SMIRKS at the scent of burning sage in the air that still lingers.

"What's that supposed to do?" he whispers. We stand in front of each other in the Kopolov family home, holding hands. We're forgoing most of the pomp and circumstance around our marriage. It's time we make this official.

"Sage," I whisper. "Wards off evil, cleanses, and all that." I shake my head and smirk back. "Your family needs a damn purification, so it's one small thing we can do."

"Ahh," he says, nodding. It's a small thing. Witchy, he'd call it. But I need to feel like this isn't just another Bratva transaction, another ceremony of duty. I need to feel like this *means* something.

I choose him.

He chooses me.

Matvei's dressed in a tuxedo, looking hot as hell in the fitted black. He looks like the devil himself come to claim me.

Rawr.

I am *so ready*.

The Kopolov men flank either side in their dark suits, wearing silent stares. Ekaterina Romanova and Polina stand on either side of them, Polina dressed in elegant gray, holding Rafail's hand. Ekaterina dressed in silver, her matching silver hair pinned like a crown around her head. She catches my gaze and winks at me as if to say *you've got this*.

I don't have parents anymore, but I've got...*family*. I look at Zoya, her wistful eyes smiling at me and Yana, graceful and poised. Rodion, with his signature smirk, and Semyon, serious as always, but welcoming, which is a lot coming from him.

Rafail steps forward. His gaze sweeps the gathering like a general preparing troops before battle. He doesn't look at me right away but at Matvei. Then he turns, and his steely eyes land on me with the weight of history behind them.

I know, I know.

"You gave everything in allegiance to this family," he says to Matvei, his voice rough with command and respect. "And we know what the old laws say. But rules," he continues, his eyes glinting, "Are written by men who fear change. Laws are rewritten by those not afraid of what lies ahead." The weight of his gaze falls on Yana. She swallows and gives him a small smile.

My chest tightens. My pulse pounds.

"We're at war," he continues. "The Irish will not stop until we're gone. Destroyed." He lifts his chin. "But the death of my parents didn't end us. We've stayed together, through every travesty sent our way. And we stand together now."

His eyes flick to Matvei. "Today, we join Matvei and Anissa together. Their vows will forgive past grievances. All of them." Matvei's grip tightens in mine. "Today signifies a joining of two people. A blood oath that fortifies. And after this, the past no longer belongs to us." He nods to me. "The Kopolov claims you as their own, Anissa. Through your union, we gain strength."

Matvei's eyes rake over me, slow and possessive. He reaches out, and I place my hand in his.

His calloused thumb strokes over my knuckles, rough and reverent.

"Do you accept this bond?" Rafail asks him.

"I do," Matvei growls. "I have always accepted it."

"And you?" Rafail turns to me, his gaze piercing through my bones. "Do you swear your blood to the Bratva? As our equal. As family."

I straighten my shoulders and lift my chin. "I do," I say, my voice steady. *"I swear it."*

There is no applause. No cheers. This is not a celebration of innocence.

This is a coronation.

Rafail nods.

Matvei pulls me against him, his hand splayed across my back like a brand as we take our vows. As he slides the thick gold band on my finger and I do the same for him.

His kiss claims me in front of everyone—possessive, bruising, hungry. He kisses me like we've already won the war, like he could devour me whole.

I let him.

Because I will burn with him. I choose *this*.

As Matvei breaks the kiss, he leans close to my ear, his breath hot against my skin.

"You're mine now," he growls, rough and low. "Not just in blood. Not just in name. In every fucking way that matters."

I smirk, tilting my head. "Earn it, big guy."

His eyes darken. "Oh, I will."

The Irish are coming.

But so are we.

THE END

BONUS EPILOGUE

WANT TO READ MORE OF MATVEI AND ANISSA'S STORY? SCAN THE QR CODE BELOW TO GET THE FREE BONUS EPILOGUE FOR *UNLEASHED: A DARK FORCED MARRIAGE BRATVA ROMANCE*!

PREVIEW

UNBROKEN: A DARK MAFIA SINGLE DAD ROMANCE

CHAPTER ONE

VADKA

An empty bottle rolls across the floor, glinting in sunlight—sunlight?

Shit, it's daybreak. Have I been up all night?

The bottle stops against the toe of my boot.

I don't move.

My knuckles ache, bruised and split beneath crusted blood that isn't all mine. I stare down at it. Hell, I think *most* of it isn't mine.

Jesus. My head is killing me.

I don't remember how many men I killed.

The air wreaks of body odor and whiskey. In the corner of the room, a woman's scuffed shoe lay, broken and crooked, shadowed by the doorway. My eyes catch on it and for a moment, something lethal twists inside.

Memory grips me. A carefree night on the town. Mariah's hand on my arm to stop herself from keeling over. Her tinkling laugh and squeal when her heel broke and she almost fell headfirst into the street. My wife, in my arms, her eyes twinkling at me. A little tipsy. Carefree.

So full of life.

I shove the memory down, out of sight, buried beneath too many feelings to name.

The Irish took my wife from me. And every last motherfucker will pay.

"Vadim."

Rafail's voice is low and rough. He hardly ever calls me my christened name. Everyone calls me Vadka, even him, when he's not pissed or serious, which is most of the time.

I don't look at him. I stare straight ahead, at nothing. Just me, here with my ghosts and demons.

"You *have* to stop this." Rafail's shadowy form steps in front of me, careful not to slip on the fucking gore that surrounds us. Dressed in a suit at the ass crack of dawn, he's either catching an international flight or hasn't gone to bed yet. "You *have* to fucking stop this," he repeats.

He crouches in front of me, serious eyes meeting mine. The eldest of his family, Rafail Kopolov only celebrated his thirtieth birthday a few years back. The youngest reigning *pakhan* in Europe, but one of the most feared. He's my *pakhan*. And my best friend.

"You're going to bring devastation I can't hold back, Vadka," Rafail says. His tone barely softens, but the fact that he's using my nickname means he's trying.

"They killed her." My voice is ragged. It never gets easier saying this out loud. *Never.* My eyes finally lift to Rafail's, my voice ragged and raw. "They killed my wife, Rafail."

His jaw flexes. "And what happens when you burn down every fucking city from here to Belfast? You think you'll find Mariah on the other side?"

The pain hits like a knife to my chest, so sharp and visceral I can't breathe at first.

"I don't fucking care," I manage to grind out. My chest heaves. "We'll find them."

"They're already coming," he snaps. "The Irish want war. Matvei is working on decoding the fucking flash drive we captured. They want blood for blood, brother, but you've given them every excuse." He leans in. "How many more innocents have to die?"

My mouth twists bitterly and I shake my head. "They want war? Good. And I haven't killed *one* innocent, Rafail." I scratch at my chest to distract myself from the undeniable thirst for a drink. My voice is hoarse. "Not one."

"Not yet," he says softly.

Silence stretches between us. Rafail drags a hand through his hair and pushes himself to his feet, pacing. I almost feel badly for putting him in this position. I didn't want war. I never wanted to shed more blood than I had to.

But that was then. This is now.

They pulled the trigger and sounded the battle cry when they killed my wife.

My wife.

Rafail's gaze travels to the broken shoe on the floor. He swallows hard. This is when he tells me about the innocent lives at stake, how hard we've worked for peace, reminds me of our limited sources. He might even pull rank.

But this time, he doesn't say any of those things. No. A flicker of genuine fear seems to run through his words when he says in a hoarse whisper, "Think of Luka."

The words hit harder than his fist would. My breath stops cold.

Luka. My boy. My miracle, asleep and safe.

Rafail presses harder. "Do you think Mariah died so you could abandon him? Or bring harm to him through your own recklessness?"

"Don't, Rafail." I drag a hand across my brow as a well of pain pushes at my chest, making it hard to breathe. *"Don't."*

"I have to. I can't let you destroy everything we've built and everything we hope for because of revenge. I can't."

I yank my hand away from my face and stare at him. "As if you wouldn't raze the fucking *earth* if someone killed Polina."

He flinches as if I slapped him. His jaw clenches, and he looks away. We both know the truth. He'd like to tell himself that he'd make decisions that would benefit the rest of his family and our Bratva. He likes to think he wouldn't cave to the temptation to murder the entire bloodline of any motherfucker who harmed a hair on her head. But we both know the truth.

He'd lose his fucking *shit*. The Rafail we all know and love would be gone and buried forever.

Just like me.

Just like me, when I lost Mariah—my last link to sanity. Without her, the world blurs and ceases to have meaning.

"I won't abandon Luka," I tell him, my voice cracking. "I will cleanse this city of every trace of the Irish before they get within breathing distance of him."

"Then pull yourself out of this fucking quagmire and act like it," Rafail snaps, his limited patience fraying. "Because right now, brother, you're *drowning*. And you're dragging the rest of us under with you."

He turns to go. The empty bottle rolls and hits my foot. I'm seized with blinding, irrational rage. Without a second thought, I grab the bottle and hurtle it across the room. Rafail watches, implacable.

The sound of glass shattering doesn't do what I hope I would. It only makes what's broken feel irreparable.

I rise slowly, my gaze on Rafail. My breath still heaves with the effort of breaking the bottle. With the effort of not falling apart.

PREVIEW

"Maybe we fucking drown them *first*."

CHAPTER 2

RUTHIE

I wipe down the bar top for the hundredth time.

"You know," Zoya says thoughtfully, tipping her head to the side. "It's really okay to only wipe that down like fifty times. It's a bar, Ruthie, not an operating room."

At nineteen years old, Zoya Kopolova is easily the youngest one here. Petite with dark brown hair and warm brown eyes, she makes the room feel warmer, the crowd friendlier.

"That's what *you* think." My voice is flat but my lips quirk up. "If you knew what truly happened at a bar, you'd realize it's not as far from an operating room as one might think." Here, hearts are broken and mended, pasts buried and surfaced. Here, couples meet and break apart. I have seen it all, and sometimes fancy myself part therapist, part miracle worker.

The Wolf and Moon isn't a popular bar for young adults, but an older bar with worn wood and comfortable seats saved for regulars. We're filled to near capacity on weeknights and weekends are barely tolerable.

There are trendier places for the younger crowd to go, but

Zoya chose here. She was always what my mother called "an old soul."

"Refill, please," Zoya asks sweetly, pushing her empty glass to me.

"Haven't you already had two?"

Zoya is everyone's younger sister. I can't help it.

"I'm fine," she says, an adorable divot forming between her brows. "Hey. Seriously. The better question is, how are you?"

"Fine," I lie.

I'm here, aren't I? The truth claws at my throat. We don't need to talk about the sleepless nights, the anxiety attacks, the memories that surface like ghosts when I least expect it.

I hate working here now. Every time I set foot in the place, I remember everything that happened that night in sordid, nightmarish detail.

"How are they?" I ask Zoya quietly, not meeting her eyes. She knows exactly who I'm talking about.

I haven't seen Vadka or my nephew in weeks. Months, even. I can't. It's too damn painful, and honestly, I feel like a piece of shit because of it. Who abandons their dead sister's husband and child?

Me, that's who.

But it kills me, every time, to look at little Luka and see my sister's eyes. To see the raw pain in Vadka that mirrors my own.

"Luka is great," Zoya says quietly. "He likes to play with Stefan."

"Ooh. Perfect."

Stefan's sister Anya married into the Kopolov family.

"Stefan is so good with him. Honestly, they all are."

A lump rises in my throat. I know. It was one of the things my sister Mariah loved best about the Kopolov family, the family she married into by proxy. Found family. Immediate extended family for her son. Something neither of us could ever offer him.

"And Vadka?"

Zoya looks away for a moment, not replying. I hate how sometimes no reply *is* a reply.

My heart aches and unbidden tears spring to my eyes.

"I don't know about Vadka," Zoya says softly, her face pained. She bites her lip as if she's said too much.

"What?" I lean in closer. "What are you talking about?"

It's been three months.

An eternity.

Yesterday.

"Well, he—he's not doing so well after Mariah's death is all. He took it hard."

How could he not? He loved her since they were both still children. They grew up together, married, bought a house and had a child. And they were *smitten*. Madly in love. I didn't believe in fate until those two met.

My nose tingles and my throat aches.

I can't think of this now. I have work to do.

So I turn halfway to the side so Zoya can't see me, even though I can't hide the husky tone of my voice. "Yeah? What's he doing?"

Zoya shrugs a shoulder. "He's kind of gone... well. Rogue, I guess you'd call it? If he wasn't Rafael's best friend..."

Rogue?

What?

My stomach knots.

"Well, is he taking care of Luka?" I ask sharply. My pulse feels too rapid, and there's a strange ringing in my ears.

Zoya flinches. "Yes, he said he hired a nanny or something? And Luka starts school in a few weeks, so..."

He does? How did I not know that?

My heart hurts. I have to check in on them. I *have* to. I turn fully away from Zoya to compose myself.

And that's when I see her. Corner table. Too young and too pretty for her own good, wide-eyed but... brittle. Next to a man leaning in too close. His knuckles are tight, whitened around the glass, flirtation barely covering aggression and violence.

I've seen this type a hundred times before. Once is too many.

Her smile doesn't reach her eyes. Her fingers worry the napkin. *Damn it.*

I know that look. I've *worn* that look. And my sister did, too, though never because of Vadka.

I'm kind of grateful for the distraction.

Without breaking stride, I cross to the stack of clean glasses behind the bar. Grab a fresh one, just like I'm minding my own business. I wink at her behind his back and jerk my chin to the women's restroom. Her eyes widen before she sits up straighter.

Inside every stall and plastered to the wall of the women's restroom is our safety protocol: a number to text if you're in trouble, or an order a woman could place. An "angel shot" means *I need help*.

I watch her excuse herself and head to the restroom. I nod to Zoya, who's watched the whole exchange. With a smile at me, she heads to the restroom a few seconds later.

Zoya loves helping a woman in distress, and she's good at it. Rafail, her older brother, would lose her mind that she's anywhere near a potentially volatile situation.

I watch the man tap his fingers nervously on the table, his jaw twitching, before he glances to the side and deftly pulls something from his pocket. *Bingo*. Son of a bitch slides the pill into her drink so quickly, anyone would've missed it if they weren't expecting this exact fucking move.

Thank fuck. You can't save a girl who doesn't want to be saved, and she hasn't called foul yet. But it's against the law to drug someone, so this asshole's just bought himself a ticket to hell.

Pulse racing, my hands stay steady enough to type a message to security.

PREVIEW

> Table six. Drugged the drink. Pull him

The response is almost instant. Seconds later, four of our bouncers close in. I watch the man stiffen, his gaze jerking up.

"Problem here?" Anton asks.

The man's face drains of color. "No, I'm fine."

Zoya exits the bathroom, the young woman behind her.

"Wh-what's happening?" She stammers.

"This piece of shit tried to drug you, darling," I say to her, my voice bright and sharp. "But not tonight." Before he can respond, Yuri hauls the man up by the collar and slams him into the side of the booth.

"You think we're blind here?" Yuri spits out.

"Yuri." My tone is tight. "Take him to the back before the Kopolovs hear about this."

Rafail's instructions are clear: anyone drugs a woman at the Wolf and Moon, we tell him and Vadka pays a visit.

My heart beats faster. I know exactly what will happen if Vadka catches wind. It isn't the man's life I'm worried about, but I don't want Vadka to get into any more trouble.

Rafail wants word to get out that predators aren't welcome in his city. Letting Vadka loose sends a loud, bloody message: This place is protected. Women here are under our watch. You try anything, you disappear. Reputation management through fear.

Rafail doesn't do it out of kindness. He's protecting his assets. His city. His reputation. But it makes him look like a protector, and he'll take that image—especially when it's Vadka's fists that do the talking.

Yuri hesitates, glowering at me. He *wants* to see Vadka deal with this motherfucker.

Sigh. So do I. But not tonight.

"*Go,*" I snap. I've got company protocol on my side, and Yuri doesn't want to lose his job.

I turn to the girl. Her hands are shaking as she clutches her purse to her chest.

"You okay?" Zoya asks softly. She comes up to us as the rest of the bar goes back to their drinks.

She nods fast. "Y-yes. I think. I—"

Zoya places a hand on her shoulder. "Hey. You're not the one who owes anyone an explanation. Do you have someone you can call?"

The girl nods and swallows.

Zoya guides her to a quiet table. The bar holds its breath, watching the scene unfold, before glasses clink and voices pick up again.

I resume my work, filling orders, when my phone buzzes with a text. I expect it to be from Anton, telling me the predator's been handled. *Handled* means he won't be back. *Handled* means tonight, the predators don't win.

But it isn't Anton.

My heart thumps hard when I see *Vadka*.

My thumb hovers. My pulse doesn't.

Stupid. It's just a name. Just a man.

Just a man with hands that could crush skulls and a voice that commands attention.

Just a man *who loved my sister*.

I go back to pouring drinks like my hands aren't shaking, trying to get my shit together. Like I'm not already answering him by pretending I haven't seen it.

Finally, when there's no one else to serve, I sigh and open the text.

> **Vadka**
> You hiding something from me, Ruthie?

I close my eyes for a beat, already tasting the fire in his words. He didn't fuck around *before* Mariah was gone, and now that she is, any semblance of politeness has vanished.

My heart beats faster and my hands are immediately clammy. Which one of those bastards ratted me out?

> I handled it without you needing to add another tat to the collage, Vadka.

The Bratva mark actions with ink. He doesn't need another murder. Not on my watch.

> **Vadka**
> You deprived me from the chance of putting a predator in the ground? Why?

"Excuse me? Anyone here to take a drink order?"

"Be right there. Sorry, we had a bit of a commotion just now I had to handle." I serve the three young women standing by the bar before I text Vadka back.

> Because you have a son and I won't let my nephew be motherless and fatherless.

Now my hands *are* shaking.

Son of a bitch.

I put my phone away and ignore the rest of the texts.

I ignore the real reason I don't want him here tonight.

Four hours later when the bar's finally closed for the night, I still have the nighttime routine to complete but I pull open my phone to check my texts.

I blow out a breath. I don't think so. I have work to do. He can wait.

I run through tomorrow's prep work and wipe the bar again. Clean enough for surgery now.

> **Vadka**
> You underestimate me.

Oh, no, I don't. That's the problem.

I grab a broom and sweep the floor, mindlessly pushing crumbs and dust into a pile. I sweep aimlessly, trying to get the job done.

I considered leaving the bar after Mariah's death, but this is the place I call home, and I hate to think I'm such a wuss I couldn't stand the pressure. Seriously. I'm an *adult*.

I turn my back to the bathroom, to the place that reminds me of Mariah. I can't think back on that night. No, not now.

I told myself that if I kept coming to work, if I kept putting one foot in front of the other, I'd eventually erase the memory of her vacant eyes and Vodka's screams of pain and devastation from my memory.

But I can't.

So this time, I don't try to. I face the vacant room and the whisper of Mariah's ghost. I let the tears fall silently and don't bother to wipe them.

"Why you?" I whisper into the stillness. If it had to be a random person, why did the universe have to pick *my sister,* the woman who was married and in love, the woman with a *child?* Why her? Why sunshine in human form, and not *me?*

I was the one who was alone, childless, and barely lovable. I was only a bartender. Single, and probably would be for life. I had no children, and even my mother, god bless her, would look at me through the haze of dementia and still call me *Mariah.*

Why not me?

I choke on a sob and let my shoulders sag.

Why? Why am I still here and the only person I've ever loved more than myself, erased from existence forever?

Why?

My phone rings. I hiccup through a sob and glance blearily at the screen.

Mom.

I let out a ragged breath and answer the phone.

I let myself hope that this time, she'll remember.

"Hello?"

"Hello? Who is this?"

"Mom. Mom, it's me. You called *me*, remember?"

"Ohhh," she says, and I cringe at what I know is coming next. "Mariah, honey, can you please bring me some groceries?"

"It's not Mariah, mom. It's Ruthie," I whisper, squeezing my eyes shut against the pain that chokes me. I don't say the next sentence that's on the tip of my tongue. I don't have the energy to explain it again. I don't have it in me to make anything harder again.

It's me, mom.

Mariah's gone.

PREVIEW

WANT TO FIND OUT WHAT HAPPENS NEXT? ORDER YOUR COPY OF "UNBROKEN: A DARK MAFIA SINGLE DAD ROMANCE" BY SCANNING THE QR CODE BELOW. AVAILABLE ON JULY 11TH!

Jane HENRY
Romance for "good girls" who love bad boys

Fueled by dark chocolate and even darker coffee, USA Today bestselling author Jane Henry writes what she loves to read – character-driven, unputdownable romance featuring dominant alpha males and the powerful heroines who bring them to their knees. She's believed in the power of love and romance since Belle won over the beast, and finally decided to write love stories of her own.

Scan the QR Code below to receive Jane's Newsletter & be notified of upcoming new releases & special offers!

Be sure to visit me at www.janehenryromance.com, too!

Made in the USA
Coppell, TX
19 July 2025

52104724R00236